The Koberg Link

A JOAN KAHN BOOK

BOOKS BY ARTHUR MALING

The Koberg Link
The Rheingold Route
Lucky Devil
When Last Seen (Editor)
Schroeder's Game
Ripoff
Bent Man
Dingdong
The Snowman
Loophole
Go-Between
Decoy

Arthur Maling

The Koberg Link

69846

Harper & Row, Publishers
New York, Hagerstown,
San Franciso, London

A HARPER NOVEL OF SUSPENSE

Designer: Stephanie Winkler
Copyeditor: Paul Hirschman

Library of Congress Cataloging in Publication Data

Maling, Arthur.
  The Koberg link.
  "A Joan Kahn book."
  I. Title.
PZ4.M25Ko   [PS3563.A4313] 813'.5'4   79-1802
ISBN 0-06-012709-0

79 80 81 82 83 10 9 8 7 6 5 4 3 2

For
George H. Emert
with appreciation and good wishes

The Koberg Link

1

Someone coughed politely. I looked up. It was Helen Doyle, my secretary.

"Still here?" I said, startled. "I thought you'd gone."

"I—I've been waiting," she said hesitantly. "I wanted to have a word with you."

I glanced at my watch. Five minutes past six. I'd promised Carol that I'd meet her at the Plaza at six thirty. But Helen's queries were always brief, so I said, "Sure. What's on your mind?"

She came across the office and sat down on the chair beside my desk. She looked unhappy. "It—it's a personal matter, Mr. Potter. I don't quite know what to do. I'd like your opinion."

I frowned. Helen had been with me for seven years. She was extremely competent. Also poised. The hectic pace of Price, Potter and Petacque didn't throw her, and she treated my erratic comings and goings without fuss. We got along beautifully. But her standards and mine didn't always mesh. She disapproved of any beverage stronger than Seven-Up and considered "Gosh darn it" an expletive, whereas in moments of stress it wasn't unusual for me to say, even in her presence, "Where the hell's the Scotch?" So we seldom exchanged personal opinions.

"O.K.," I said, guessing that she'd finally decided to invest some of her savings. Although she worked for a stockbrokerage firm and spent five days a week in an atmosphere that fluctuated with every move of the financial indexes, she didn't, as far as I knew, own a single share of any company.

My guess was wrong, however. Helen clasped her hands tightly in her lap and said, "You see, Mr. Potter, it's a moral decision. I want to—I think I should—intervene in someone's life, but I'm not sure it's wise."

I clasped my hands too. I didn't like the way the conversation was starting out. "Generally," I said, "it isn't."

She nodded. Her expression went from unhappy to very unhappy. "I tend to agree with you. In this case, though, it's someone I care a great deal about, and I'm terribly uneasy. Terribly."

"Andrea?"

Helen nodded.

Andrea Doyle was her one living relative and the only person about whom she'd ever spoken freely to me. She'd helped raise the girl and put her through school, and Andrea was a source of pride and pleasure to her. As, it seemed to me, she would be to anyone. I'd only met her a few times, when she'd come to the office to pick Helen up, but I liked her immensely. Pretty, bright, cheerful—she lit up a room.

"You've had experience with private detectives, Mr. Potter," Helen said. "I want to know if you think they're—well, effective."

"Effective?" I was astonished. I'd only had dealings with one private detective, a Chicago investigator named Philip Quick, and my dealings with him had been limited. But Helen had always wrinkled her nose whenever his name was mentioned, and she'd referred to him as "that person," even though she'd never met him. "I don't understand."

"I mean, do they do what you want them to, and how much do you have to pay them?"

"But, Helen—why?"

She unclasped her hands, but immediately clasped them again. "Andrea's getting married."

"My best wishes! I'm delighted for her!"

Helen's face showed no joy. "On the twenty-first of this month. And I thought that Mr. Quick might be . . . available."

"Available? What for?"

She looked away.

I felt a pang of sympathy. She was a proud woman. This couldn't be easy for her. "Suppose you just relax, Helen, and tell me what it's all about."

She didn't relax. Instead, she stiffened. "I want somebody to investigate those people, Mr. Potter."

"Which people?"

Her eyes came back to mine. "Robert McDonald and his father."

"Robert McDonald's the man Andrea's going to marry?"

Helen inclined her head.

"And you don't like him?"

"Well . . ."

I studied her. Questions surfaced. An able secretary she certainly was. Composure she definitely had. A good appearance she always made. But what else was in this package that for seven years had been sitting in the office adjoining mine without my really examining it? In her youth she must have been quite attractive, yet she'd never married. She'd had several brothers and sisters, but only one of them—Andrea's father—had lived past the age of twenty-one. She occasionally spoke of having been to a play or concert, but not of having been to it with anybody. She kept up with what was going on in the world, but took a dim view of most of it.

She had a keen sense of responsibility—that much I knew. She took things seriously. In addition, she was generous, yet inflexible; narrow-minded, yet kindly; pleasant, yet aloof.

Helen Doyle, I suddenly realized, was just like everyone else I knew—a stack of contradictions. Even her manner was contradictory: both maternal and pinched.

Most of the time she was probably lonely. And now her loneliness was going to deepen, for she was losing the one person in the world to whom she felt a close attachment. Losing her, moreover, to a man who undoubtedly had a normal assortment of

3

what Helen considered masculine vices.

"It's not Bob I object to," she said presently. "It's his father."

"Oh?"

"I mean, Bob is nice enough. He's good-looking and considerate and he has prospects—he's working on his Ph.D. But, as the saying goes, the apple doesn't fall far from the tree."

"And his father is someone you don't approve of?"

"No, I don't, Mr. Potter. There's something about James McDonald that frightens me."

"Frightens you?"

"He never smiles."

"Come now, Helen."

"I mean it, Mr. Potter. I met him for the first time the other night and . . . I want someone to investigate those people."

A good-looking, considerate young man with prospects, I thought. Andrea is fortunate. "You'd be making a mistake," I said firmly. "The fact that people don't smile, or that we don't like them, doesn't entitle us to go around having them investigated."

"But—"

"There are no buts, Helen. It's wrong to pry. Yes, I've used Philip Quick on several occasions, but that was business, and what you're talking about isn't."

"Nevertheless—"

"No, Helen. You'd be making a mistake." I glanced at my watch again. Carol's boss had given her two tickets for a benefit performance by the ballet, and I'd promised to take her to dinner first. "Definitely." I stood up.

"You wouldn't like him either," Helen persisted. "He hates rich people."

"Andrea's prospective father-in-law?"

Helen nodded. "Simply hates them."

"I don't like all rich people myself." I smiled. "I only like the nice ones. I wish I had more time, Helen, but I'm supposed to meet Miss Fox and I'm late."

Reluctantly, Helen rose. "Well, thank you, Mr. Potter. I appreciate your giving me your advice. But James McDonald—"

"Give him a chance. You may end up liking him." I went to the closet and got my coat. "The twenty-first is only a couple of weeks from now."

"I know. They've been going together for a long time, but I didn't know they were serious. Andrea just broke the news to me the other day. It's going to be a small wedding, at my apartment, and I have hardly any time to get ready, and I want to have squabs."

"Squabs are nice." I headed for the door.

Helen followed me and turned out the light. "So you think—?"

"Yes. Definitely a mistake. And look at it this way: you won't be losing a niece, you'll be gaining a nephew."

Helen heaved a shuddering sigh.

I patted her arm and hurried down the corridor.

2

Carol took a sip of coffee and put down the cup. "It *would* be nice," she said wistfully.

"What would?" We'd been talking about any number of things, and I didn't know which she was referring to.

"If you did something for them."

I got the drift. "For Helen's niece and her fiancé?"

"Yes."

I'd told her about the conversation with Helen that had delayed me. She didn't know any of the people involved—to her Helen was simply a voice on the telephone, one that said, all too often, "Mr. Potter's in conference." But in spite of that, Carol had been interested. To her, marriage was an irresistible topic.

"I'm planning to," I said. "I'm going to buy them a bond."

"Besides that, I mean. After all, the woman's been your secretary for years."

I looked at her. Both of us were merely repeating what we'd said at the beginning of the meal. "Like what?"

"I don't know. Something personal." Carol was gazing at the coffee cup with a slight frown, as if considering various possibilities.

I wondered whether it was really Andrea Doyle she was thinking about or herself. And I began to feel uncomfortable.

At one time Carol and I had spent a lot of time analyzing our relationship, but we no longer did. For one thing, Carol had started going to a psychoanalyst, and relationships were his specialty. For another, we'd decided to let well enough alone. Or at least I had. As relationships go, it seemed to me, ours was nothing spectacular, but it was better than what a lot of couples had. And, given our particular deficiencies, it was the best we could do.

We weren't married and were reasonably certain that we never would get married. Carol had her apartment, on Fifth Avenue near Ninth Street, and I had my house, two blocks away, on West Eleventh, near Fifth. She had her work, and I had mine. When things were going well between us, which was about two-thirds of the time, she spent weekends at my place, and an occasional night in the middle of the week, as well. We liked each other and enjoyed being together. The essential ingredient for marriage was lacking, however. We weren't in love.

At times we came close. We reached the border. But we weren't able to cross it. Sex and love, Carol pointed out, were two different things; we had the former but not the latter. And I had to agree. It wasn't her fault, and it wasn't mine. In that respect, we were well matched. Neither of us was capable of total surrender.

Basically, I was satisfied. But every now and then Carol would decide that we were at a dead end and should break up, and there would be nothing I could do to change her mind. But our separations never lasted, because when we were apart we missed each other.

Still, getting married and having children were never far from the surface of Carol's mind, and I knew it. I was therefore sorry that I'd told her about Andrea, and by way of changing the subject I said, "We have to hurry. The curtain's in twenty minutes."

Carol appeared not to have heard me. She continued to gaze at the coffee cup. Suddenly her eyes brightened. "I know! A small dinner party. It doesn't have to be elaborate. I'll do the cooking."

I was amazed. Carol was an excellent cook, but she hardly ever volunteered. "You will?"

"I'll do a chicken casserole. Or do you think pepper steak?"

7

"It really isn't necessary." I signaled the waiter for the check.

"Of course it isn't necessary. But it would be nice. After all—"

"—the woman's been my secretary for years."

"Well, she has."

The waiter brought the check, and I gave him my American Express card. Carol went on with the proposed menu. Rice and the watercress-and-mushroom salad I liked so much and of course a wedding cake.

The waiter returned with the receipt, and I signed it. I started to get up.

"I'm not finished," Carol said. And she wasn't. Not with her coffee, or with the party plans. I sat down again.

She concluded with a "What do you think?"

I thought it would be an unpleasant reminder to both of us. "We'll see," I said vaguely.

"Oh, for heaven's sake, Brock!" she exclaimed with irritation. Then she resigned herself. "Well, think about it and let me know. But I'm leaving on the twentieth, don't forget."

With that, we began to talk about my lack of Christmas plans. Carol was going to Minneapolis, to be with her family over the holidays. We'd agreed that it wouldn't be a good idea for me to go with her, because her parents wouldn't understand. In the past, when I hadn't spent Christmas with her, I'd spent it with one of my partners—Mark Price or Tom Petacque. But this year the Prices were going to Palm Beach, where Mark's in-laws had a house, and Tom was taking his wife and son to Sugar Bush to ski. And everyone else in my little realm had plans of one sort or another that didn't include me. I had nothing lined up.

"What about Brian?" Carol suggested, in the taxi. Brian Barth was one of my researchers, and unattached.

"He said something about going down to Virginia to see his mother."

"But if he doesn't?"

I shrugged. "Something'll turn up."

We arrived at the theater three minutes before curtain time and hurried through the lobby. We were just settling into our seats when the house lights dimmed.

"Which ballet are they doing?" I whispered to Carol.

"I've forgotten," she whispered back.

It turned out to be *Sleeping Beauty*.

And the best part of *Sleeping Beauty* is the wedding scene.

"Wasn't it lovely?" Carol said, on the way out. "I'm so glad we came."

I stopped humming long enough to say that I was too.

"Imagine a wedding like *that!*"

I stopped humming again, but this time I said nothing.

Carol took my arm. "I still wish you'd do something for Helen's niece."

Silently I blamed Tschaikowsky. But then I told myself that it wasn't really his fault. Carol would have persisted even if we hadn't seen the ballet. She simply wanted, vicariously, to be a prospective bride.

I looked at her, and something inside of me gave way. If it would make her happy, why not? And Helen would appreciate the gesture. Furthermore, it would be nice to see Andrea again and to meet the man she was going to marry. "Well," I said tentatively.

Carol gave my arm a squeeze.

"If you don't mind the work."

She drew closer to me.

"Pepper steak would be best, I think."

She completely encircled my arm. "So do I," she said softly.

3

Every Monday morning the research department has a staff meeting, at which we exchange the information we've picked up during the preceding week and discuss the action of the market as a whole. The facts and opinions that come out of the staff meeting form the basis of the market letter I send to our customers on Tuesday afternoon. So at the beginning of the week I'm always at the office, and the traveling that I do—some 100,000 miles a year—is done on Wednesdays, Thursdays and Fridays.

But since Thanksgiving everything had been different. For I'd decided that we should provide our customers with an additional service: an annual forecast. It would include our predictions of trends in interest rates, Gross National Product, capital spending—the whole bit. A special section would be devoted to specific industries and companies; we would predict which industries would outperform the averages, and which companies within those industries. The whole thing would be printed rather than photocopied, and we would mail it on the last business day of the year.

Back in March, when I'd first proposed doing the forecast, Tom and Mark had been skeptical. My staff wasn't big enough, Tom had said. And Mark had agreed with him, adding that an annual forecast wasn't necessary—we made forecasts every week. But I'd talked them into it.

Each of us—Tom, Mark and I—owns one third of Price, Potter and Petacque, a brokerage firm that sells stocks and bonds to large purchasers like mutual funds and banks. Since we don't deal with the general public, we're able to operate with relatively few employees. As we see it, that's an advantage. There's no dead weight. We can move fast. And we do move fast. Even our competitors acknowledge that we're hard to keep up with.

Our own roles in the company haven't changed since the day we started in business. Tom is in charge of sales. Mark handles the financing and runs the office. I'm chief securities analyst and head of the research department. Each of us has the final say over the day-to-day operations of his own bailiwick, but we make major decisions as a team.

We often disagree, and sometimes our disagreements are sharp. But we never really fight, because, no matter how much we may differ on an issue, we differ from a solid base of respect and affection. Tom and Mark are not only my partners, they're also my best friends. Tom and I have been close since long before Price, Potter and Petacque was in existence. And while we originally included Mark in the partnership not because we liked him but because he was a multimillionaire and we needed money, we soon came to appreciate him for what he is—an oddball, but an oddball with a brilliant mind, total dedication to the company and a rare sense of decency.

The researchers themselves, as I'd anticipated, were wildly enthusiastic about the forecast. For nine months they'd been talking about it and acting like a bunch of squirrels—burying morsels to be dug up later.

The research staff is made up of five people, aside from myself: Irving Silvers, Joe Rothland, George Cole, Harriet Jensen and Brian Barth. Irving is my chief honcho; he supervises the other four when I'm not around and occasionally writes the Tuesday letter from my notes. All five of them are scrappy and competitive, so highly motivated that at times it's hard for me to restrain them.

11

Throughout the spring, summer and fall they'd been popping into my office at odd moments with ideas that they thought would make the forecast better. I'd finally had to tell them that if we incorporated all their suggestions, Price, Potter and Petacque's annual forecast would have more pages than the *Encyclopaedia Britannica*. And now that we were into the actual writing, they realized that, even within the limits I'd set, it was a tremendous undertaking. More time-consuming than any of us, myself included, had imagined. I was beginning to feel that Tom and Mark were right—a mere six people couldn't do it.

The one thing in our favor was the fact that it was December and we didn't have much else to do. Tom's department was busy. The funds, as always, were trying to get in as good shape as possible by the end of the fiscal year, and the salesmen were on the telephones constantly. But the researchers, if they hadn't been working on the forecast, would have been twiddling their thumbs. The people they normally called on for information didn't want to be bothered during the month of December; they were preoccupied with office parties, their kids' school vacations and trips to the Caribbean. It was a bad time to find out what was going on behind the scenes; and frequently, during the holiday season, not much did go on behind the scenes.

So instead of meeting only on Mondays, the research department was meeting every day, and segments of it were getting together, usually in my office, even oftener. The traditional bickering over who should cover which companies had stopped. Now everyone was bickering over stenographic help, of which there wasn't enough to go around.

And it was a minor dispute over the services of a stenographer that caused the outburst, on the morning after the ballet, which tore the entire department to pieces.

I should have realized that pressure was building. The researchers traveled as much as I did. They weren't accustomed to being together five days a week. Irving had his own office and his own secretary, but the other four shared an office and had to make do with such assistance as they could get from the two young women who made up what we called our secretarial pool. The office was adequate for four people who were rarely in it at the same time, but it was too small for the use they were currently giving it. Furthermore, Sylvia Klein and Norma Calder—the pool—had been hired not because they were skilled but because they were willing to work for what Mark was willing to pay. Neither of them was capable of doing anything more difficult than eating lunch. Norma couldn't even take dictation. I'd spoken to Mark about hiring a couple of good stenographers, but he hadn't made any move in that direction, and I didn't think he would. Although he's worth maybe fifteen million dollars and stands to inherit another fifteen or twenty million when his father dies, Mark can best be described by an expression my mother used to use: tight as Dick's hatband.

Harriet had requested a meeting with me, and I'd scheduled it for ten o'clock that morning. She was working on one of the key sections of the forecast, the balance of payments. She wanted my opinion, she'd said. Later I'd asked Irving and Brian to sit in. Irving is our steel and automotive expert, and Brian's specialties are chemicals and oil. Finally, as an afterthought, I'd included Joe. He reports on the utilities and some of the conglomerates, and a number of the conglomerates he follows have extensive foreign interests.

The meeting got off to a good start, with Harriet passing around a few graphs. She'd been drawing graphs for months, and these, she claimed, were the culmination of her efforts.

But almost immediately Irving said that, while they were nice graphs, he didn't agree with what they showed. The balance of payments wasn't going to be that bad, because his study of the steel and automotive industries pointed to declining imports of those items due to higher foreign labor costs.

I sensed that I'd walked into a trap—that Harriet and Irving had already discussed the matter and Harriet had asked for the meeting with me in the hope that I'd support her findings. By then it was too late, however. Heated words were being traded, with Joe and Brian chiming in. Joe said that just yesterday he'd met Louis Glass having drinks in a bar on Third Avenue with another man, and Glass also felt that foreign labor costs were in for a rise. She didn't give a damn what Louis Glass said, Harriet retorted. Louis Glass was one of the smartest men in the entire business community, Irving proclaimed. The hell he was, Brian countered, and what difference did that make anyway?

The meeting quickly degenerated into a free-for-all. We'd had acrimonious meetings before, but this one reached the level of personal insult, with the nastiest remarks being exchanged not between Harriet and Irving but between Harriet and Joe. I couldn't figure out what was going on between those two, but I decided that it didn't matter—the meeting had to end.

"We're getting out of control," I said.

No one paid any attention.

I raised my voice. "Cool it."

The dispute continued.

"Shut up, damn it!"

There was silence.

"We're getting out of control," I repeated, in a more moderate tone. "Let's break this up for now. We'll get together again tomorrow, after everyone's had a chance to simmer down."

The four of them filed sullenly out of my office.

I took a couple of deep breaths and summoned Helen. I wanted to dictate some thoughts I had on one of the sections which I was contributing to the forecast: the anticipated price-earnings ratio for industrial stocks in general.

Notebook in hand, Helen settled herself in the chair beside my desk.

"Price-earnings ratio," I began, staring at the blotter. Then I looked up. "Oh, and by the way, Helen, I'd like to do something for Andrea and her fiancé before the wedding. I thought perhaps I'd have them and you and one or two other people over for dinner. Do you think they'd enjoy that?"

Helen's "Good morning, Mr. Potter" had been cooler than usual, and I'd guessed that she was embarrassed by what she'd said the evening before. But now she thawed. In fact, she almost melted. "Why, Mr. Potter, that would be lovely! I'm sure they would."

"Great. How about this coming Sunday?"

"I'm not sure of their plans, but I think it will be all right. We aren't making much of a fuss, so there isn't a lot of entertaining—parties and showers and all that. Yes, Sunday will probably be just fine."

"I'll count on it, then, unless you tell me otherwise. Miss Fox will be there, and you, and . . . perhaps Andrea's fiancé's father would like to come?"

Helen's smile faded. "I presume so. And, if you wouldn't mind, Bob's aunt and uncle. They're the only other family he has. They raised him."

"Glad to have them, if they can make it."

"I'll ask." Her smile returned. "Really, Mr. Potter, it's awfully nice of you."

I started to say I hoped she'd definitely given up the notion of hiring a detective, but decided that it would be tactless. I simply said, "I'm looking forward to meeting the lucky man," mentally thanked Carol for her bright idea and went back to the price-earnings ratio.

At twelve thirty I finished dictating and went down to the coffee shop on the ground floor for a quick lunch. But the quick lunch took longer than I'd expected, because I had to stand in line for a seat at the counter, and then, as I was finishing my coffee, Mark sat down on the stool next to mine and wanted to talk.

He'd just finished signing the bonus checks, he said, and while signing them he'd had an inspiration. Instead of sending Christmas cards with the checks, we would send letters. He couldn't understand why the idea hadn't occurred to him before—there would be quite a saving.

"How much do the bonus checks add up to?" I asked.

"A hundred and twenty-eight thousand nine hundred and fifty-three dollars."

"And how much would we save on the cards?"

"Almost twenty dollars."

I gave him a look.

"Well, twenty dollars is twenty dollars, Brock."

"No, it isn't. It's ten dollars. Uncle Sam pays half."

15

"But the stationery is already paid for."

"Let's not worry about that. We'll use it up."

We were still discussing the matter when we got back to the office.

And as we were crossing the reception foyer, the outburst occurred.

4

A man bellowed, "God damn you!" His voice was so full of rage that I couldn't identify it.

A woman screeched, "Don't you dare!" The woman sounded like Harriet.

Sylvia Klein scurried out of the researchers' office, clutching her notebook, and took refuge in the ladies' room.

Another man—Brian, I thought—said loudly, "Give them back."

I took off down the corridor to see what the trouble was. But just as I got to the researchers' office, Joe came charging out and collided with me. His face was the color of claret, and he had a sheaf of papers in his hand.

The impact sent me staggering against Mark, who had followed in my wake.

"What's the meaning of this?" Mark demanded of Joe.

At that moment Harriet raced out of the office and grabbed Joe's sleeve. "Give me my graphs!"

Joe yanked his arm, and Harriet spun against the wall.

Brian barged into the corridor. "Give her her graphs!"

Joe raised his arm as if to swing at Brian. Mark stepped between them.

George Cole appeared. "Stay out of it, Brian!"

"I'm going to slap your face!" Harriet shrieked at Joe.

Irving emerged from his office, across the corridor, and yelled, "Hey!"

"Stop this!" I shouted, moving into the thick of things.

Harriet ignored me and flung herself at Joe. George caught her by the shoulders and pulled her back. Ward Carlton, Tom's second-in-command, came out of the salesmen's office and halted abruptly, some yards away.

"Stop this!" I shouted again.

Brian thrust Mark aside and snatched at the graphs. Joe gave him a push, then wadded up the graphs, threw them at Harriet's feet and stormed down the corridor to the reception foyer and disappeared.

The rest of us just stood there.

Finally Harriet knelt, picked up the papers and, without a word, returned to her desk. Brian went with her.

I took George's arm. "I want to talk to you," I said, and led him into my office.

Mark came with us. Irving too.

"O.K.," I said to George, closing the door, "suppose you tell me what the hell's going on around here."

Joe had given Sylvia some work to do, George explained, but before Sylvia had had a chance to complete it, Harriet had taken her off the job. Harriet had given Sylvia some dictation earlier and felt that what she'd dictated should be typed first. Joe, as far as George could determine, hadn't known about Harriet's dictation and felt that in any case Harriet should have consulted him. One word had led to another, and tempers had flared.

"A bunch of children," Mark observed.

George said nothing, but a spot of color appeared in each cheek, which was as close as George ever came to showing anger. He was a tall, ascetic-looking man who gave the impression of having been born centuries too late for his true vocation—illuminating manuscripts in a Benedictine monastery.

"Not really," Irving said, and explained that Sylvia and Norma simply couldn't handle all that was being thrust on them. He'd had to lend the other researchers his secretary from time to time, even though he needed her himself.

"And I've had to lend Helen," I added.

"Lack of proper organization," Mark said.

"The hell it is," I snapped. "I've been telling you those girls are no good."

"Norma can't even take dictation," Irving said.

"And Sylvia can't count past ten without taking off her shoes," George put in. It wasn't just today, he went on; trouble had been brewing for over a week. Not just between Harriet and Joe, but among all of them. And this noon Harriet had been in a particularly bad mood.

"My fault," Irving murmured.

"Not at all," I said. "Mark's fault."

"I've been saying all along that an annual forecast is unnecessary," Mark reminded us.

"We should have been doing it for years," Irving said. "Everyone else does."

"You're damn right," I said, beginning to get angry. "If Mark weren't so—" I checked myself. I didn't want to embarrass Mark. But he got the idea. "Very well," he said stiffly, "I'll see what I can do." He left the office.

I felt better. Once Mark realized that a particular expense was necessary, he incurred it. Promptly. But I was still aggravated. "You should have let me know that things were this bad," I told Irving.

"Honestly, Brock, I didn't think they were," he replied.

"O.K., O.K.," I said, "let's forget it. Back to work, you two."

They went back to work, and so did I. But I found it hard to concentrate. I was genuinely upset. The one thing I'd always harped on was team spirit. Regardless of how capable an individual was, I maintained, he was of no value to an organization if he couldn't subordinate his interests to those of the organization itself. I didn't want stars; I wanted a championship department.

And I thought I'd succeeded. The researchers did have team spirit. They quibbled over everything, but when the chips were down, they went to bat for one another. If one of them had a problem, the others helped. Sometimes it seemed to me there was actually too much team spirit, for when I criticized one, all of them banded together against me. But I preferred it that way.

And on those occasions when I was the one with the problem, they rallied round like embattled warriors defending their last outpost.

Within the group, there were alliances. George and Joe were friends from way back, and their wives were friendly too. Brian and Harriet, perhaps because they were younger, also tended to stick together. At one time Irving and Brian had disliked each other intensely. They'd got over their dislike, but they were still chary of each other. Irving and Harriet, on the other hand, got along very well.

In addition to being bright and aggressive, all of them were remarkably tenacious. They got what they went after. Yet, to outsiders, none of them came on very strong. Irving, who was no more than five feet five inches tall and whose top weight was a hundred and twenty pounds, appeared to be about as threatening as a bantam rooster. But he had the instincts of a falcon. George, although he looked like a simple monk, had more in common with a Richelieu. Joe, who'd been a first-string offensive tackle at college and still had the physique of one, seemed to the unwary like a big, dumb ox, but his IQ almost matched his weight. Harriet, a beautiful, petite blonde who attracted men of all sorts, enjoyed men most as rivals. She could match wits with the best of them, although they seldom realized that, at first. As for Brian—well, I called him my piranha. A plump, smooth-skinned Virginian with innocent blue eyes and a deferential manner, he seemed utterly without defenses. But he was capable of absolutely obliterating an opponent, and I'd seen him do it.

There was really nothing to worry about, I assured myself. Individually and as a group, the members of the team had demonstrated deep loyalty to me and to one another. Moreover, they had a great deal in common and liked their jobs. They were simply out of sorts today. By tomorrow everything would have blown over.

But when I thought back to the scene in the corridor, I wasn't so sure.

And, as it turned out, I did have something to worry about.

5

The next day was Friday, and at nine thirty I called another meeting. This time I included George. I wanted to resolve the balance-of-payments issue, if we could, and to remind everyone that there were only eight days left before the final, wrap-up meeting. But mainly I wanted to pour oil on the department's troubled waters.

My first two objectives were reached. Harriet agreed to adjust her figures and her graphs. And there appeared to be no problem as far as the deadline was concerned.

I didn't succeed in calming the waters, however. Everyone was excessively polite, but directed his remarks solely to me. The members of the department, aside from Irving, wouldn't speak to, or even look at, one another. After a while I decided to give one of my we're-a-family pep talks, and gave it. But nothing changed.

The meeting ended after only thirty-five minutes.

At eleven o'clock Mark came into my office to tell me that he'd spoken to an employment agency and on Monday morning the pool would have a third girl. I thanked him.

No sooner had Mark left than George came in. He wanted to know whether I'd have lunch with him. Just the two of us, he said. His expression was unusually grave. I said that I would, and he suggested an out-of-the-way restaurant that none of us ever went to. He also suggested that we go there separately. So at a quarter past twelve I made a quiet exit.

George was already at the restaurant when I arrived. He still looked grave. I didn't ask him what was on his mind. I waited.

The wait was short. He began as soon as we were seated. "I'm about to do something I don't make a practice of doing," he said. "Betray a confidence."

"Joe's?"

He nodded. "In his own best interest." He stopped, struggled with himself, then went on. "He didn't come back yesterday afternoon, except to pick up his coat. He went to see Louis Glass."

I raised an eyebrow.

"Glass offered him a job."

I wasn't surprised. The members of the research department were always receiving job offers. Some of them I knew about; others, I supposed, I didn't. That was the way of the world. But in the state of mind Joe had been in . . . "You think he'll take it?"

"I think he might."

The waiter came for our drink orders. We gave them to him.

Louis Glass had been trying for some time to hire Joe, George explained. Interamerican Marine, of which Glass was president, had several economists on the payroll; he wanted to put Joe in charge of them. "I think that's just a come-on, though," George concluded. "Glass is always hungry for information about other companies. He'll squeeze all he can out of Joe, then toss him overboard."

A typical George Cole deduction, I thought. And one hundred percent correct. "That would be a shame," I said.

"Yes, it would."

Neither of us spoke again until after the drinks had been served. Then George gave me a detailed account of the friction that had been growing in the department. There was no major issue; all of the causes were petty. A window that one wanted open and another wanted closed. A telephone conversation involving one member of the department which interfered with

22

another's attempt to concentrate. And, above all, conflicting needs for stenographic help.

The picture became unmistakably clear. Four fierce competitors, egged on by me, had been trying to excel at a new task and had got in one another's way. Now they were enemies.

I told George that I'd see what I could do to straighten things out; I didn't want Joe to quit, or any of the team to remain at odds. But as we walked back to the office after lunch, I wasn't sure that the damage was repairable. Time healed some wounds, but not all; and small wounds could lead to deadly infections.

Joe first, I decided. And with the decision came an idea.

At two thirty I called him into my office to discuss the over-all capital needs of the utilities companies, and I jotted down some of his ideas. Then, as he was leaving, I said offhandedly, "Oh, and by the way, I'm giving a small dinner party Sunday night for Helen's niece, who's getting married. I'm not having any of the other members of the department, but I'd like you and your wife to join us, if you can."

He looked surprised and pleased. He said that he didn't think his wife would be able to come—she'd been in bed for the past three days with a strep throat—but he himself would be delighted.

"Good," I said with enthusiasm. "Seven o'clock, at my house."

Irving would understand, I thought. So would George. Brian and Harriet would be resentful, but I could deal with them later.

Joe left my office smiling.

6

On Saturday Carol and I went grocery shopping in the morning, then spent a lazy afternoon. After dinner I did some writing on another of the sections I was contributing to the forecast—the insurance industry—while Carol listened to my old recording of *La Traviata* and gave herself a manicure and pedicure.

On Sunday we slept late, but by noon Carol was already in the kitchen, preparing the vegetables. I set the table while she did her fancy slicing and chopping, but when she came into the dining room to inspect my work she didn't like it and did it over again. I didn't have the touch, she said. It seemed to me that she was going to more trouble than was necessary, and I said so; but Carol pointed out that we were entertaining a couple that was Getting Married and that these days not all couples Got Married—those who did were Special. Her implication was plain enough: such couples, unlike ourselves, were to be envied.

By one thirty she was beginning to show signs of irritability. She wished I'd quit watching her and she wished I'd get Tiger out of the kitchen. Tiger is my dog, and he was underfoot. So I took him for a walk.

Tiger isn't a large dog. He's a toy poodle, not quite eight inches high. People who see us on the street at opposite ends of a leash are inclined to snicker. We don't look right for each other. But actually we are. Both of us like to move around a lot, are friendly until given cause not to be, and have more than average curiosity.

I hadn't chosen him. As a puppy he'd been foisted on me by Brian, who'd felt that because he was away so much he couldn't take care of him properly. Since I had a housekeeper five days a week who could puppy-sit during my absences, I'd agreed to give him a home.

But how Tiger had come into my life was no longer important. He was there, and I was fond of him, and he returned my affection. In fact, he seemed to think of himself not as my dog but as my kid brother. I probably encouraged him in this by sometimes telling him what was on my mind. And now, as we waited at the corner of Fifth Avenue and Ninth Street for the light to change, I found myself doing it again.

"Carol doesn't know it," I said, "but Joe is more important than Helen."

Tiger regarded me with what I interpreted as agreement.

The heavy-set man who was standing beside me nudged the woman beside him and pointed at us.

The light changed. We crossed Ninth Street.

Carol was annoyed with me for inviting Joe. He was part of neither the bride's family nor the groom's, she'd said, and he didn't belong. I hadn't told her about the intradepartmental crisis and didn't intend to. I'd merely told her that Joe's wife was sick, and that in any event it was too late to retract the invitation. Which had prompted Carol to call me insensitive.

Tiger paused to sniff a piece of chewing gum that someone had discarded.

"Everything will work out," I said hopefully.

Tiger wagged his tail.

We continued toward Washington Square.

And, as it happened, Joe was the one who made the party a success.

He did it by attaching himself to James McDonald and keeping him absorbed, so that the rest of us could have a good time.

My initial reaction to James McDonald was negative. For

Helen had been right—he was a man who didn't smile. A man who didn't have much to say, either.

I judged him to be in his middle to late fifties. He was attractive in a saturnine way, with dark, wavy hair, high cheekbones and brooding black eyes. As a young man, I guessed, he'd been quite handsome. But his expression was so unwaveringly grim that I couldn't help wondering whether he was angry about something.

The entire family arrived together—Helen, Andrea, the two McDonalds and Dick and Rosemary Knight, the uncle and aunt. I sensed immediately that this was a party that could go either way, and made the first round of drinks a stiff one. For everybody but Helen, that is. "Just a little ginger ale," was all she wanted. But the elder McDonald downed his three-ounce shot as if it were a mere dram, and I began to worry. Helen might turn out to be a wet blanket, and Andrea's prospective father-in-law was liable to pass out before Carol could get dinner on the table. But then Joe showed up, and things took a turn for the better.

The Knights were a nice couple. Helen had introduced him as Dr. Knight, but he explained that he wasn't a medical doctor—he was a Doctor of English Letters and, as he put it, one of the survivors in the English department at City College. His survival, he added, was really a miracle, because his specialty was Shakespeare, and Shakespeare, like the Age of Johnson, was a highly overcrowded field. His wife, Rosemary, was a pretty woman with no apparent interest in English literature but a keen appreciation of her husband's wit and an obvious soft spot for her nephew. She was James McDonald's sister.

Carol came out of the kitchen long enough to get acquainted. She was pleasant to everyone, but there was no doubt that she was mainly interested in the bride- and groom-to-be. She could hardly take her eyes off them. At one point she even pulled me aside to exclaim, in an undertone, "Isn't he handsome!"

"She's not a bad dish either," I said.

To which Carol replied, with a grin, "If you like upturned noses and freckles."

They were indeed a stunning pair. Bob was tall and looked much as I imagined his father had at that age. The black-framed glasses he wore, instead of detracting from his appearance, enhanced it. He was soft-spoken and like his father in that his expression was serious. But, unlike his father, he did smile occasionally, and his smile indicated that there was another facet to his personality—a sense of mischief.

Andrea, in addition to the upturned nose and freckles, had gorgeous auburn hair, green eyes and extraordinary animation. I was even more drawn to her now than I'd been before.

The two of them were so clearly in love that I had to work at not being jealous. They were capable of a depth of feeling that I'd never experienced. But I didn't have time to dwell on the matter—I was too busy playing host.

I made the second round of drinks weaker. When I gave James McDonald his, he drank it as quickly as the first.

"Weather's turning cold," I said, trying to start a conversation with him.

He nodded.

"But then, it's that time of year."

He nodded again and regarded me with suspicion.

"I understand your son is working on his Ph.D."

"Yes."

"He and Andrea make a swell-looking couple."

"Yes."

I kept at it for a while, but eventually gave up. He simply wasn't a talker. I moved on to his son, with better results.

Bob admitted that he'd been influenced in his choice of career by his uncle: he hoped to be a professor of English. But he wasn't going to City College; he was going to Columbia. And he wasn't specializing in Shakespeare but in the eighteenth- and nineteenth-century poets. He was at the dissertation stage. His subject was William Blake. He was attempting to establish a relationship between the images in Blake's poetry and those in his engravings. "What I'm hoping to do," he explained, "is synthesize him."

"Why Blake?" I asked.

He gave me one of those mischievous smiles. "I like madmen."

I laughed and told him that if he liked madmen he ought to get a job in the securities business.

"Oh, no," Andrea said. "According to Aunt Helen, you're all

terribly sane. And terribly profit-minded. To you, everything is balance sheets."

"Come on, now," I said. "We're as crazy as everybody else."

"Who's as crazy as everybody else?" Dick Knight asked, joining us.

"Stockbrokers," I said.

"Impossible!" he exclaimed. "English professors have a monopoly on nuttiness."

I glanced around to see who needed a fresh drink. Except for Bob's father, no one did. And Bob's father seemed to be doing all right without it. Astonishingly enough, he'd begun to talk. With Joe, of all people. And he was looking less somber.

Rosemary went over to them, and James McDonald brightened even more. There was, I noted, a strong resemblance between him, his sister and his son. All three of them had the same bone structure and coloring.

Helen was sitting by herself, I saw. I approached her. "A little more ginger ale?" I offered.

She shook her head. Her eyes were on James McDonald. "If only he'd smile," she said in a low voice.

"He seems to be doing all right," I said. "He and Joe have taken to each other."

She sighed.

Carol reappeared and announced that dinner was ready.

And during dinner the unexpected happened. Helen got drunk.

Or almost drunk. High. For she consented to have a glass of wine in honor of the occasion, and one glass was all it took. Her voice rose, and she became the life of the party. She couldn't keep anything to herself. "Oh, dear," she cried repeatedly, "I do believe the wine is going to my head!" But that didn't stop her from nudging Dick Knight, who was seated next to her, and asking him whether he'd mind if she took off her shoes. And confiding loudly to him that she was wearing a new girdle which was even tighter than her shoes, and that she thought it was terrible that young women today wore so little underwear.

It wasn't what she said that was so funny, but the fact that she was the one who was saying it. And when she told a long, rambling anecdote about the choirmaster in the church she'd gone to as a girl, Andrea and Carol laughed so hard that they almost fell off their chairs. Because the choirmaster had been, in Helen's words, "an incurable feeler" who'd never passed up an opportunity to touch various parts of the sopranos' anatomies. For some reason, Helen recalled, he preferred sopranos to altos, and she herself was an alto. "But," she concluded, "it's not as if I didn't know what was going on."

"Too bad your voice wasn't a notch higher," Dick Knight observed, with a straight face.

"I know," Helen confessed. "I tried. I just couldn't get it up there."

Even James McDonald appeared to be amused. But for the most part he and Joe kept up the quiet discourse they'd begun before dinner, oblivious of the rest of us. Carol had seated them beside each other, and the arrangement couldn't have been better. They were having their own party within a party. And James McDonald was talking freely.

I couldn't hear what they were saying, but I was pleased that they'd hit it off. McDonald's eyes were brighter, and he was no longer radiating gloom. Watching him, I wondered why Helen had expressed such misgivings. It probably had to do with his drinking, I supposed. There was no doubt that he could put away a lot of booze. Yet the alcohol didn't seem to affect him. After two bourbons and twice as much wine as anyone else was having, he was still perfectly sober. Whereas Helen . . .

I smiled, and drank some more wine myself.

There was, I conceded, something odd about him. He was obviously ill at ease among strangers. Even now, talking with Joe, his posture was stiff. He didn't unbutton his coat while eating and he kept his left arm in his lap, self-consciously. Also, he was exceedingly careful when he lifted his fork, as if he was afraid that something might fall off. All in all, I thought, he was rather like a child at a grownups' party, trying not to make a mistake.

Can't relax, I decided. Afraid of disgracing the family.

In a way, I felt sorry for him.

Carol brought in the dessert. It was a surprise, even to me.

She'd bought a chocolate cake; but without my knowing it, she'd also bought a big white wedding bell with a white satin bow, and she'd put that on top.

"How lovely!" Helen exclaimed in a voice that could be heard a block away.

Andrea gave Carol a kiss.

I poured champagne. Everything was turning out great, I thought.

After dinner Helen suggested that we sing. When she was a girl, she said, people always sang at parties, and now they didn't anymore, and it was a shame. But I don't have a piano, so I put on some records, and instead of singing we danced. It wasn't easy, on the carpet, but we danced anyway. All except Joe and the elder McDonald, who went on a tour of the house to inspect my paintings. McDonald was interested in art, Joe explained; his wife had been something of a connoisseur.

At eleven o'clock Andrea began to yawn and couldn't stop. Then Helen too began to yawn. And by eleven thirty Joe was the only one who was left. He seemed to be in excellent spirits and in no hurry to go home. I was delighted. Without even mentioning Louis Glass, I felt, I'd counteracted the job offer.

"One for the road?" I suggested.

"Sure," Joe replied amiably.

So Carol, Joe and I had nightcaps.

"You were terrific," I told Carol.

She smiled. "I was, wasn't I?"

"Nice people," Joe commented.

"You and McDonald seemed to get along just fine," I said. "What were the two of you talking about all evening?"

Joe shrugged. "One thing and another. Mostly about the years he spent in Chicago."

"Chicago?"

"He lived there for a while. You know who he was married to? The granddaughter of Augustus Koberg."

"The Koberg Chemical Koberg?"

Joe nodded.

I was amazed. Koberg Chemical had once been a very large

company, and was still good-sized. "You mean Andrea's marrying into money?"

"Well, no," Joe said. "Not into money, but into the family." He paused. "Jim's mother-in-law, I gather, didn't approve of him."

"Well, money or not," Carol said, "they're a beautiful couple, and it's a good thing they're getting married."

"Yep," I agreed, "they sure are."

We finished our drinks, and Joe decided that it was time to leave.

I began collecting the glasses.

"Why don't you leave them for Louise?" Carol said. Louise is my housekeeper.

I shrugged.

"Let's have another drink."

I didn't really want another drink. "I ought to let Tiger out," I said. I'd locked him in a bedroom, but I knew he wasn't happy about being there.

"It won't kill him to stay put a little longer. I'd like another drink."

I gave in, and over drinks we rehashed the evening. "I can't get over the fact that Bob is Augustus Koberg's great-grandson," I said presently.

"Which means," Carol said, "that the baby will be Augustus Koberg's great-great-grandchild."

"Baby?"

"Couldn't you tell? Honestly! Men! Of course. Andrea's at least four months pregnant."

"Are you sure?" I hadn't noticed a thing.

"Positive."

"I wonder if Helen knows."

"I doubt it. A woman like that—I don't think Andrea will tell her until she has to. . . . It would be nice to have a baby, don't you think?"

"They'll have a good-looking kid, that's for sure."

"I'm not talking about them. I'm talking about us."

"A baby?"

Carol nodded.

"We're too old, for Christ's sake."

Carol turned pale. She put her glass down slowly, but even so she almost missed the table. "You may be, but I'm not."

"Come off it, Carol. You're thirty-five."

That did it. What had been a happy evening came to an unhappy end. For one word led to another, and in no time at all Carol threw the keys to my house at me and said she never wanted to see me again. What's more, she was in tears.

Suddenly I found myself staring at the door she'd slammed on her way out.

7

Helen, my paragon of virtue and undeviating rectitude, had a hangover. She didn't refer to it as such. She merely told me what a nice party I'd had and how much she appreciated it. But I noticed a glass of water on her desk, and at noon I caught her popping aspirin tablets. "A slight headache," she explained.

I didn't feel so hot either. On account of Carol.

There wasn't time, however, to dwell on Helen's distress or my own. In the morning I had the usual Monday staff meeting, even though, after all of our previous meetings, there wasn't much left to discuss. And in the afternoon I put together such notes as I could for the Tuesday letter, handled the mail and dealt with several tough questions put to me by customers and by our own salesmen.

The tension among the researchers seemed to have eased. Joe was back to normal, and so was George. Harriet's nose was still slightly out of joint, and Brian was frostier than I'd ever known him to be, but I thought I could bring them around.

Mark had eliminated the main irritant. No sooner had I got my coat off than he'd appeared in my office to introduce a young Filipino woman named Maria Magdalena Alvarez, the new addition to our stenographic pool.

All in all, it seemed to me, everything was under control.

At four o'clock Helen asked whether it would be all right if she left a few minutes early; she had a fitting for the dress she'd bought for the wedding. Then, she added, she was meeting Andrea for an early dinner, and the two of them were going back to Helen's apartment. Andrea had a friend who was a florist, and he was coming over to give them some ideas for flower arrangements. I told her she could leave whenever she wanted.

At a quarter to five I called Carol. The switchboard operator at her office, when I gave my name, informed me that Carol was out. I was sure that that wasn't true. Carol had said on Saturday that she intended to work late on Monday.

She'll get over it, I thought. But I wasn't certain.

After that, I spent some time studying the notes on the price-earnings ratio that Helen had typed. I began to wonder whether my estimate wasn't too low. It all depended on interest rates, I decided. And interest rates were Harriet's specialty—she reported on financial institutions. So I went looking for her, but I discovered that she wasn't around. The only one in the researchers' office was Brian. He was doing some computations on his pocket calculator.

"Has Harriet left for the day?" I asked.

"They all have," he replied without looking up. There was a distinct chill in his voice.

I guessed that he was angry because I'd invited Joe to my house but not him. "How late do you intend to work?" I asked.

"Until I'm finished."

"Well, I'm working late too. Why don't you have dinner with me?"

Brian continued to punch keys. "I'm not hungry yet."

"Neither am I. But when we do get hungry."

He shrugged.

"Come on," I said. "Unbend."

He gave me a startled glance.

I smiled and said, "Six thirty."

And at six thirty I returned, wearing my topcoat. "Ready?"

Brian was still working with the calculator. "I suppose." Grudgingly he put the calculator away.

"How about the Elephant and Castle?" I suggested as we

walked to the elevator.

"Never heard of it."

"It's on my street. We'll stop at my house first and have drinks." I was counting on Tiger to help me smooth the ruffled feathers.

Which was exactly what Tiger did. He was so delighted to see Brian and responded with such enthusiasm to the games Brian played with him that after a few minutes Brian forgot his hurt feelings. A couple of Scotches completed the process. By eight o'clock Brian was sitting on the floor of my den with a tuckered-out dog on his lap and an expression of good will on his face.

I was tempted to avoid any reference to the problem at the office, but decided that it would be better to clear the air. So toward the end of dinner I asked Brian what had been bugging him.

To my surprise, it wasn't what I'd thought. Brian had found out about the party, all right, but he didn't mind not having been invited. What bothered him was that he'd overheard Joe telling George that at my house he'd met someone named McDonald who was connected with Koberg Chemical. Brian considered chemicals to be his exclusive domain. He suspected me of going behind his back. If I wanted to know anything about Koberg, he felt, I should have asked him to find it out for me.

I set him straight. James McDonald was merely the father of the young man Andrea Doyle was going to marry, I explained. At one time he'd been Gus Koberg's son-in-law, but he was no longer associated with the company.

Brian was vastly relieved. Blushing—he blushes easily—he apologized for his suspicions. He added that he really didn't know much about Koberg; it wasn't one of the companies he followed.

"It isn't a company that anyone follows," I said. "It's yesterday's news."

Still blushing, he admitted that during the afternoon he'd spent a few minutes checking. Koberg's stock had recently been doing rather well, he'd learned. That, he'd thought, was why I'd become interested.

"What do you mean by 'rather well'?" I asked.

"The last trade was at six and an eighth."

"And prior to that?" I didn't follow the company either. It hadn't been listed in years.

"Between three and four. Since the beginning of time, practically. But for the past few months it's been climbing. Could one of the funds be stepping in?"

I considered. "Anything's possible, I suppose. It isn't likely, though. Nobody's recommended it, or even mentioned it, as far as I know."

Brian nodded and changed the subject. "M.M.'s a champ."

I looked at him. "M.M.?"

"Maria Magdalena. That's what we're calling her. If they ever decide to include a typing event in the Olympic Games, she'll win. She types faster than anyone I've ever seen."

"It's an ill wind . . ."

Brian smiled. "Sometimes."

I brought the conversation back to the McDonalds. I told him about Andrea's fiancé and his dissertation on Blake. Brian was interested. One of his brothers, he said, had done a paper on Blake. Brian had no full brothers or sisters, but he had a whole phalanx of half-brothers and -sisters and step-brothers and -sisters. I couldn't keep them all straight. I knew only that they ranged in age from six to twenty-six and that they kept Brian broke—he was always helping one or another of them through some financial crisis.

"Which brother is this?" I asked.

"Greg."

"The one who got the scholarship to Virginia Polytechnic?"

"No, that's Keith. He's majoring in biology. Greg's the one at William and Mary."

"More coffee?"

"Sure."

We drank coffee and talked about Brian's family until almost ten o'clock.

Brian walked me home. I invited him in for a nightcap, but he said he was tired, so I took some magazines up to my bedroom and settled down to read. I'd been so busy that I hadn't even looked at the last two issues of *Forbes* and *Barron's*.

The first article to catch my eye was one titled "Toward the Ionosphere." "Interamerican Marine Soars," the subhead stated, "as Louis Glass Pilots It into the Wild Blue Yonder."

I felt a twinge of annoyance. George was right, I thought; Glass would have wrung all the information he could from Joe and then discarded him. Glass had antennae out in all directions. He was a walking radar screen. Yet I couldn't condemn him; I too was always seeking information. And he was indeed piloting Interamerican Marine into the wild blue yonder. I'd recommended its stock twice in the past six months, and I intended to recommend it again; it was nowhere near its peak.

My mind wandered. Should I call Carol? She was certainly at home by now.

Carol. Christmas. Life in general.

What was it all about, really? How much was I getting back in relation to what I was putting in? Three-quarters of my waking hours were spent at work. More than three-quarters, in fact, for a good part of my eating, drinking and kibitzing was also business-related. I was past forty. Where was I going? True, I loved my work. I loved the people I worked with. My standard of living was far above average. Hell, my paintings alone were worth more than many people earned in a lifetime.

Why, then, did I sometimes have a feeling of emptiness? Why at this very moment, although I knew I'd put in a productive day, was I vaguely, naggingly depressed?

Because you're never satisfied, something said.

Because Christmas is coming and you have no place to go, said something else.

Because I'm just plain tired, I answered. What I need is a vacation.

But Tom and Mark had already made their plans. And someone had to mind the store.

I began to get sleepy. I moved the magazines to the bedside table and unbuttoned my shirt. Another day, another . . . how many dollars?

The ringing of the telephone jolted me.

Carol, I thought exultantly. She wants to make up.

I snatched the telephone from its cradle.

But the voice at the other end of the line wasn't Carol's. "Mr. Potter!" it cried. "Oh, Mr. Potter, please come right away! Something terrible's happened!"

The voice was so high-pitched, so hysterical, that I didn't recognize it. "Come where? Who is this?"

"It's me—Helen. Please come." She began to make strange sounds. I couldn't tell whether she was sobbing or gasping.

"Where are you, Helen? What's happened?"

The sounds continued. Finally Helen managed to say, "At a Hundred and Sixteenth Street and Broadway. Oh, please come, Mr. Potter. It's horrible."

"A Hundred and Sixteenth Street and Broadway? Helen, what—?"

"Please come, Mr. Potter. It's ghastly. Someone's killed Bob McDonald."

8

The taxi let me off on the east side of Broadway. I spotted Helen immediately. She was across the street, huddled against one of the telephone booths outside a Chock Full O'Nuts coffee shop, in what appeared to be a bizarre costume. There were a number of people at the intersection, waiting for the light to change, but no one was paying any attention to her.

Dodging cars, I hurried across Broadway and went up to her.

"Oh, Mr. Potter!" she moaned.

I put my arm around her, and she almost collapsed. She was shivering uncontrollably. She wasn't dressed for outdoors. The costume was a full-length housecoat and a red-and-black afghan, which she was holding around her like a shawl. On her feet she was wearing quilted pink house slippers and no stockings, and the hands that were clutching the afghan were also clutching a pocketbook and a large tapestry knitting bag.

I opened my topcoat and enfolded her in it, but she continued to shiver.

"It—it—it's around the c-c-corner," she stuttered. "Oh, Mr. P-Potter!"

"You're freezing, Helen. We've got to get you inside." I began to guide her down 116th Street. "Tell me what happened."

She tried, but she was so distraught that she didn't make sense. She kept repeating the same facts. Someone had shot him.

This friend of his had called her. She hadn't had change for the taxi driver—she'd had to give him a ten-dollar bill. She'd seen the body and she'd been afraid that she was going to faint. Poor Andrea. Poor, poor Andrea.

From time to time I glanced at her. My competent, poised Helen had completely come apart. She couldn't even tell me how to get to the building. All she could do was point with her pocketbook and stutter, "Th-th-that way."

But when we came to Claremont Avenue, I needed no further directions. Halfway down the block were a covey of police cars and a sizable crowd. I headed toward them.

One policeman had stationed himself in front of the entrance to the building and was keeping people out. He tried to keep us out too.

"B-b-but I'm Andrea's aunt," Helen protested. "And this is Mr. P-Potter."

The policeman eyed Helen's outfit.

"She's a relative of the victim's," I said.

He hesitated a moment, then let us pass.

There was also a crowd in the lobby. A man I took to be a plainclothes detective was questioning a young man in jeans and a pajama top. Helen nodded toward a door at the right, next to the automatic elevator, and drew closer to me. I led her over to it and knocked. A man opened it.

For an instant I had the same reaction Helen had had—a sudden lightheadedness and a feeling that I was going to black out. I leaned against the jamb of the door to support myself.

"Don't touch that!" the man said sharply.

I quickly moved my hand and swallowed a couple of times. I stared at the body on the floor.

I'd seen dead people before, but this was different. More horrible, somehow. Bob McDonald lay flat on his back, one arm flung out, his face covered with congealed blood which had streamed from his nose, his mouth and a terrible wound in his forehead. His eyes were open, and he seemed to be gazing at the ceiling. His glasses had come partly off and were hanging from one ear.

"My God," I said hoarsely, and at that moment a flashbulb exploded.

Helen uttered a cry.

The police photographer moved to a different spot.

Helen began to whimper.

The man who had opened the door took notice of her. Evidently he knew who she was, for he said, "Oh, it's you. She's next door. Apartment Three."

The police photographer took another picture. I steered Helen to the apartment next door and knocked.

No one answered, but a moment later we were joined by the young man in jeans and pajama top. He too recognized Helen. "She's inside," he said, opening the door and preceding us into the living room.

Andrea was slumped in a big, ragged chair, her head resting on one of its arms. She was motionless.

Dropping her knitting bag and pocketbook, Helen rushed over to her. "Oh, my poor darling!"

Andrea didn't move.

"I'm Dan Chapin," the young man said to me.

"Brock Potter," I replied.

He recognized the name. "You're the one she ran out to call."

I nodded.

He explained that his telephone had been disconnected because he hadn't paid his bill. Then he said, "The goddamn police. A bunch of fascists, all of them."

I gestured toward Andrea.

His expression softened. "I know. I have beer. I tried to get her to drink some, but she wouldn't."

"How about coffee?"

"That I have." He left the room, and presently I heard the banging of a pot.

I went to Andrea and tried to rouse her. She looked at me. She was dry-eyed, but her face was the color of skimmed milk. "He's dead," she said dully, and put her head back on the arm of the chair.

I felt utterly helpless.

41

Chapin returned, drinking from a can of beer. "Coffee'll be ready in a minute." He too seemed pale, and the hand that held the beer can was none too steady.

I took him aside. "What happened?" I asked in a low voice.

"How should *I* know?" he replied irritably. "I wasn't here." He had a part-time job in a cafeteria, he explained. He'd come home shortly after ten o'clock and had been getting ready for bed when he'd heard screams. He'd rushed out and found Andrea standing in the doorway of McDonald's apartment and, beyond her, the body.

"Christ!" he exclaimed, and took a quick swig of beer. "Christ, it was *awful*. And he was such a damn nice guy."

"Yes, he was. What do the police say?"

"The police! A bunch of fascists is what they are." He drank some more beer. He'd called the police from McDonald's apartment, he continued, then brought Andrea into his own apartment. She'd been in a state of shock. He'd thought someone ought to come and help him with her. He'd got her to give him Helen's name and telephone number. By that time other neighbors had congregated in the lobby. Iverson, the history instructor, had been among them. Iverson lived on the second floor. Chapin had called Helen from Iverson's apartment. She'd arrived within twenty minutes, not long after the police, but she'd been of no use. All she'd done was hyperventilate and talk about Mr. Potter. Finally she'd rushed out to find a telephone. "Maybe *you'd* like a beer," Chapin concluded.

I shook my head. "But I'll have some coffee."

He went into the kitchen and returned a moment later with two cracked mugs of steaming coffee. He gave them to me. I put one on a table and took the other over to Andrea.

I was still trying to get her to take the first sip when there was a knock at the door. It was the detective who'd been in McDonald's apartment.

"Feeling better, miss?" he asked Andrea.

She looked up. "He's dead," she replied in the same dull tone as before.

The detective nodded. His expression was mildly sympathetic. Just mildly. "Tell me again what happened."

"Here," I said to her, "drink some coffee."

"Who're you?" the detective asked me.

Helen rose from her kneeling position by the chair. "That's Mr. Potter," she said.

"What's your connection?" he asked.

"He's my employer," Helen informed him. And apparently for the first time she noticed that she wasn't properly dressed. "Oh, dear! I'm not wearing stockings."

"I knew McDonald," I told the detective.

He became interested, and introduced himself. "Detective O'Brien," he said. "Homicide." Then he asked me about McDonald.

I gave him such information as I could, including the information that Bob and Andrea were to have been married the following Monday, which no one else had thought to tell him. But when I explained that I'd met Bob for the first time the night before, his interest waned and he again turned his attention to Andrea.

Helen, with some embarrassment, was trying to arrange the afghan into something resembling a toga.

Chapin, glowering at O'Brien, finished his beer.

Haltingly, Andrea told her story. She'd met Helen at Bloomingdale's at five o'clock. Helen had had a fitting of the wedding dress. They'd had dinner at Schrafft's. Then they'd gone to Helen's apartment. A friend of Andrea's who was a florist had come over, and they'd talked about flowers. He'd stayed until almost nine o'clock. Then she and her aunt had discussed the wedding luncheon menu. She'd taken a taxi from Helen's to Bob's. She didn't know exactly what time it had been—a little after ten, she thought. She had a key to the building and a key to Bob's apartment, but at first she hadn't used them. She'd rung the bell. But when there had been no answer . . .

At that point, unable to go on, she stopped.

O'Brien began to question Chapin. Chapin said that he'd already given all the information he could to the other guy.

"I want to hear it too," said O'Brien.

But before they could go into details, the other guy appeared. O'Brien introduced him as Detective Nelson.

Nelson was the one I'd seen in the lobby. He gave O'Brien a rundown of what he'd learned, which wasn't much. Several of the tenants had heard what might have been a shot, but none of them had given much thought to it, and each claimed to have heard it at a different time. The nearest Nelson could come was somewhere between eight fifteen and eight thirty. No one had seen the assailant enter or leave the McDonald apartment, although three or four people had seen strangers in the lobby at one time or another during the early part of the evening. That wasn't unusual, however, for there was always a lot of coming and going in the building.

Nelson finished by telling O'Brien that two teams were questioning the tenants of the adjacent buildings, and O'Brien nodded. He looked as if Nelson had told him more or less what he'd expected to hear. "Maybe Fingerprints will come up with something," he said. Then, indicating Chapin and me, he added, "We've got to get these two, too. They touched things."

I offered Andrea the mug of coffee. This time she took it and drank some.

Helen became aware of her knitting bag and pocketbook on the floor. She picked them up and placed them on a table, then perched on Andrea's chair and put a protective arm around her.

Chapin repeated his account of the discovery of the body, and Andrea explained to the detectives who Bob was and where his family lived. Nothing said by either of them was new to me, except that over the years Bob had held a number of part-time jobs around the university and that his father lived with the Knights, a few blocks from Claremont Avenue on Riverside Drive near 113th Street. And that Chapin, a graduate student in the department of archeology, was something of an expert at deciphering Mayan hieroglyphics.

Chapin and I were eventually taken to McDonald's apartment, where the fingerprint men were at work. The photographer was no longer there, and neither was the body—but a chalked outline on the rug indicated where it had been. Chapin didn't like the

44

idea of being fingerprinted, and neither did I, but both of us submitted.

Shortly after that, the ordeal ended. I glanced at my watch and was surprised. It seemed as if I'd been in the building for a very long time, but actually I'd been there for only an hour and a quarter.

O'Brien offered to have Andrea driven home, but I said I'd take her. Helen said we should take her to *her* apartment, and I agreed that that would be best. Nelson asked for Helen's address and telephone number, which she gave him. He said that he and O'Brien would be around to see them again in the morning. Meanwhile they would break the news to McDonald's family.

In the taxi Helen began to regain her composure. All the way back to her apartment she apologized to me for her behavior. She was so sorry that she'd put me through such a terrible experience. She didn't know why she'd done it. She'd simply panicked. She supposed that she'd felt the need for strong moral support, and I was the first person she'd thought of. It really wasn't like her to lose her head that way.

I kept assuring her that I understood, but the more I assured her, the more she apologized.

Andrea sat between us, hugging herself, saying nothing. I put my arm around her, but she didn't seem to notice.

When we reached the building in which Helen lived, she helped Andrea from the taxi. I volunteered to escort them upstairs, but Helen said I'd already done enough.

With a lump in my throat I watched the two forlorn figures cross the sidewalk.

It was a pathetic sight.

9

The next day I wasn't good for much. I just couldn't get with it. I kept seeing Bob McDonald's body sprawled on the floor, Andrea slumped in the chair, Helen huddled against the telephone booth. No matter how hard I tried to rid my mind of those images, they wouldn't disappear.

I told Clair Gould, our switchboard operator, that Helen wouldn't be in, and why. But she already knew; she'd read about the murder in the morning paper. So, apparently, had others, for as I was going out to lunch, Rose Nye, Mark's secretary, stopped me and asked when and where the funeral was going to be—the girls in the office had taken up a collection for flowers. And throughout the day everyone who came into my office for any reason began by asking about the murder. I had to repeat the story a dozen times.

The one who appeared to be most upset by the news, naturally enough, was Joe. He'd met Bob. He'd seen Bob and Andrea holding hands, exchanging fond glances. To him the tragedy was real. He sat in the chair beside my desk, the chair Helen usually sat in, shaking his head sadly and repeating, "It doesn't seem fair, it just doesn't seem fair."

"No, it doesn't," I agreed. "It sure doesn't."

But that was as far as my thoughts could go. The unfairness of the thing. The unexpectedness. The perversity. What shouldn't happen, does; what should, doesn't. Happiness is as transient as a flash of lightning; for an instant it brightens your life, then it vanishes.

I tried to tell myself that the murder of someone as remote from me as my secretary's niece's fiancé shouldn't disturb me to the point where it interfered with what I had to do. After all, my own life wasn't going to be affected. I'd only met the man once. But that was the trouble. I *had* met him. I'd liked him. And twenty-four hours after our meeting, I'd seen him dead.

In a fashion, I did function that Tuesday. Although I let Irving write the weekly market letter, I made detailed notes for him to work from. Because Helen wasn't there to screen my calls, I talked on the telephone even more than usual. I borrowed M.M. from my staff for long enough to handle the most urgent mail. But my thoughts wouldn't stay fixed on what I was doing—they kept straying off to the two adjacent apartments on Claremont Avenue, to the sights and sounds of the night before.

I wondered who the killer was, but I had no theories. Upper Broadway, I'd read, had a huge population of former mental patients; between one and two hundred thousand of them were living there, supported by welfare agencies and kept rational by medication. Perhaps the murder had been committed by a psychotic. But then again, perhaps not. I really didn't know. All I knew was what I'd seen, what I'd heard and what I was now feeling—shock and sadness.

Late in the afternoon I called Carol, and this time I got past her switchboard operator. "I thought you might want to know," I said, "that Bob McDonald was shot to death last night."

"Bob McDonald?" Carol asked after a stunned silence. "Andrea Doyle's fiancé?"

"Yes."

"Shot to death?"

"Yes."

"Oh, God! I can't believe it! Poor Andrea!"

"I thought you might want to know," I said again.

"Yes. Thank you for telling me." And Carol too inquired about the funeral.

"I have no idea," I replied. "There might have to be some sort of inquest or something first. . . . Still mad at me?"

"No, not mad. Defeated."

I was about to ask her what she meant by defeated when she hung up.

With an unhappy sigh, I went back to what I'd been doing before—staring at the wall. You ought to call Helen too, I told myself. You ought to ask if there's anything you can do.

But I decided to pay her a visit instead. After dinner. And meanwhile, since I wasn't operating on all cylinders anyway, to go home.

10

The building in which Helen lived was located on West End Avenue and had once been considered quite posh. But that was during the 1920's and '30's. Now the big money was on the other side of Central Park, and the building in which Helen lived was twenty-odd stories of grandeur gone to pot.

The stonework around the entrance was chipped and had graffiti written on it in spray paint. The bracket that held the house phone had come loose from the wall, and the phone looked as if it was about to fall off. The palms in the lobby seemed to be hanging their heads in shame, perhaps because the glass doors to the two elevators were cracked and one of them had a hole in it the size of a man's fist.

Yet I knew that Helen paid an indecently high rent. And as I rode up to the twelfth floor in a wheezing elevator, I felt an expanding sympathy for her. Manhattan was hard on its Helen Doyles; it squeezed them dry.

But the sympathy I felt in the elevator was nothing compared to the sympathy I felt when Helen greeted me. For overnight she'd aged five years.

She was alone, she explained; Andrea had gone over to the Knights'.

"How's she taking it?" I asked.

Helen's eyes filled with tears. "Poor child." But then she drew herself up and forced a smile. "You've never been here, Mr. Potter. Come, let me show you around."

And with some of the old dignity, she did show me around, pointing out pieces that had belonged to her mother and grandmother, explaining how she'd reupholstered the sofa herself and how she'd found the two floor lamps at Macy's, on sale. In general, I thought, the furnishings reflected the woman—prim but nice. When we got back to the living room, I tried not to picture it as it might have looked set up for the wedding.

Don't mention the wedding, I cautioned myself. But the subject came up anyway when Helen said, as we sat down, "I wish I had something to offer you to drink, Mr. Potter. I know you do like a drink now and then, but there wasn't time after you called. . . ." I protested that I didn't need a drink at the moment. Suddenly she brightened. "Come to think of it, I do have something. There's some champagne I bought for the . . . party. Let me get a bottle. It isn't chilled, I'm afraid, but I think it's a good brand—the man recommended it."

I continued to protest. She insisted, however. But then she couldn't get the wire off the cork, so I did that. And as I sat there drinking the wine that had been intended for a happier occasion, I asked whether there was anything I could do for Andrea or herself. Helen said no, and began to apologize for not being at work when she knew there was so much to be done. I told her not even to think of the office, but she said that she felt derelict in her duty, adding that because of police procedure, which was quite beyond her, the funeral was being delayed and wouldn't take place until Saturday morning. By Monday, though, she would be back at her desk.

Having apologized for her absence in a time of need, she went on to apologize for her performance the night before. She didn't know what had got into her, or what I must be thinking. Running out of the apartment in her dressing gown. Calling me up like that. Being so . . . so . . . so uncontrolled. Really, she'd never done such things in her entire life.

"But it's entirely understandable," I said. "You'd had a terrible shock."

It might be understandable to me, Helen replied, but she couldn't forgive herself. She hadn't even been wearing her good house slippers—she'd been wearing her old ones. She'd thrown them away this morning; she should have thrown them away long ago. And her knitting bag—she couldn't account for that at all. Well, maybe in a way she could. She'd been knitting when the telephone rang. In her distraught condition after the telephone call, she'd grabbed her knitting bag instead of her pocketbook, become aware of her mistake, gone back for the pocketbook and somehow ended up with both. She went on and on, reproaching herself for each detail of her appearance and behavior, explaining it, reviewing it, expressing the hope that it wouldn't cause me to think less of her.

After a while I began to wish she would stop—she was overdoing the whole bit. But then her monologue took a slightly different turn, and I realized what was really bothering her. She regretted that she'd talked to me about hiring a private detective.

She approached the matter obliquely, saying that she hadn't been herself ever since Andrea had broken the news that she intended to get married. Then, a few words at a time, she drew closer to what she wanted to say, and finally, with downcast eyes, she came out with it. "I'm terribly ashamed of myself for what I told you the other day, Mr. Potter. I hope you'll forget it."

"Told me?"

"About consulting Mr. Quick. You were right. A person shouldn't pry."

"Under the circumstances," I began. I was going to say that, under the circumstances, it might not have been such a bad idea.

But Helen didn't give me a chance to finish. "Andrea's all I have," she interrupted. "I'd always hoped—well, I'm prideful, Mr. Potter. I'd always hoped that she'd make a good marriage. In my opinion, the McDonalds . . . Well, anyway, I'm ashamed of myself."

"I'll forget the whole thing, Helen. But—"

"Pride's a dreadful sin. I know that. I've fought against it all my life, but somehow . . . I've saved a little money. I've been saving for years. I hoped that someday I could give Andrea a nice wedding, the kind of wedding that I—the kind of wedding that a girl should have. A church wedding, with bridesmaids and white candles and a ring-bearer and all the pretty things that I—that a girl should have. And a lovely reception afterwards. You know what I mean. But all of a sudden Andrea announced that she and Bob were going to get married in just a few weeks and they didn't want any fuss—only the immediate family—and they were going to Florida for a week's honeymoon during Bob's Christmas vacation from school, and then they were going to live in his little apartment up there in that dreadful neighborhood until he got his degree, and, well, I was disappointed. I'd hoped for something better for her."

"Things seldom turn out the way we plan," I said. Everything was clearer to me now.

Helen nodded. "I know." Then suddenly she began to cry.

I patted her hand.

"Oh, Mr. Potter, I don't know what to do. Andrea's going to have a baby."

"No!" I hoped that I sounded sufficiently surprised.

Helen nodded and sobbed simultaneously. "A baby. That was why . . . why . . . they didn't want a . . . a big . . . wedding."

I offered her my handkerchief. She covered her face with it and went on crying. But presently she pulled herself together. She blew her nose and, clutching the handkerchief, said, "Excuse me. I didn't mean to give in like that. But all day we've been . . . You see, it's too late to—to stop things. And Andrea says that she wouldn't even if she could. She wants to *have* the baby. And the baby won't have any father. It—it'll be . . . illegitimate."

"But somebody will take it. Somebody will give it a good home. There are agencies."

"No. Andrea insists she won't give the baby out for adoption. She's going to raise it. She—" Helen began to cry again, but this time she stopped almost at once.

"A lot of women are doing that these days," I said. "It isn't like it used to be."

"I know that, Mr. Potter. I know what's going on in the world. I watch television. I read. I—sometimes I even think that some of it is right. When I was growing up, we—well, it wasn't as good then. I can't bring myself to approve of all that's going on now, but when I remember how it used to be, I have the feeling that I ought to. Oh, it's so difficult, Mr. Potter. I always thought I knew what was right, and now I'm not sure anymore. Some things *aren't* right, but others *are*, and I'm not sure which are which. What Andrea wants to do—"

"It isn't her fault, Helen. They were going to get married. . . . You didn't know?"

Helen shook her head. "Not until today. Andrea was afraid to tell me. She thought I wouldn't understand. And that's what's so awful, you see. It means that Andrea thinks I'm different. But I'm still a woman, Mr. Potter, and I would have *tried* to understand. I really would have *tried*. And I certainly wouldn't have called Mr. Quick."

"You mean you *did* call him?" I was astonished.

Helen avoided my eyes. She looked utterly miserable. "Oh, dear. I didn't mean to let it . . . Oh, dear. Well, I won't lie about it." She made an effort to meet my gaze. "Yes. I called him. His telephone number is in our file. He charged me five hundred dollars. But I wanted the information. Please don't tell Andrea, though. Promise me. Please."

"I promise. But why, Helen? What information did you want?"

Helen twisted the handkerchief. In her face there were lines I'd never seen before. She'd suddenly gone from middle-aged to elderly, I thought. "Well, I won't lie," she said again. "The information about James McDonald. He's been in jail, you see."

My jaw almost hit my chest.

"I wanted to tell you," Helen went on quickly, "but I didn't know how. And you were in such a hurry that night, and you seemed so against the idea of a detective. It was a long time ago, when Bob was a little boy. But I wanted to know what his father had gone to jail *for*. Andrea's all I have. . . . Now I know I was wrong. Bob told Andrea in confidence—he wanted her to know the whole truth about himself. And she told me in confidence—she wanted me to know the whole truth too. She didn't think I'd betray her confidence. But I did. To Mr. Quick. Promise you won't tell anyone, Mr. Potter."

"Trust me, Helen."

"That's what I feel so terrible about, you see. Andrea doesn't know I spoke to a detective, but *I* know. In the back of my mind, I think—I want to be truthful—in the back of my mind, I think, I wanted to *separate* Andrea and Bob. That's a dreadful thing to want to do, Mr. Potter—to want to separate people. And all because I'm prideful."

I recalled James McDonald sitting at the table in my dining room. His dour expression. His guardedness. Now I could understand. "If I'd known," I said, and stopped. If I'd known, what would I have done? Advised Helen to go ahead and hire a detective? It wouldn't have made any difference—she'd hired one anyway. "What did Quick tell you?"

"It happened in Chicago, you see—that's why I thought of Mr. Quick; he lives there—a long time ago. Over twenty years ago. That's how Bob came to live with the Knights. His mother was dead, and his father was in jail."

"What did Quick find out?"

"James stole some money from a store he was working in. He got caught and sent to jail."

"Have you told this to the police?"

"Oh, no. I wouldn't dream of it. Not now. What difference would it make? Bob's dead." Her chin quivered. She bit her lip.

"Have you told Andrea?"

"I'd rather die first! And if you—"

"I won't."

"Promise?"

"I promise."

She noticed that she was still holding my handkerchief and gave it back to me.

"I do think you ought to tell the police, though," I said.

"No. I've done enough harm already."

"You haven't done any harm at all, Helen. Don't confuse the thought with the deed."

"But it's the thought that's important, Mr. Potter. I know what was in my heart, and I'm ashamed."

I saw no point in arguing with her. In one respect, she was right. Bob McDonald was dead; nothing she told the police about

54

his father could alter that fact. Furthermore, the police would undoubtedly question James McDonald—they'd learn about his past. "Well," I said, "I wish there were something I could do to make things easier for you, Helen."

She smiled, and for a moment she looked younger again—the Helen Doyle I'd always known. She's going to be all right, I thought. It's only a matter of time. "You've already done a great deal, Mr. Potter. You were there last night when I needed you. And you've listened to me. I feel better now. It's keeping it all inside that's so terrible. I'm grateful to you. I am indeed."

I finished my glass of champagne and left. I hoped that my visit had done some good. At least it had given Helen a chance to unburden herself.

Catharsis, I thought as I climbed into the taxi. At one time or another everyone needs it. Because no one, to himself, is entirely innocent.

11

After that, however, my mental stabilizers began to operate and I regained my balance. I didn't forget about Helen; the disarray in my office was a constant reminder of her absence and the reason for it. But the tragedy of Bob McDonald's death no longer haunted me. There was too much that had to be settled before the final meeting on the annual forecast, which was scheduled to begin at nine o'clock on Saturday morning. The pace became even more frantic than it had been before. I worked late three nights in a row, and so did every member of my staff.

The quarrel that had divided the research department had been more or less patched up. Harriet still wouldn't speak to Joe unless she absolutely had to, but in general team spirit had been reestablished. I resolved to take Harriet out to dinner one night after the forecast was at the printer's and have a talk with her, but in the meanwhile I didn't feel that hard feelings were the number-one problem. I was more concerned with our conclusions about what the economy would do during the coming year.

The choice of a Saturday for the meeting had been dictated by the printer's deadline. Monday was the last day on which he could accept our material and still have it ready by the end of the year. I hadn't seen anything extraordinary in our working on a day when the office was usually closed. But apparently others in the company did. To them we were doing something very special, and they wanted to be included.

The first indication I had of this was when Mark said casually on Friday morning that he thought maybe he'd join us on Saturday. The second was when Tom, less than an hour later, said exactly the same thing. The third and fourth were when Ward Carlton and Milt Radison, who is Ward's chief rival for Tom's favor, approached me ten minutes apart to ask whether they too could attend.

I didn't mind having Mark and Tom at the meeting; Price, Potter and Petacque was their company as much as it was mine. But I did object to having Ward and Milt. I was afraid that a couple of gung-ho salesmen, such as they, might make use of the material in the forecast before it was published. So I told them that they couldn't come.

Then I had second thoughts. If I couldn't trust Tom's people, what right had I to expect him to trust mine? There was enough friction between the sales department and the research department as it was; sometimes it was as if the two departments weren't part of the same company. So I reversed myself later in the day and told Ward and Milt that they'd be welcome. Which caused the other two salesmen, Al Cahill and Dean Marks, to come clamoring into my office for invitations, and Lucy Janeen, our comptroller, as well.

I went through the same no-yes routine with them. At least with the salesmen. To Lucy, I said no, period. Nor did I say it as diplomatically as I might have. I told her that I'd schedule a private working meeting, not a public forum. With the result that Lucy has been cool toward me ever since.

And so the stage was set for a minor miracle. For on Saturday twelve people who were frequently at odds with one another became, at least temporarily, the best of friends.

12

In the past, all meetings of the research department had taken place in my office. But when I arrived that Saturday morning, I found that someone had set up the conference room.

The conference room had never really been off-limits to the research department; we just didn't have any need for it. It was Tom's territory—he used it when he wanted to impress customers. But there it was, all lit up, with twelve chairs around the table—the eight regular chairs and four extras—twelve scratch pads, twelve pencils. Furthermore, someone—Tom, I guessed—had arranged for a large urn of coffee to be on the side console, along with a platter of Danish pastries and a stack of styrofoam cups.

I began the meeting by reading the introduction to the forecast, which I'd written, based on the views of all six of us. Then I called on Irving to follow with his contribution.

Each of the researchers read what he'd prepared, and Harriet's graphs were passed around, as well as charts and tables of figures that the others had put together, and I concluded with a summary of the investments most likely to do well during the next twelve months.

After that, there was a discussion. And from the very outset it was a remarkable one. Nothing like it had ever taken place in our firm, or, I suspected, in any other firm. But twelve bright, scrappy, competitive human beings suddenly became high-minded and selfless on the same day.

I'd known everyone in that room more or less well over a period of time. I'd been close to some of them for years. There wasn't one I didn't consider good at what he did. But as the discussion progressed, I realized that, high as it had been, my opinion of everyone hadn't been high enough. The Price, Potter and Petacque gang was even more concerned with the welfare of the firm and its customers than I'd given it credit for being.

Many opinions were expressed. Some were opinions that had never been expressed before, at least by the people who were voicing them. And not all of the opinions coincided. But no one was on the offensive, and no one had to defend himself. Everyone was willing to listen and learn.

The traditional animosity between the sales department and the research department disappeared. The long-standing antagonism between Ward Carlton and Milt Radison was nowhere in evidence. There was no hint of the hostilities that had divided the research department. Joe and Harriet were like Tristan and Isolde, damn near.

We talked about everything—one topic led to another. But we talked more about food and fuel than anything else, since these, we felt, were the key problems. With the world's population growing as it was, and its resources dwindling as they were, unless solutions to these problems were found, half the world would die of cold while the other half died of starvation. Conservation wasn't enough. New sources had to be found. Of energy. Of nutrition. But could they be found as long as people were fragmented into opposing blocs? With most of the world tilting away from private ownership, yet demanding the high standard of living that had never been achieved except under a system of private ownership, was a period of anarchy inevitable? If so, what would follow it? And which was more important—human rights or a good meal? As things stood at the moment, the countries that had the most human rights also had the best meals. But would that always be the case? How did you get rid of a dictator, once you'd elected him? At what point does protection become oppression? Where should law-making stop?

The companies which the research department studied and the sales department sold shares in dealt with such questions daily, we agreed—even the philosophical questions. They had to, in order to survive. And some of them, we further agreed, were liable to come up with answers. But which companies, and what kind of answers? Moreover, what would the answers lead to—the end of civilization or a better civilization than had ever existed before? Either was possible. None of us really knew. Perhaps Al Cahill and Irving summed it up as well as anyone could.

"Every coin has two sides," Al said. "You're never sure, when you toss it, whether you'll win or lose. But the chances are fifty-fifty; and when you stop to think about it, fifty-fifty isn't so bad."

"People aren't coins," Irving said. "Their chances would be better than fifty-fifty if they just realized how much they need one another."

Shortly after that exchange, the meeting came to an end. I'd anticipated that it would last until twelve, but it was now a quarter to three. The coffee and Danish pastries had long since been consumed, but no one had said a word about lunch. Suddenly, however, everyone admitted to being famished. And with all our newfound good will, we decided to eat together. But no one could think of a place in the neighborhood that was open for lunch at three o'clock on a Saturday afternoon; most weren't open at all on Saturday.

Someone suggested we try the World Trade Center. Someone else suggested we go uptown.

Utopias are fragile, and ours began to fall apart over the issue of where to eat.

The uptown faction won, and we decided to go to the Brasserie, in the Seagram Building. The Brasserie was always open. So we piled into four taxis and took off for 53rd Street.

Who rode with whom was a matter of who was standing next to whom at the curb, and I happened to be standing between Ward Carlton and Joe.

Our conversation in the taxi was desultory. Ward spoke of a problem he was having with his older son—his son wanted a motorcycle, and Ward didn't approve of motorcycles. Joe mentioned that his daughter was taking lessons in figure skating. I said that I'd seen a remarkable performance of ski jumping by a young Austrian, on television.

Then, out of the blue, Joe asked whether anyone from the office had gone to Bob McDonald's funeral.

I said that some of the girls had been planning to go—I'd heard Clair Gould and Rose Nye talking about it.

"I still can't get over the fact that he was Augustus Koberg's great-grandson," he said.

"Who?" Ward asked. "The fellow who was shot?"

Joe nodded.

Ward frowned. "The Koberg Chemical family?"

"Yes."

"Strange," Ward said. "Just yesterday Hardin was asking Tom about Koberg Chemical."

I perked up. "He was?" Hardin Webster worked for Amalgamated Investors Services, our largest customer. He was plenty smart. "How do you know?"

"Tom mentioned it to me. He doesn't think much of the company. Do you?"

"It would be a great investment," I said, "if this were 1925."

Ward chuckled, then said, "I didn't know that Helen's niece was marrying money."

"She wasn't," Joe told him. "All the guy had was what he'd managed to scrape together from part-time jobs while he was going to school. But his grandmother was Elissa Koberg."

"Hm," Ward mused. "Funny about some of those families. The blood thins, and the money thins with it."

The taxi came down the ramp that skirted Grand Central Station.

None of us spoke again until we pulled up in front of the restaurant.

Some of the group were already there. The hostess was putting together several tables to accommodate us. We distributed ourselves around them. The last taxi load arrived—Tom, Harriet and Irving. Brian was seated at my right, and Joe opposite me. Tom took the seat at my left and immediately went into his host act. He does more entertaining than anyone else in the company and is marvelous at it. In no time at all, what might have been an ordinary lunch became a party. A round of drinks helped, of course. No one had eaten for hours, and the alcohol worked quickly. We became noisy.

It was the in-between hour, and the restaurant wasn't crowded. There were maybe thirty people in the place, aside from the staff, and our table was the center of attention. Every time we erupted in laughter, heads turned. People on their way in or out paused on the stairs to look at us.

And without my noticing, one of them came over to us.

Milt Radison had just finished a hilarious story about his neighbor's cat. His neighbor, it seemed, owned a prize Burmese that he was anxious to mate with another prize Burmese, which was owned by someone who lived in Stamford, Connecticut. The two owners had corresponded and had made arrangements to bring the cats together at Milt's neighbor's for a weekend of dalliance. But Milt's neighbor's cat took an immediate and totally inexplicable dislike to her intended and wouldn't have anything to do with him. In fact, she went to such lengths to avoid him that Milt found his neighbor on a ladder at seven o'clock in the morning frantically trying to coax his cat down from the roof of the house while the rejected suitor stood at the foot of the ladder, shrieking.

I was still laughing when I heard a voice behind me say, "Price, Potter and Petacque must have had a good year."

At first I didn't turn. But then I noticed that Joe had stopped laughing and was staring over my shoulder. I looked behind me.

"For Pete's sake!" I exclaimed. "Louis Glass!"

"I don't want to interrupt the festivities," Glass said. "I just want to say hello and tell you I appreciate the nice things you've been saying about me."

I'd met Glass on a number of occasions, but I didn't know him well. In general, I admired him. My emotions at the moment were mixed, however. I didn't like the idea that he'd been trying to hire Joe. "Don't thank me," I said. "Thank yourself."

He smiled. "We try." Then he looked at Joe. "And how is Mr. Rothland?"

Joe was obviously embarrassed. "O.K.," he said. "Just fine, thanks."

I wondered whether Joe had told him that he wouldn't be taking the job, after all. Glancing from one to the other, I couldn't tell.

Tom didn't know Glass, but, ever hospitable, he said, "I'm Tom Petacque. Pull up a chair, why don't you?"

"Ah, thank you," Glass replied, "but I'm with a friend. We were just leaving. I merely wanted to express my appreciation for your company's favorable remarks about my company." He directed his attention once more to Joe. "I hope you'll be coming around soon. You're always welcome."

"Well, sure," Joe said, reddening.

"Maybe next time I'll come with Joe," I said. "I'm sure I'd learn something."

Glass bowed slightly and moved away. I watched him as he crossed the room and went up the steps. He joined a good-looking man in a camel's-hair polo coat who'd been waiting for him, and they went through the revolving door.

"Extraordinary man—Glass," I said to Joe.

His face was still red. "Very aggressive," he replied.

"He's an egghead egghead," Brian observed.

I glanced at him.

"An egghead in both senses of the word," he explained. "Intellectual and Humpty Dumpty."

I laughed. I hadn't thought of Glass in those terms before, but Brian was right. Glass's head, bald and perfectly oval, did resemble an egg. And he was a genuine intellectual. Everyone who knew him said so.

"But I wouldn't trust him"—Brian gestured toward the counter, which could seat at least fifty people—"as far as I could throw that counter."

"No?" I said. "Why not?"

He shrugged. "Something about him."

"The man he was with," Joe said, "that's the man he was with in the bar."

"The bar?" For a moment I didn't know what Joe was talking about. Then I remembered the discussion in my office before the big blow up. "Oh, yes. Now I recall."

"The same man," Joe affirmed with a slight shrug.

"The guy with the Julius Caesar haircut?" Brian asked. "Who was he?"

Joe shrugged one shoulder. "He didn't introduce me. And when Glass and I started talking, the other guy left."

"I didn't like *his* looks either," Brian said.

"You're turning negative," I told him. I thought back to the man who'd been standing at the top of the steps. Gray hair. Early sixties. And Brian was right about the haircut—all the man needed was a crown of laurel leaves. I was certain that I'd never seen him before.

"No, I'm not," Brian said. "I'm young and naïve and optimistic and butter wouldn't melt in my mouth. I'm not the least bit negative. Isn't that right, Joe?"

"You're young," Joe admitted. "As for the rest of it . . ."

Brian ignored him. "But there are some people I dislike at first sight. Whatever that makes me."

"Scary," Joe said, and the three of us laughed.

I noticed that I still had some martini left and drank it. "Tell us more about your neighbor's cat," I called down the table to Milt.

"She eloped with a worthless alley cat," he called back.

Brian nudged me. "Smart cat," he murmured. "She wasn't taken in by a big reputation."

"Honest to God," I told him, "sometimes I think I overtrained you."

13

If Saturday was a high, then Sunday was a low.

I moped about the house for the better part of the day, bored, restless, out of synch. There was nothing to do. The vague depression that I'd been aware of on Monday evening descended again.

I called Carol twice—in the morning and in the early afternoon—but didn't get anywhere with her. She was willing to talk to me, but not to reconcile. It was just as well, she said, that things had turned out as they had, when they had, because at last she knew how I really felt; and while I might think she was too old to begin a normal existence, she didn't think so; and there was still time for her to find a man who agreed with her. She wasn't angry at me, but she did feel defeated by me—I didn't see her as she saw herself, she realized now, and I never would. So thank you very much, Brock, for all the nice things, but I have to hurry or I'll miss my plane—and the rest of my life.

Presumably she didn't miss her plane, for when I tried to call her a third time, there was no answer.

It wasn't, I told Tiger, going to be much of a Christmas.

For a while I watched the football game, but the Jets were having as bad a day as I was. In the middle of the second quarter I turned off the television set and went upstairs to take a nap.

I couldn't sleep, however, and after trying all known positions

I finally gave up and took a magazine from the bedside table—only to discover that it was one I'd put there on Monday night. "Toward the Ionosphere" caught my eye for the second time. My thoughts drifted away from Carol. I found myself thinking about the Brasserie—about what Brian had said, about the expression on Joe's face, about my own mixed emotions.

Brian, despite the ruthless impulses that sometimes got the better of him, was basically friendly and outgoing. It wasn't like him to express distrust of someone he didn't know.

On the other hand Joe's instincts about people were as good as Brian's. He wouldn't even have considered going to work for Glass if he hadn't respected the man.

As for me—well, mixed emotions were nothing new. I had them frequently. In this case, Glass had annoyed me by trying to hire one of my staff. But he hadn't succeeded, and I could afford to be generous.

I did admire him, I decided. He was, as everyone said, a sort of genius. Not only a brilliant businessman, but a sophisticated scientist. Which was all the more remarkable when you considered that his formal education had been nothing special.

An egghead egghead.

I smiled, and began to make a mental collage of the bits and pieces I knew about Glass.

For a man who'd risen to the heights he had, his introduction to the business world had been a peculiar one. He'd started as a used-car salesman.

But he hadn't remained a used-car salesman for long. By the time he was twenty-three he'd already made the first of the many moves that were to characterize his what sociologists love to call upward mobility: he was sales manager of a small company that did metal plating. When that company was taken over by a larger one, Glass was absorbed into the parent firm and promoted. After a while he moved on to a still larger company, in an unrelated field—aircraft. By then he was in his early thirties. He became a vice-president, in charge of sales.

Altogether, he moved at least a dozen times, higher within a company or from one company to another. But his big move was when he accepted the presidency of Interamerican Marine.

Interamerican Marine at one time had been a manufacturer of smallcraft and smallcraft engines, and it still was. There were Incan cruisers and sport fishermen and houseboats in marinas all around the country. But pleasure boats represented only a fraction of what the company was now involved in—and had already been involved in when Glass took over as president. It had expanded into aircraft engines, advanced hardware for the military and other items. Its largest customer was the United States government, and its next largest customers were whichever foreign governments the United States government would let it sell to.

Glass continued the company's aggressive policy of expansion and acquisition, and stepped up the pace. But he scored his greatest coup when Interamerican took over Cort Technologies. The coup was great for several reasons. First, Cort was larger than Interamerican—the little fish swallowed the big one. Second, Cort was less government-dependent than Interamerican, so Interamerican became better balanced. And, third, Cort didn't want to be taken over; it had liked being independent. Its management had been asleep at the switch, though. It didn't realize until too late that Interamerican, with the aid of several banks, had bought up enough Cort stock to gain control. The Cort management sued, in a belated attempt to save itself, but lost the suit.

A number of former Cort executives were still looking for jobs. However, the public at large—especially that segment of it which had owned Cort stock—was better off. Cort stockholders had become Interamerican stockholders, and the price of Interamerican had gone up. Furthermore, Glass was making better use of the Cort research and development people than the Cort management had done. New products were coming out in a steady stream—everything from microwave ovens to antisubmarine weapons—and were good. The housewives were happy, and so were the admirals.

What was so extraordinary to me was Glass's ability to learn. He hadn't begun with any particular scientific background; he'd picked up his knowledge along the way, from the people he worked with. But he really did understand the principles of physics and chemistry and could talk to members of the National Space Administration or the Nuclear Energy Commission or the Environmental Protection Agency as knowledgeably as he could talk to bankers, salesmen—and, of course, used-car buyers.

Plenty of businessmen whom I'd met dealt in a wide range of products, many of which were highly complex. The more honest of them admitted that they didn't know beans about sound waves or electric circuitry—all they knew was whom to hire. But Glass not only knew whom to hire but what they were up to after he hired them, and how much rope to give them. Which was of immense importance, for, while the scientific journals were always full of great ideas, it took a particular talent to know which ideas were workable and right for present conditions. Glass had that talent.

My completed collage suggested a man of superior intelligence who was quick to spot ability in others and to take advantage of it.

That didn't make Glass unique, though, I thought. Most of the people I dealt with had similar qualities. My partners, my staff, our customers . . .

Amalgamated Investors Services. Hardin Webster.

My thoughts went off in a different direction.

Amalgamated Investors Services had placed over $300,000,000 worth of business through Price, Potter and Petacque during the past twelve months. Partly because of me—the big deciders up there in Boston, where the fund had its headquarters, liked my advice. But even more because of Tom's ability to get along with Hardin. Hardin's reputation for toughness was well deserved. Tom knew how to handle him, though—they'd been friends for years. Someone had once said that Tom Petacque was the only person in the world who could go into a negotiating session with Hardin Webster and come out smiling.

What had prompted Hardin to ask Tom about Koberg Chemical? Had he heard something? If so, why hadn't I heard it too? Was I slipping?

Suddenly I got off the bed. The thud of my feet hitting the floor roused Tiger, who'd been dozing in his basket. He came up to me.

"Enough of this,' I told him. "We're going visting."

14

I hadn't picked the best time to show up. The apartment was wall-to-wall skis, poles, boots, parkas and miscellaneous gear that was being assembled for the trip. But my relations with the Petacques were such that I knew I was welcome anyway. Not only was Tom my partner and best friend, but Daisy—his wife—and I were very close, and Jerry, Tom's and Daisy's son, was my godchild.

Tom greeted me in a pair of ski pants that he was holding up with one hand. "My God!" he exclaimed. "You've brought the dog!" And he called over his shoulder, "Hey, Jer, get a load of this. Brock's brought his dog." Then he frowned and said to me, "It *is* a dog, isn't it?"

"You know damn well it is," I replied.

Jerry came tearing out of the bedroom, followed, more sedately, by his mother. He hadn't seen Tiger lately. "Holy cow!" he cried, dropping to his knees to get reacquainted.

Daisy kissed me.

I handed my end of the leash to Jerry, and he and Tiger made their way through the clutter to the farther reaches of the apartment, where they could be alone.

"It's so nice to see you, Brock," Daisy said. "You've been quite a stranger the past few weeks."

"Our annual forecast," I explained.

69

"Tom's been telling me. How's Carol?"

"That's a sensitive subject. She hasn't been speaking to me lately, and she left for Minneapolis this afternoon before we could make up."

Daisy sighed.

Tom changed hands. "These goddamn pants won't close. I've gained weight."

"For goodness' sake, darling," Daisy told him, "take them off and go out tomorrow and buy yourself a pair that *will* close."

"But I've gained *weight*."

"You'll lose it. Now go change."

Tom, clutching the pants, went into the bedroom.

"But with Carol away," Daisy said to me, "what are you going to do for the holidays?"

"Where's the Scotch?" I said ruefully.

"You know perfectly well where it is. Help yourself. And while you're at it, pour me a little vermouth on the rocks—half sweet, half dry."

I made the drinks and almost fell over a ski pole as I was bringing them back to the living room.

Tom joined us, wearing a different pair of pants. "These are tight too," he complained. "I'm going to have to go on a diet."

"Have a drink while you're thinking about it," I suggested.

"Good idea," he said, and went off to make himself one.

"Why's Carol angry?" Daisy asked.

"I told her she's too old to have a baby."

"I don't blame her, then. Really, Brock!"

"It just slipped out."

She shook her head sadly.

Tom, returning with his drink, tripped over the same ski pole, and moved it. "Good meeting yesterday, huh?" he said.

"Great," I agreed. "You've got some bright boys working for you."

"That's what I keep telling you." He sat down in his favorite chair.

"I know. But I mean I was really impressed."

He nodded.

"That's one of the reasons I came over," I said. "Aside from just feeling sociable, that is. Ward said something yesterday as we were going uptown that's been bothering me. He said that Hardin asked you on Friday about Koberg Chemical. Any special reason?"

Tom took a sip of his drink. "You know how Hardin is. A new idea every day. The biggest problem I have with him is getting him to stay on one track. No, no reason in particular, as far as I know. I told him to forget it. I was meaning to mention it to you, though. Have you heard anything?"

"No. But Hardin must have."

"He did say the stock's been moving lately. Up."

"So I've learned. It's around six now. But I wonder who called Hardin's attention to it."

Tom shrugged. "We're not the only company he does business with."

There was no doubt about that. Amalgamated Investors Services' portfolio amounted to a tidy $4,500,000,000. "Um," I said.

"Afraid you're missing a boat?" Tom asked.

"I'd hate to think I'm slipping," I admitted.

"You can check it out if you want to," Tom said. "But after yesterday I wouldn't worry about slipping if I were you. You guys have done a hell of a job."

"For our number, we cover a lot of ground," I said. "But there are so few of us. Some things get overlooked that shouldn't."

"Don't look so worried," Daisy said. "Nobody's perfect. It's like I'm always telling Tom, people can expect only so much of themselves."

"Yes," Tom said, "but, as I'm always telling Daisy, how much is 'so much'?"

I finished my Scotch. Tom volunteered to get me a refill. I let him.

"What's Koberg Chemical?" Daisy asked while he was out of the room.

"An old, old chemical company," I said. "From before the turn of the century. Makes Aragon paint."

She brightened. "I've heard of that."

"Been making it for eighty, ninety years. Also does a little with plastics. But the company sort of went down during the Depression and never really came back. Still in business—just not important anymore."

"We all get older, dear."

"Yes, but in different ways. Du Pont's managed to get older without losing its zing."

Tom came back with my drink. "What's this about Du Pont?"

"It's still alive and kicking," I said.

"You might say that," he conceded. "How about staying for dinner?" He turned to Daisy. "We *are* having dinner, aren't we?"

She smiled. "Presumably. But I haven't the vaguest idea what it's going to be. I wonder if Brock likes poached ski wax. I know we have some ski wax."

"Love it," I assured her.

"Then you're on," she said. "I'd better go take a look in the kitchen and see what else is around."

So I stayed for dinner, and we didn't have ski wax—we had hamburgers. Very good hamburgers, as a matter of fact. And we spent a couple of pleasant hours.

But I couldn't get Koberg off my mind, and around eight thirty, as I was about to leave, I asked Tom to find out from Hardin who'd been talking about the stock.

"I'd be glad to," Tom said, "but unfortunately Hardin left for Nassau Friday night. Took his wife and kids down. Christmas vacation, chum." He paused. "If you think it's important, I can call him down there—I know where he's staying."

"Lord, no!" I protested. "It would be making a mountain out of a molehill. And I'd lose face, besides. No, I'll poke around on my own. If there's anything to be found out, I'll eventually get to it."

"I'm sure you will. But why the sudden concern? Nothing Koberg does is likely to be news."

"True enough. I don't know. The fellow that Helen's niece was going to marry was a Koberg descendant—that was what brought it to mind. And the stock *has* gone up. And Hardin mentioned it to you. . . ." My voice trailed off.

"It's Christmas, Brock. Why don't you take it easy for a few days? Take some time off. Go away. Come up to Sugar Bush with us."

"Thanks, Tom. One of us has to stick around the office, though. You're going to be away, Mark's going to be away. I really shouldn't."

"I suppose you're right. But don't knock yourself out, at least. Daisy's right, you know. We can expect only so much of ourselves."

Daisy had come up behind him. Jerry too. "Daisy's always right," Daisy said. "And in case I don't see you before, Merry Christmas, dear."

"Merry Christmas," I said, and kissed her. Then I shook hands with her menfolks, collected my dog and rang for the elevator.

I felt somewhat reassured, but not entirely. My question still hadn't been answered.

"We'll go home by way of Brian's," I told Tiger as we reached the ground floor.

15

It was only a few blocks from Tom's apartment, at 69th Street and Third Avenue, to Brian's, at 62nd and Lexington. But distance isn't everything. Tom owned seven rooms in a high-rise that included among its amenities a doorman who smiled, a receiving room for packages and a lobby with two Miës van der Rohe chairs. Brian occupied a room with an alcove and a Pullman kitchen on the fourth floor of an elderly four-story building that had a pet shop and a discount drugstore on the street level.

That apartment had been all Brian could afford when I'd hired him, but he was now earning three times what he'd been earning then. As his salary had gone up, however, so had the number of his siblings who were in college. Brian, I thought as I approached the entrance, was a one-man scholarship fund.

"Relatives," I said aloud.

Tiger wagged his tail.

The tiny vestibule smelled as if someone had recently spilled vinegar in it. I pushed the button beside the slot marked "Barth." Brian answered, and when I said, "Brock," he buzzed me in.

Clad in baggy jeans and a sweatshirt, he greeted me with an astonished "I thought someone was playing games with me."

"No games," I said. "The real thing—an unprovoked social call."

"Well, come on in, for gosh sake. Both of you." He picked Tiger up and got licked on the chin.

I walked into the combination living room/dining room/bedroom. There was part of a pizza on the table in front of the convertible sofa and an almost empty wineglass beside it.

"Want some pizza?" Brian offered.

"No, thanks. I just ate, over at Tom's. No, Tiger!"

Tiger had headed straight for the table with the pizza and was sitting up, begging. He gave me a baleful look.

Brian deposited himself on the sofa and said he was glad I'd decided to stop in—he'd had a dismal day. A reaction, he guessed. Weeks of excitement and then, suddenly, nothing.

Same with me, I told him, and I suspected that all of us were experiencing a similar feeling.

We rehashed the meeting and talked about how our forecast was likely to compare with everyone else's. Then we got onto the subject of holiday plans. Brian confirmed that he was going down to Virginia to be with his family. I was disappointed. He'd been my last hope. Now, with Christmas falling on a Friday, I would have not one empty day, but three. Maybe Tom had a good point. Maybe I ought to go away, at least for the weekend.

I put the idea out of my mind.

But Brian reinstated it. "As long as you're not doing anything special," he said, "why don't you come with me? You'd meet the darnedest family you've ever seen."

"Down to *Virginia?*"

"It's not that far. And the folks would get a real charge out of meeting you—they know all about you."

"I couldn't."

"Why not?"

I made up some reasons. They weren't very good ones.

Brian continued to urge, and I continued to resist. Finally I thought I'd better change the subject. "I said this was an unprovoked call, but that's not quite true. I have something on my mind."

"About Christmas, though—"

"No, honestly. Let me tell you." And I related what Ward and Tom had said about Hardin's inquiry.

The focus of Brian's attention shifted. He raised his eyebrows. Then he began to look pleased. "As a matter of fact," he said, "I've been doing some checking the past few days. I was going to bring Koberg up at the meeting tomorrow. Why are you smiling?"

"Because I thought that's what you might have been doing."

Brian blushed. "Well," he said. "I had a few minutes."

We compared notes. I knew nothing about Koberg's recent history, but I did know about its early years. Brian was vague about the early years, but had gathered some information about the company's current activities.

Augustus Koberg had been a German immigrant. A carpenter by trade, he'd begun to experiment with the manufacture of paint shortly after his arrival in the United States, in the 1880's, and had founded a small paint factory. His brand name was Aragon, and it soon became widely known. For decades Aragon was considered the best housepaint on the market; it was in demand by builders all over the country. Koberg expanded into related products. By the turn of the century Augustus Koberg was a multimillionaire and Koberg Chemical was a giant.

But in those days giants were smaller than they are now. And Koberg was no longer a giant even by the standards of the early 1900's. For, while Aragon was still an excellent product, other companies had come along with paints that were just as good, and cheaper.

The real trouble, in my opinion, began in 1916, when Augustus Koberg died. His heirs took no active interest in the business. They left the running of it to hired hands, who were uninspired. The hired hands couldn't cope with the Depression. They went on making expensive, top-quality paint, didn't modernize the plant, didn't reinvest profits, and profits dwindled. World War II gave the company a shot in the arm. The military used a lot of paint during the war years, and much of what it used was Aragon. Furthermore, the company received government contracts for other items, notably life rafts and life jackets. But when the war ended, so did the contracts. Koberg didn't continue its subsidiary lines—there was little demand for them—and didn't come up with new ones. It reverted to being simply a maker of paint and a few plastic items, and, while the giant didn't become a pygmy, it did let itself be dwarfed by younger, more aggressive competitors. Until finally it was delisted by the New York Stock Exchange. Not because it was bankrupt or in disrepute, but because there wasn't enough trading in its stock. The public had lost interest.

The company's cash position, according to Brian, was good. That, he said, was part of the trouble. The old management never spent the money it made. Part it paid out in dividends, the rest it put into Treasury notes and bonds and other fixed-income securities; but with inflation, their value was shrinking.

"It would have been smarter," he concluded, "to plow the profits back into the business. And that's what the new management has started to do."

"New management?" I wasn't aware of any changes at the top.

"Not really new," Brian explained. "But six years ago the old guard, who was represented by a guy named Dwight Wilson, retired. The Wilson family had run the company ever since old Koberg died. First the father, then the son. But the son had become an old man, and he finally gave up the reins to a young guy named Paul Carmichael. Carmichael made a clean sweep. He's the first breath of fresh air they've had in the place in sixty years."

"That's all news to me. I remember the name Wilson, but Carmichael . . ."

"Evidently he's been turning things around. He's brought in a lot of young blood, modernized the old plant and built a new research facility."

"Any new products?"

"Not to my knowledge. It's still Aragon paint, as far as I've been able to learn, and petroleum-based plastics, but you never know. With a new research facility . . ."

"Right. Where's this facility located?"

"Outside Chicago. The headquarters is in downtown Chicago, the old plant is in Joliet and the new one is in the general area. A place called Barrington. What are you smiling at now?"

"At you. How, with all you had to do last week, did you manage to dig all this up?"

"Oh, it was easy. I just asked."

"Asked who?"

Brian's eyes widened. I wasn't supposed to put such questions to him. Of all the members of my staff, he was the most secretive when it came to revealing the names of his sources. We'd quarreled over the issue in the past, and I'd lost. But his information was always accurate, and there was no way I could force him to tell me where he got it, short of firing him. Now, however, he said, after a moment's hesitation, "Darryl Otis."

I was flabbergasted. Darryl Otis worked in the research department of Sperling, Bradenton—one of our competitors. "You mean—?"

"I don't make a practice of it," Brian hastened to assure me. "And when I do, I get more than I give. This wasn't a Price, Potter and Petacque inquiry, I told him; it was personal. Otis is good when it comes to some of those out-of-the-way companies."

"But don't you realize that your 'personal' inquiry may have started a rumor?"

This time, instead of merely turning pink, as it usually did, Brian's face turned beet red. "You mean, you think Darryl told Hardin I was interested?"

"Could be."

"I'll kill the son of a bitch!"

I got up and began to pace. Tiger, who likes socks and had found one under the bed, abandoned it and came over to me. He didn't know whether I was getting ready to leave, or what.

"You say the cash position is good?" I asked. My mind was working rapidly now.

Brian recovered. "Yes. And of course the stock is probably cheap in relation to book value. You're thinking—a takeover?"

I nodded. A medium-sized company with a good name, a strong cash position and low-priced stock. It was possible that Koberg could be bought with its own capital. A familiar pattern. And the stock had started to move. This could be one of those special situations—a chance to make really big money.

"I wonder who's been doing the buying," Brian said, his thoughts keeping up with mine.

"I don't know, but I'm going to speak to Mark about it tomorrow." Mark's contacts with the banks were excellent. "He may be able to find out something from the transfer agent. And maybe, if I can get an appointment with Carmichael, I'll take a run out to Chicago this week."

"Wait a minute," Brian protested. "Chemicals are *my* thing."

"You're going to Virginia."

"Not until Thursday." He thought it over. "I suppose, though . . ." Suddenly he brightened. "You could fly from Chicago to Virginia. Meanwhile I'll talk to Keith."

"Keith?"

"My brother. He may be able to find out something."

I couldn't imagine what Keith could find out. But then, I didn't try very hard. "Really, Brian . . ."

I began to waver. There was no reason not to go to Virginia. It would be nice to meet Brian's family.

Ten minutes later, with my consent, Brian placed a call to his mother and told her to expect one more for Christmas dinner.

And with that matter settled, I began to make plans for the rest of the week.

16

Helen was at her desk on Monday morning, as promised. She was meticulously dressed and coifed, but looked awful. My heart went out to her.

Her self-control was back to normal, however. She handled the accumulated mail by arranging it in two neat stacks—one designated these-I-believe-I-can-answer-for-you-Mr.-Potter; the other, you'll-probably-want-to-answer-these-yourself. She was right on all counts, and within fifteen minutes my desk was clear.

There was no trace of the hysterical woman who'd summoned me to 116th Street and Broadway on Monday night, and she was plainly reluctant to discuss the event. When I asked her how Andrea was, she replied with a formal "As well as can be expected," and when I said I was sorry I hadn't been able to attend the funeral, she gave me a similarly formal "I quite understand."

She'd already made arrangements for the forecast material, she said. She'd collected it from the cabinet where I'd stored it over the weekend and had called the printer—he would be around at ten thirty to collect it; meanwhile she'd taken the liberty of having a photocopy made. I thanked her and refrained from asking how she'd known where I'd stored it—I guessed that my habits were as predictable to her as hers were to me.

Before starting the staff meeting, I had a brief talk with Mark. I told him about Koberg Chemical and asked him to see what he could find out from the transfer agent. He said he would, adding that if he couldn't learn anything from the transfer agent, he would track down the man who made the market in Koberg.

The staff meeting itself was the dullest I could remember. We'd used up all our material, and no one had anything new to contribute. Not even Brian, who could usually be counted on to liven things up by springing one or two items he'd been withholding.

I thought that Saturday's mood of total cooperation might have been a fluke, and while the group was assembled in my office I looked for signs of lingering hard feelings. I couldn't detect any that were overt, but I sensed that Harriet was still a bit out of sorts, and when the meeting broke up, at a quarter to eleven, I invited her to have dinner with me after work. She thanked me, but asked for a raincheck. Christmas shopping, she explained.

After the meeting I spent a few minutes thinking about Koberg. Did I really want to make the trip? I was less prepared to interview Paul Carmichael than I usually was when I went on the road. I didn't know him and had no specific questions in mind. All I knew was that Koberg stock had been going up.

It would be a fishing expedition, I decided. And I was without bait.

But stocks didn't rise for no reason. Especially stocks which had been dormant for years.

I decided to go. And, having made up my mind, I immediately placed a call to the Koberg offices in Chicago.

"Mr. Paul Carmichael," I told the switchboard operator who answered.

"Who shall I say is calling?"

"Brockton Potter, of Price, Potter and Petacque, in New York."

She connected me with Carmichael's secretary, who asked the same question and one more—what did I want to speak with Mr. Carmichael about? I told her that I wanted to make an appointment with him.

There was a longish silence. Finally a man said, "Paul Carmichael speaking."

"My name is Brockton Potter," I said, putting a friendly smile into my voice. "I'm with Price, Potter and Petacque. We're a stockbrokerage firm. We—"

"I know who you are, Mr. Potter. I've read about you."

"Really? Well, I'm going to be in Chicago the middle of this week, and I'd like to make an appointment with you. Our firm is preparing a survey of chemicals companies, and Koberg is one we'd like to include."

"I'm flattered. But I'm afraid that I won't be here the middle of this week."

The pause between the two sentences was just long enough to arouse doubt in my mind. "Oh?"

"Christmas, you know."

"I see. How about the following week, then?"

"I'm afraid that won't be any good either."

"Well, in that case why don't you suggest a date that'll be convenient for you, and I'll adjust my plans accordingly."

"I can't say for sure, Mr. Potter, just when I'll have time. Why don't we leave it this way: when something opens up, I'll call you."

Like in five years, I thought. "That depends," I said, keeping the smile in my voice, with difficulty. "We're working against a deadline of sorts, and I have my own schedule to consider. You know how it is. Our clients have their needs, and there's quite a bit of interest in chemicals companies at the moment."

"I wasn't aware of that."

"Gosh, yes. There *always* is, but lately we've been getting even more requests for information than usual."

"Not about Koberg, certainly."

"Why, yes. Among others."

Carmichael said nothing.

"So you see my problem," I said at last.

"Yes, I do. But I'm afraid I don't have any time just now, Mr. Potter. I'll call you when something opens." And with that, Carmichael hung up.

I put down the telephone and swore.

"Such language!" Irving said.

I hadn't seen him come into the office, but he was standing just inside the doorway, grinning.

I swore again.

"Would you rather I came back?" he asked.

"No, Irv. Come on in. What's on your mind?"

"Nothing. I thought I'd go to lunch, and I thought maybe you'd go with me, but I guess I picked the wrong day."

"It's only a quarter past eleven."

"I know. But I have nothing to do."

"Well, I'll give you something to do. Sit down and tell me what you think of me."

"I beg your pardon?"

"I want to know what you think of me. My reputation, I mean. I believe it's beginning to get in my way."

Irving shook his head. "I'd rather go out to lunch."

We debated the matter, and both of us won. I agreed to go out to lunch with Irving, and he agreed to tell me what he thought of my reputation. Seriously, I insisted. Seriously, he promised.

And, as it turned out, we had rather a good time. The restaurant wasn't crowded, there was pumpkin pie on the menu, and Irving's comments about my reputation weren't too upsetting.

Basically, he said, I was one of the five best securities analysts in New York. Some people considered me *the* best. But the publicity I'd got had hurt me. A number of folks thought I was a glory hound and dangerous.

I didn't know about being *the* best, I told him. I didn't even know about being one of the *five* best. But I did believe that I was ranked pretty high. He was right, though, about the publicity. It made certain types wary of me. And what was so unfair was I hadn't sought the publicity; it had been thrust on me.

No one knew that better than he, Irving replied. I was anything but a publicity-seeker. But, still and all, I couldn't go around exposing criminal fraud and getting people into trouble, no matter how much they deserved it, without attracting attention—and arousing curiosity as to my motives.

It was too bad, I said. Corruption and greed weren't universal, but they did exist, and a fellow couldn't help stumbling across them occasionally. My misfortune was that I'd stumbled across a few particularly flagrant examples and, instead of walking away from them, I'd rushed in to do battle. In the long run, the public had benefitted from my actions. But I certainly hadn't done myself any good.

Irving nodded, and asked, "If you had it all to do over again, would you do anything different?"

"I don't suppose I would," I replied, after a moment's thought. "If I did, I'd end up hating myself. I can't be an ostrich, Irv. I just can't."

Irving smiled. "No. An ostrich you'll never be."

"All I can hope is that I'll never be put to the test again."

"Amen. But tell me, Brock, why the introspection all of a sudden?"

"Because I was trying to get an appointment with a man named Paul Carmichael and he turned me down. He said he'd read about me, and that was that."

"Who is he?"

I told him, and gave him a rundown of the conversation. "I don't believe he's going out of town this week," I concluded, "because when I tried to get an appointment with him for some time later, he put me off. I think he's afraid of me."

"Maybe it's not you he's afraid of. Maybe he's afraid of all securities analysts. After all, he hasn't had much experience with people like us. We haven't been interested in him."

"Could be, I suppose. But I don't know. . . ."

"Why Koberg?" Irving asked. "And why you? Brian'll be furious."

I explained the situation. My talk with Brian. What Ward and Tom had said. The manner in which Koberg had come to my attention in the first place.

Irving looked thoughtful.

"See what I mean?" I said.

"That casts a different light on it," he said finally. "What are you going to do?"

"I'm not sure. I have half a mind to go to Chicago anyway. Where there's smoke, there's fire. And when someone is evasive . . ."

My chief honcho nodded. He knew the signals as well as I, and evasiveness was as much a signal as the unexplained movement in the price of Koberg's stock.

We dropped the subject, for there was nothing more to be said. Each of us knew what the other was thinking. Koberg's stock was rising. Koberg's president wanted to avoid me. For those two reasons alone, Koberg merited investigation.

For some minutes I considered not going to Chicago, but by the time we left the restaurant, I'd made up my mind: with or without Carmichael's cooperation, I would find out what the company was up to.

My eyes met Irving's, and, without speaking, we agreed.

"What's the first step?" he asked as we walked back to the office.

"A condolence call," I replied.

17

Dick Knight lit a fire in the fireplace. Rosemary brought out a decanter of sherry, a bowl of apples and a plate of cheese squares with colored toothpicks in them. The crackling fire and the assorted refreshments on the coffee table gave the room a semblance of cheer, but the expressions of the three people who faced me across the coffee table dispelled it. The Knights and James McDonald looked like a trio of new arrivals in purgatory.

I'd expected it to be bad, but I hadn't expected it to be that bad, and I didn't know how to get started. When I tried to express sympathy, tears slid down Rosemary's cheeks, while Dick nodded miserably and McDonald glared at me with hot, what-do-you-know-about-it eyes. And my attempts at general conversation fared no better.

After a while I decided on the direct approach. I focused my attention entirely on McDonald and said, matter-of-factly, "Joe Rothland tells me that you used to work for Koberg Chemical."

The remark had been directed to him, but all three of them reacted. For a moment, wretchedness was replaced by surprise. Rosemary started to speak for her brother, but before she could say anything, he spoke for himself. "What about it?" he demanded, his eyes becoming even angrier.

"I'm somewhat interested in the company at the moment," I

replied. "I'm thinking of making a study of it. I was wondering if you could give me the name of anyone who's connected with it."

Surprise, resentment and now suspicion. "Where'd you get that idea?"

"It was more in the nature of a hope."

"Well, you can stop hoping. I don't know anyone."

"It was such a long time ago," Rosemary put in quickly.

I didn't look at her. I kept my gaze on him. "You not only worked for Koberg, as I understand it; you were married to old Gus Koberg's granddaughter."

"So what?"

"Have some more sherry," Dick offered nervously, although my glass was still full.

I shook my head.

"Is that why you came here?" McDonald asked harshly. "To get names?"

"That's one of the reasons."

"You rich people are all alike."

"Oh?"

"All you care about are yourselves."

"Now, Jim," Rosemary said, sounding like an indulgent mother speaking to a wayward child.

"Maybe we ought to change the subject," Dick suggested.

I ignored both of them. "Actually," I said to McDonald, "my motives aren't altogether selfish. My studies go to some of the pension funds that send monthly checks to retired workers and to trust officers that look after widows and orphans and all kinds of other people who can't look after themselves."

"And you get rich off them."

"Now, Jim," Rosemary said again.

McDonald turned to her. "Well, he does. You've seen his house. You've seen how big it is. He's got paintings all over it, too—paintings and etchings and statues. Stuff worth a fortune. He buys, he sells, he tells other people what to buy and sell—he's rich."

"You're right," I said. "But let's get one thing straight, Jim. I wasn't born rich. I started out as poor as you've ever been, and whatever I have now I made for myself, and made honestly, so I don't feel I have to apologize for it. So why don't we just dispense with the class warfare?"

"Class warfare?"

"Or whatever you want to call it."

"I don't want to call it anything. It was nice of you to give that party for Bob and Andrea, even though you were really doing it for your secretary and not for them—but that doesn't give you the right to go poking around in my affairs."

"I'm not asserting a right, Jim. I'm asking for help."

"Well, you're asking the wrong person."

I hadn't anticipated that I'd lose my temper—or even that I'd be provoked. But that was what was happening. And I said the first thing that came to mind. "What's bugging you, McDonald—the fact that you got sent to jail?"

The three of them just stared at me.

"Yes," I said. "I know about it."

Rosemary was the first to recover. "May I remind you," she said coldly, "that this is a house of mourning?"

"I know that," I told her, "and I'm truly sorry. I only met your nephew once, but I liked him. He was a fine young man. I'm sorry I didn't get to know him better. I think his death is a real tragedy, and I feel for you—for all of you. But I did hope that in spite of your grief you'd be able to help me. It didn't seem that I was asking anything unreasonable."

"You're raking up unpleasant memories," Dick said.

"Very," McDonald added. But he didn't look as resentful as he had before. It was as if I'd lanced an abscess and some of the poison had drained. In fact, he smiled. "You shouldn't have come yourself, Potter. You should have sent Joe Rothland. I like him better than you."

"Why?" I asked, genuinely curious.

"He's not a boss."

This was the first time I'd seen him smile, and the smile improved his appearance. He was at his worst now, I realized; he hadn't shaved in a couple of days, the lower lids of his eyes were red, and his face seemed to have lost whatever little fullness it had had. But it crossed my mind, as it had when he was at my house, that he must have been quite handsome when he was younger. "I gather that you really don't like us bosses," I said, doing the best I could to return his smile.

"I don't like anybody who makes life hard for other people."

"Neither do I."

We looked at each other and came to an understanding of sorts.

"It's all Elissa's fault," he said.

"Elissa?"

"My ex-mother-in-law. *Née* Koberg, as she used to put it." There was arsenic in his tone.

"What is?"

"Everything."

"Now, Jim," Rosemary said soothingly, "you'll only make yourself feel worse. I'm sure Mr. Potter doesn't want to hear about all that."

"A few minutes ago I was Brock," I told her. "And I *do* want to hear about all that."

McDonald got up and went into the dining room. A moment later he returned with a bottle of bourbon and a glass. Sitting down, he poured himself at least four ounces of the whiskey. "He wants to hear," he said to his sister, then turned to me. "That's what you came for, isn't it—to hear?"

"All I wanted were some names of people you might know at Koberg," I replied, "but yes, I'm interested."

He took a long swallow of bourbon, and Rosemary sighed.

"What was your wife's maiden name?" I asked.

"Cadbury. Bonita Cadbury. Bonnie."

"She was the granddaughter of Augustus Koberg?"

McDonald nodded. "Elissa Koberg had been her mother's maiden name before she married her first husband. But she had Bonnie, the only child she ever had, by her second husband, and his name was Cadbury. He was an English lord. Lord Abingdale. Bonnie didn't remember him. She was only two when her mother and father divorced. And when I met her, her mother was married to her third husband, the Duke of Hess-Bandenburg."

"Tell me about her mother," I said.

His face darkened. "She was still rich."

"Still?"

"In spite of all the money she'd spent. She'd always spent a lot of money. That's all she was good for—spending money. That and getting married. She's now married to her fifth husband. She's a terrible woman, Mr. Potter. She's always been a terrible woman. Even Bonnie never liked her."

"Who else was there in the Koberg family?"

"By then, nobody. Both her parents had been dead for a long time—her mother died before her father. She'd had a brother, but he was dead too—he'd died as a kid. So, as far as America was concerned, the Koberg family was extinct. There was nobody left except Elissa, and she wasn't what you'd call an American. She'd lived in Europe most of her life. She'd gone to school over there—one of those boarding schools in Switzerland. Then she'd married a French marquis, then Bonnie's father, then the German duke, and after him a Spaniard, and now she's married to another Frenchman, the Count de Garonne. All her husbands have been members of some big-name family. That's what she went in for—titles. Would you believe it? Titles! Aristocrats! In this day and age!" His face grew even darker. "That's why she was so against Bonnie's marrying me. I wasn't an aristocrat."

"What were you?"

"What do you mean, what was I? I was a man. A plain American man. But I was educated, believe it or not. Our folks saw to that, didn't they, Rosie? They saw to it that we had an education. And it wasn't easy for them, either. But that's what I was. A man. An American ex-GI."

"How did you meet Bonnie?"

A log disintegrated, sending a shower of sparks against the firescreen.

"At the Wilsons'," McDonald said. "The Dwight Wilsons'. He was president of Koberg. He did a lot of his work at home. I was asked to take some papers out to his house for him to sign. And Bonnie was there."

"Dwight Wilson was your boss?"

"Not my direct boss. I was in purchasing. But he was head of the company, so he was everybody's boss."

"Did Elissa ever come to the office?"

McDonald shook his head. "She never cared about the company. All she cared about were the dividends."

"So you met your wife at the Wilsons'," I said. "Go on."

He drank some more bourbon, and for the better part of a minute he remained mute, staring at the tabletop. Then he began to speak again, but his viewpoint had shifted. He now approached the story of his marriage from the other side—the Koberg side. And some of the bitterness left him. He became almost detached. A historian.

The last decade of a monarchical Europe. An American heiress, spoiled, alienated, neurotic. A boarding school catering to members of a society that was about to die but didn't know it. Elissa had opted for membership in that society, had clung doggedly to it through its lingering demise—and was still clinging to its desiccated remains.

Manor houses and antique-filled apartments in half a dozen countries. Maids who curtsied. All-day sessions in the fitting rooms of the leading couturiers. Elissa had rolled meaninglessly and self-indulgently through young womanhood, maturity and middle age, never gathering the moss of self-knowledge and eventually rolling into alcoholism. Avoiding, all the while, a daughter she hadn't wanted, couldn't love and didn't know what to do with.

Bonnie, apparently, had always been in the way. And had from infancy been turned over to governesses, boarding schools and elderly gentlewomen who took select groups of girls on art-appreciation tours of Italy. Her father had no more interest in her than her mother did, and her stepfather was all but a stranger to her, as were the various men who occupied her mother's time and boudoir between marriages. A beautiful, shy, self-contained girl, Bonnie never really had a home. Or, for that matter, a country. She was being raised to follow in her mother's footsteps. And undoubtedly that was what she would have done if Hitler hadn't decided to devour Europe.

Elissa, then newly married to her first husband, the marquis, had remained in France throughout the First World War. But she returned to the United States for the duration of the Second. According to McDonald, Hess-Bandenburg was a Nazi. At any rate, he was called into the German army. And in the spring of 1940, shortly before the invasion of France, Elissa, with Bonnie in tow, made the difficult journey across the Continent to Portugal and from there to the United States. Not, McDonald said, because she had anything against Hitler, but because she realized that Europe was going to become less comfortable than it had ever been, and because she hoped to get an American divorce—Hess-Bandenburg had been unwilling to give her a divorce in Germany.

She took an apartment on Lake Shore Drive in Chicago, the city of her birth and the only American city with which she was acquainted, and for the next five years Chicago was the base of her operations. Bonnie entered Northwestern University.

For Elissa, five irritating years of feeling lost and out of place.

For Bonnie, five years of the first real happiness she'd ever known.

And for Jim McDonald, one long revelation.

"I'd gotten my discharge the end of '43," he explained. "A Jap grenade. And I'd gotten a job with Koberg. I was doing well, too. Wilson liked me—I thought. But Elissa managed to talk him into firing me."

"Firing you?"

He nodded grimly, and finished the bourbon. "After I married Bonnie."

Instant attraction, Bonnie and the ex-GI. A passionate but troubled courtship. Marriage, despite Elissa's fiery objections. And a steady downhill slide into disaster.

McDonald's account of his courtship and marriage contained gaps. But he told me enough so that I could fill in the gaps for myself.

He was exactly what Elissa most despised in people: he was ordinary. Her whole life had been spent in the pursuit of those who had something special in the way of heritage. But Jim McDonald could claim nothing of that sort. His father had been a department-store clerk in Omaha, Nebraska—and no one in the family had ever been more than that. Jim's mere existence was a challenge to every belief Elissa cherished, and the fact that someone such as he would be her son-in-law was intolerable to her.

She and Bonnie quarreled bitterly over him. And for a while Elissa's will prevailed—Bonnie stopped seeing him. But he was the first man Bonnie had ever loved, the first human being to whom she'd ever been deeply attached, and the separation from him was too much for her. They began keeping company again, furtively. And early in 1945 they eloped and were married in Crown Point, Indiana.

Elissa was livid—and unforgiving. She cut Bonnie out of her life, disinherited her and arranged for Jim to be fired. Thus avenged, and free at last from Hess-Bandenburg—not by divorce, but by a shell fragment at Tobruk—she took off for Europe in 1946, and her daughter and son-in-law never saw her again.

They notified her of the birth of her grandson, but received no acknowledgment. They heard of her only indirectly, through a Chicago friend of hers, Dorothy Whitcomb, who encountered her from time to time in Europe. She'd married again, Dorothy informed them—a Spaniard—and was dividing her time between Madrid and Marbella, where she'd built a new house.

Young love had triumphed, but the price had been stiff. Too stiff.

It seemed strange to McDonald that he couldn't get a decent job. The good jobs simply eluded him. Later he learned why. Elissa had not only arranged for him to be fired; she'd also arranged for him to be slandered. It was reported, through the personnel office of Koberg Chemical, that he'd been fired for taking kickbacks. When he tried to confront Wilson with what he'd learned, Wilson refused to see him; and the personnel director denied everything. But the rumor persisted.

Employed at low wages, married to a wife who could identify the work of every major artist from Giotto to Matisse but who couldn't cook or do laundry, who'd never known what it was not to have money, McDonald did his best, but his best wasn't good enough. Bonnie wasn't able to manage. Debts accumulated. And Bonnie began to suffer from depression. After she gave birth to Bob, her depression grew worse.

"And pretty soon she died," he concluded abruptly.

"Suicide?" I asked.

McDonald didn't answer, but his brother-in-law did. "Locked herself in the kitchen and turned on the gas."

In the ensuing silence, I thought of my father. He too, overwhelmed by a poverty he hadn't been prepared for and couldn't cope with, had killed himself. His death had been, and still was, like a bone that was stuck in my throat.

I felt somewhat shaken. But evidently McDonald felt even more shaken, for suddenly he got up and strode out of the room, and presently I heard a door slam at the other end of the apartment.

"You see what you stirred up," Rosemary said. She was no longer the charming wife of the witty professor, as she'd been at my house. Nor was she the grief-stricken aunt who, in spite of her sorrow, had tried to be a gracious hostess when I'd arrived at the apartment. She was angry.

I nodded.

"And I suppose you also want to know why he got sent to jail," she went on accusingly.

I said nothing.

"Well, I'll tell you. He was six thousand dollars in debt. He had a child to look after and no wife. He took a day's receipts from the cash register at the store he was working in and he got caught. He'd intended to pay the money back, but no one believed him. And ever since then—all these years—only the most menial type of jobs, because of his record—when he could get a job at all. Trouble, that's all he's had. Trouble and discouragement. And now . . . now . . . ." She couldn't finish.

"He's had a pretty rough time," Dick said, reaching for his wife's hand.

But she didn't want to give him her hand. She wanted to make two fists instead. "And all because of that—that witch!" she exclaimed, bringing the fists down hard on the cushions of the sofa. "I hope she gets what she deserves. God, how I hope she gets what she deserves!"

There was another long silence.

Finally Rosemary pulled herself together. "Excuse me. I'm not being very nice, am I?"

"Understandable," I murmured.

"She didn't even come to her daughter's funeral," Dick said disgustedly.

"And Bob, her grandson—no interest whatsoever?" I asked.

"Well . . ."

Rosemary spoke up. "She showed a little interest a couple of times. Once, when Bob was about ten, her lawyer sent a letter. She wanted Jim to send Bob over to Spain to visit her. But Jim was still in prison, and Bob was living with us, so it was up to us to make the decision, we thought—and we didn't think it would be good for Bob to go. The woman was already separated from her Spanish husband, you see, and . . . well, she was living with a man she wasn't married to. We didn't feel that that was a very suitable environment for a child at an impressionable age."

"And then later on," Dick amended, "the lawyer wrote again. The same sort of letter. She was married to the Count by this time, and it probably would have been all right; but Bob himself didn't want to go. He was just finishing his freshman year at Columbia and he was having a good time and—well, he just didn't want to."

"Quite rightly, in my opinion," Rosemary said tartly. "Jim was willing to forgive and forget, but not I. I may have been wrong, but I don't think so." Suddenly her shoulders sagged, and her voice softened. Tears again welled up in her eyes. "Now it doesn't make any difference."

Once more her husband reached for her hand. This time she let him take it.

I looked at the two of them sitting side by side on the sofa, a pair of bereft surrogate parents. Leave them alone, I thought; you've distressed them enough. "Well," I said, "I guess I'd better be going."

Neither of them made any attempt to detain me, and I got up from the chair. Dick accompanied me to the door.

"By the way," I said as he handed me my coat, "would you happen to remember the name of Elissa Koberg's lawyer?"

"Why, yes," he replied, startled. "Fisher. Amos Fisher. But he won't be able to help you. He's dead now. Been dead for several years."

"What about Dwight Wilson? Is he dead too?"

Dick said he didn't know anything about Wilson—tonight was the first time in years that the man's name had been mentioned in the house.

"And Dorothy Whitcomb?"

"Dorothy Whitcomb?" Rosemary said, joining us in the hall.

"I was asking if she was still alive," I explained.

"Who knows?" Rosemary said. "But if you're interested in the company, she's not the one to ask. She was merely a friend of Elissa's."

I expressed my condolences again, and left.

But when I got home, I did the very thing I'd advised Helen not to do. I called Philip Quick.

I asked for information about Dwight Wilson, Amos Fisher and Dorothy Whitcomb.

18

I'd just got settled at my desk when Mark appeared with an armload of Christmas cards. "It's your turn," he said, depositing them on my desk.

I picked up the topmost card. On the outside was a picture of a dove with an olive branch in its mouth. "Peace on Earth," was the caption. And the message inside was equally brief: "Good Will Toward Men—Season's Greetings." Mark had signed the card, and so had Tom.

"Better than a letter," I said, reaching for my pen, "but not very original."

"The store was crowded," he replied. "I still think letters would have done." He noticed the suitcase beside my desk. "Where in the world—?"

"Peace on earth, Mark."

"But it's—"

"Good will toward men. Chicago. The twelve-o'clock flight. I need some expense money."

"Chicago?"

"Sit down and I'll tell you."

He sat down and I told him. It was interesting to watch his expression change. From a sort of puzzled annoyance it went to thoughtful consideration, with a moment of surprise in between.

The surprise came when I said I'd called on Andrea Doyle's would-have-been father-in-law.

But, with characteristic acuteness, he immediately saw through to the crux of the matter. "It might be a sleeper," he said, "but you have nothing to go on. You're fishing."

"And I may not catch anything," I admitted. "But if I do catch something, we'll be the first with it—no one else is suspicious yet." Then I thought of Darryl Otis and added a cautious "Or so it would seem."

Mark nodded. "And if Hardin asked once, he'll ask again." He paused. "I'm abashed. I've been remiss. I haven't yet tackled the transfer agent."

Abashed. Remiss. I tried not to smile. At times Mark sounded like the late President Franklin D. Roosevelt—they'd attended the same schools, a couple of generations apart. "O.K.," I said, "let me know as soon as you find out anything. Meanwhile I need five hundred bucks."

Mark left, and I signed the Christmas cards, then went into Tom's office.

Tom was talking alternately into two telephones, one of which was tucked between his ear and his shoulder, and punching away at his telequote machine with his free hand. He looked decidedly harried. But he managed to smile when he saw me.

I waited for the excitement to die down, then said, "I just dropped in to wish you a nice trip and a Merry Christmas, chum. I'm off to Chicago."

Tom's reaction, when I explained the purpose of my trip, was different from Mark's, but just as typical. "Honestly, Brock," he said, with real concern in his voice, "you're pushing yourself too hard. Mark's going on vacation, I'm going on vacation, and you're carrying on as if it wasn't even Christmas. I feel guilty."

"Don't," I replied. "I'm too old for Christmas. Anyway, I told Brian I'd stop off in Virginia on my way home."

He shook his head sadly and was about to speak, but just then one of his telephones rang, so I gave him a cheerful wave and went on to Irving's office, where I spent twenty minutes discussing the Tuesday letter. It was, Irving and I agreed, going to be skimpier than we would like.

The Christmas cards were still on my desk. I buzzed for Helen and asked her to take them to Mark. She picked them up and then stood there hesitantly, holding them.

Her "Good morning, Mr. Potter" had had more life to it than the one the day before, and she'd seemed less haggard. She'd noticed the suitcase and taken an interest. When I'd told her that I was going to Chicago, she'd asked whether I needed reservations. I'd said that I'd already made them, but the fact that she'd asked had seemed a good sign.

Now she was looking troubled again, however. Her eyes, her mouth, her posture—she was a woman with a problem. "Er— Mr. Potter," she said awkwardly. "I—er—"

"Yes?"

"Well, I received a telephone call a few minutes ago. From Rosemary Knight."

"Yes?"

"She said that you were over there last night. She said that you're—uh—looking into the Koberg company."

"That's right."

"Well, what I want to say is I hope that you're not doing so because of Andrea and me."

"Why, no. Whatever gave you that idea, Helen?" But I knew the answer: Rosemary had given her that idea. "I'm going because there's been some interest lately in Koberg's stock."

"Oh, I'm glad," she said with relief. "I thought perhaps—"

"One thing has nothing to do with the other."

"I wouldn't want to feel responsible."

"You're not."

"Because I know how you are."

"Oh? How am I?"

"You know what I mean. You go *into* things."

I smiled. To an extent, I knew, Helen shared the opinion of those who thought I enjoyed wading in troubled waters. But she was ambivalent about it. My activities sometimes worried her, but she was rather proud of them. "It's my going into things that helps pay our salaries," I said.

"Oh, I didn't mean—"

"I know what you meant, Helen, and I appreciate your

concern. I can assure you, though, that this has nothing to do with you."

"I'm so glad. Because Rosemary . . ." She didn't finish.

"Rosemary is disturbed," I finished for her.

"Rather."

"I got that impression last night. She thinks I'm interested in her brother's past. Well, I'm not. I'm just looking for a gopher to dig me a hole into the president's office."

Helen came as close to smiling as she'd done in over a week. "A gopher," she said. "I'll tell her that." And she went on her way, with the Christmas cards.

I leaned back in my chair. Bits and pieces of James McDonald's story came back to me. Life had been tough on the guy. A wife who committed suicide. A prison term. And now a son murdered. Fate could be malevolent.

But Helen was right, in a way. If it hadn't been for her and Andrea, I never would have met James McDonald. And if the researchers hadn't quarreled, Joe wouldn't have met him either and the Koberg company might not have come to my attention.

The chain of events, I thought. Always the chain of events.

I began to make plans. First an unannounced call on Paul Carmichael. Then Wilson and the Whitcomb woman.

Something inside me stirred, tentatively. A sort of excitement. And it occurred to me that, no matter what I said or thought to the contrary, I liked what I was about to do. Situations with unknown outcomes appealed to me.

I glanced at my watch. Twenty minutes to eleven. Time to be going.

On the way out, I stopped in the researchers' office to wish everyone a happy holiday and tell Brian what time I'd arrive in Richmond. Then I went in to see Mark. He had the expense money ready for me. Also some information.

"I wasn't able to find out much," he said, "but I did find out something. The main purchaser of Koberg stock lately has been a bank—the Central Markham and Retailers. Whether they're acting for their own trust accounts or for someone else, I couldn't discover. But there's something else. Koberg Chemical has started buying up its own stock."

"In the open market?"

Mark nodded.

"Interesting," I observed. "Well, have fun on the golf course."

"Good luck, old man."

We shook hands, and I left.

The sense of excitement that had stirred earlier intensified as the taxi carried me along the East River Drive and across the Triborough Bridge. Skiing was nice, I decided. So was golf. But it seemed to me that at the moment I was the luckiest of the three Price, Potter and Petacque partners: I was going fishing.

19

It was snowing in Chicago. Not hard—just hard enough to make the pavement slippery under my rented Oldsmobile. But even with the snow and the hazardous road conditions, I was glad to be back. Chicago was a city that I visited fairly often and liked.

At the moment, however, because of the poor visibility, it seemed to have vanished. I was almost downtown before I spotted the dim outlines of the John Hancock Center and the Sears Tower, the two black spindles that always served as my compass when I was in the area. By then it was after three o'clock, so, instead of first checking into the hotel, I went directly to the Koberg offices, which were located on South Michigan Avenue.

I knew South Michigan Avenue from the old days when it was the address of such companies as Standard Oil of Indiana, International Harvester, IBM and Pullman, all of which had since moved into new quarters; but I hadn't had occasion to go there in recent years. The neighborhood, I noted with some sadness, now had an air of neglect. The buildings were still there, but the people weren't. And even the buildings were beginning to look shabby.

The Koberg Building couldn't have been beautiful even when it was new, which, according to the carving on the lintel, was in

1908. It was ten stories of red brick without any adornment—a lot of bricks, a lot of windows and a plain glass door that was in need of washing. Furthermore, with its prosperous neighbors gone, there was something left-behind and lonely about it.

The lobby was no better than the exterior—plain gray marble, chipped in places, with a directory on one wall and a single sand-filled ashstand under it. Carmichael, Paul, I saw on the directory, had his office on the eighth floor. I stepped into one of the automatic elevators, which appeared to be newer than anything else in the building, and pushed "8." The elevator rose swiftly.

The spacious reception foyer on the eighth floor was paneled with oak and had Cupids and bunches of grapes bulging from it at strategic points, and the receptionist sat behind a glass window. The receptionist's duties included the operation of a large switchboard of a vintage that the Illinois Bell Telephone Company had pretty much done away with in most places. She was busy.

I walked over to the window, which was partly open, and eavesdropped.

"Just a moment, and I'll connect you. . . . Mr. Jenkens is out at the moment, may I take a message? . . . Certainly, Mr. Fowler, I'll get him for you."

It was some little time before she noticed me, and by then I'd heard what I'd wanted to hear: "Mr. Carmichael is in conference, can he call you back?"

We exchanged smiles, and she said, "May I help you?"

"I'd like to see Mr. Carmichael," I said.

"Mr. Carmichael's in conference, but if you'd care to give me your name . . ."

"Potter." I omitted my first name.

"Do you have an appointment?"

I shook my head.

She eyed me with uncertainty and decided to consult with higher authority. Shoving a plug into one of the holes and flicking a lever that was almost too big to be flicked, she reported, "There's a Mr. Potter to see Mr. Carmichael. He doesn't have an appointment."

Silence reigned while the higher authority considered the information, or passed it on to Carmichael himself.

"I'm sorry," the receptionist told me finally, "but Mr. Carmichael won't be able to see you, Mr. Potter. He'll be tied up for the rest of the day."

"Will he be in tomorrow?"

"Why, yes—as far as I know. But if you want an appointment, I suggest you call first."

"Thank you," I said. "I'll do that. Meanwhile, I'd like to leave a message. Tell Mr. Carmichael that Brockton Potter is at the Drake Hotel and would appreciate a call."

She wrote it down, and I turned to leave.

As I did so, the door of one of the elevators opened, and a man stepped out.

I recognized him instantly. He was the man who'd been at the Brasserie with Louis Glass. Same Julius Caesar haircut, same camel's-hair polo coat, same everything.

And apparently he recognized me too, for when our eyes met, his face registered shock and he quickly backed into the elevator before the door closed.

"Who was that?" I asked the receptionist.

"Who was who?"

"The man who just got out of the elevator."

She shook her head. "I didn't see any man."

She probably hadn't, I thought. I'd been standing in the way.

I crossed to where the elevators were. The elevator that had taken the man in the polo coat up stopped for me as it went down. But he wasn't in it.

I returned to my car, brushed some snow off the windshield and got in.

Twenty minutes later I was at the Drake. It was no more deserted than any other big-city hotel during the week before Christmas, but that wasn't saying much. I had the feeling that maybe ten percent of the rooms were occupied. The bellman who took me up to my room seemed pathetically grateful to have something to do.

As soon as the bellman left, I threw my topcoat on the bed and grabbed the telephone.

It was too late to reach Harriet at the office, but I reached her at home.

"I have an assignment for you," I said. "An important assignment."

"Honestly?" She sounded almost as grateful as the bellman, and I had the feeling that by giving her what I called an important assignment I was doing more to cement relations than I would have done by taking her to dinner.

"How good are your sources at the Central Markham and Retailers?" I asked.

"Quite solid."

"Wonderful. Central Markham has been buying stock in Koberg Chemical. I want to know if they're a front for Interamerican Marine, and if there's any connection between the bank and Louis Glass. I think I may have stumbled onto something."

20

I'd set my watch back an hour when the plane landed in Chicago, but I hadn't been able to set myself back; I woke up on New York time. I stayed in bed, waiting for dawn to break, but this was one of those days when dawn didn't break. The sky went from black to dark gray and that was that.

At seven thirty I rang for coffee, and evidently I was the only one in the hotel who wanted anything, for the coffee arrived within five minutes. I stood at the window, sipping, and watched the cars moving north and south along Lake Shore Drive. It was too early to make plans or to speculate, so for a little while I let go of my identity. It was kind of transcendental and nice.

But at ten minutes to eight the telephone rang, breaking the spell. I put my coffee cup on the windowsill and rejoined the rest of humanity.

"Potter?" said the grating voice at the other end of the line.

"Hi, Quick," I answered. He was punctual as always.

"It took longer than I thought. It took almost the whole day yesterday. Lucky this is my slow season."

"Right." What he was getting me ready for, I surmised, was a sizable bill.

"Number one—the lawyer. Amos Fisher. He *is* dead. No doubt about that. Died two years ago last August nine, aged eighty-seven."

106

"A ripe old age."

"Yeah. Anyway, he was with a firm called Koenig, Koenig, Dempster and Fisher, and you're right about him handling the Koberg estate. That's all he did handle. It was his life's work. So I guess he didn't practice much law—just looked after that one family's investments. Kind of a cushy job, if you ask me."

"There were a lot of investments."

"Even so. Anyway, he lived in Winnetka, had a wife, who died just after he did, and—"

"None of that matters. Who's handling the estate now?"

"You didn't say you wanted *that*, Potter. I can find out, but it'll be extra."

"Never mind. I can find out for myself, if I need to know."

"O.K., so number two—Wilson. He's still among the living, but pretty old. Eighty-four. You want his address and phone number?"

"Yes."

Quick gave them to me, and I wrote them down. Wilson too lived in Winnetka. "Were Fisher and Wilson neighbors?" I asked.

"Half a mile or so, I'd say. Anyway, he's a widower. His wife died three years ago. Had two sons, but both of them are dead too. One a long time back, in World War II; the other, eight years ago, after some heart surgery. Anyway, a widowed sister, Abigail Henning, moved in with him after his wife died. She keeps house for him. He retired as president and chief executive officer of Koberg Chemical Company six years ago this coming December thirty-first. He banks with City and Southern. Savings account in the low sixes, checking account in the fours, most of the time. Used to be a big shot in the Boy Scouts and the Chamber of Commerce and some clubs, but no more. Used to like trout fishing and golf, but no more of that either. Too old. And his health ain't so hot, I hear. Anything else you want to know?"

"Is he senile?"

"Nobody said he babbles. And he does his own banking."

"What about the Whitcomb woman?"

"She's also among the living. Your nextdoor neighbor, in fact."

"My nextdoor neighbor?"

"She lives at the Drake Tower. Has damn near since the building went up."

"Well, what do you know!"

"I thought you'd like that. Anyway, she's sort of a society dame—or at least she used to be. She's pretty old now too. Eighty-three. She's from the Whitcomb Rug family. Never married."

"Really?"

"I know the kind. I've had them as clients. Still have mother's tea service and ride around in thirty-year-old Rolls Royces. Never remember where they put their pearls and think the maid stole them. She's worth a couple of million, I'd say. At least. Anyway, she doesn't give a dime to any charity I've been able to find out about, and has arthritis, and never misses the opening of the opera. Here's her phone number."

I wrote it down, then asked, "How'd you find out about the arthritis, for God's sake?"

"A friend in the catering business. Good people to know—caterers. You thinking of becoming a private detective, Potter?"

"If things ever get tough. I wonder if Miss Whitcomb and Dwight Wilson are friends. I should imagine they would be."

"You planning on using one to meet the other, or something?"

That was exactly what I *was* planning. "Maybe."

"You'd probably be safe. The Whitcomb dame belongs to half the clubs in Chicago, and some of them are the same ones Wilson belongs to, or his wife did. Chances are it'd stand up." He paused. "Er—Potter?"

"Yes."

There was a silence. I sensed uncertainty, and it wasn't like Quick to be uncertain. About anything.

"Nothing," he said presently. "Anything else I can do for you?"

"Not just now, but I appreciate what you've given me."

"O.K., then. I'll send my bill on the first. Nice talking to you." He hung up without giving me a chance to reply.

I went back to the window. The coffee was cold, but I drank it anyway. Quick's brief uncertainty bothered me. What had he wanted to ask?

Suddenly it came to me. Helen. She'd asked him about McDonald. Quick had no doubt run across the fact that McDonald had been married to the Koberg granddaughter. And here I was, two weeks later, inquiring about the men who'd managed the Koberg estate and the Koberg company. Quick had been curious about the connection, but hadn't wanted to betray Helen's confidence.

Satisfied, I considered the information he'd given me, and how to use it. Actually, I thought, he hadn't told me much that I wouldn't have been able to find out for myself, given enough time. But he'd provided me with what I needed: a shortcut. And two survivors out of a possible three wasn't bad. Provided that those two were in town—and liked the sound of my voice.

At nine o'clock I made a final attempt to get an appointment with Carmichael. It didn't work. I wasn't surprised, but I was annoyed. I gave his secretary my room number at the hotel and added irritably, "Tell Mr. Carmichael that he's making a mistake."

She offered no comment.

I then dialed the Wilson number. A woman answered.

"Is Mr. Dwight Wilson there?" I asked.

"He's having his breakfast," she replied.

I heard a man's voice in the background, frail and querulous. "Who is it, who is it, who is it, Abby?"

"Who is this?" Abby asked me.

"Brockton Potter. I'm with Price, Potter and Petacque. I'd like to make an appointment with Mr. Wilson."

She passed the information along and received her instructions. "Mr. Wilson hasn't been well," she told me. "What do you wish to see him about?"

"I'm a securities analyst. I'd like to talk to him about Koberg Chemical."

This time I couldn't hear anything—evidently she'd covered the mouthpiece.

"We have a doctor's appointment this morning," she said presently, "but if you'd like to come at four, Mr. Wilson will have had his nap by then."

"I'll be there," I said gratefully, and hung up before she could change her mind.

Hoping that my luck would hold, I immediately dialed the Whitcomb number.

My luck did hold. The lady of the house herself answered, and on the first ring.

I told her who I was and said that I was a friend of Dwight Wilson's. I was in town for a couple of days, I added, and wanted to meet her.

"Why, how very nice!" she exclaimed eagerly. "Would you like to have lunch? Let's do! How about today?"

I was so taken aback by the eagerness that I didn't know what to say. "Well, uh, sure," I managed.

"Oh, dear! You sound shy. I hope you're not shy. I hate shy men."

I got hold of myself. "I'm not really," I assured her. "Where shall we make it?"

"At Le Perroquet. I love Le Perroquet. Twelvish, if that's all right with you. I'm having my hair done at two."

"Suits me fine."

"Splendid. Twelvish, then. At Le Perroquet. And promise you won't be shy."

"I promise." I wondered what I was getting myself into.

"Don't be late, now. I'm having my hair done at two. À bientôt, chéri." She hung up.

"Good Lord," I said aloud. But I felt pretty chipper. Two yeses in succession.

I ordered another pot of coffee from room service, and when it came, I signed the check with a flourish.

21

Twelvish, to Miss Whitcomb, meant twenty minutes after.

Mink-clad, she limped out of the tiny elevator, leaning heavily on an ebony cane, spotted me, the only person at the three-stool bar, and headed in my direction.

"Mr. Cotter? How very nice to meet you. Why don't you bring your drink to the table? I'm having my hair done at two and I dasn't be late." She cocked her head. "But, *mon cher*, you're good-looking. You didn't *sound* good-looking."

"Potter," I said. "It's nice to meet you too, Miss Whitcomb."

The maitre d', who had the air of a diplomatic envoy of some sort, recognized her, greeted her warmly and led us to a table. It took her a while to get settled. The cane had to be disposed of, the coat removed, the gloves peeled off. When all that was finally accomplished, she turned to the diplomatic envoy and said, "If that's a Tanqueray martini my friend is having, I'll have one just like it. And I think he could use another—he's shy."

The diplomatic envoy departed. The old lady and I studied each other, smiling politely. I tried to fit her into some known category and failed. Somewhere along the way she'd had a face-lift; from the shoulders up she was fifty-five. But the surgeon hadn't been able to do anything about her hands; they showed her true age. And she was considerably stooped—her head came

111

at you before the rest of her. What confused me most, however, was the way she'd got herself up. The green eyeshadow, scarlet lipstick and store-bought eyelashes said one thing; the old-fashioned brocade dress and black velvet headband said something else.

She finished her inspection before I finished mine. "It's so nice to meet a friend of dear Dwight's," she said. "Is he better? I must call him."

"He was going to the doctor this morning," I replied.

"Poor lamb. But I'm delighted to meet *you*. I get to meet so few people these days. There's no one left to lunch with."

"That *is* a problem, I suppose."

"You have no idea! One clutches at anything."

I laughed. "I'm not exactly 'anything,' Miss Whitcomb."

"Of course you're not, *mon cher*. But you know what I mean. And do call me Dolly. Everyone does."

A lesser dignitary brought our martinis and a pair of menus.

"To you, *mon cher*," Dolly said, raising her glass. She tasted the drink, nodded approvingly, then, with some care, fitted a 100-millimeter cigarette into a six-inch ivory holder. I lit the cigarette for her. "*Merci*," she said. "*Très galant.*" And without further ado, she revealed the reason she'd been so easy to meet. What it amounted to was that she was giving a party on Saturday and was rather desperate for guests—so many people were sick or out of town. "I do hope you're staying over," she said. "I'd adore having you."

I was pleased that I'd passed her inspection so satisfactorily. "I'm afraid I'm not," I said. "I'm going to Virginia tomorrow night."

"Can't you change your plans? I'll send my car for you."

"That wouldn't be necessary. I'm right next door to you, at the Drake. But I really can't."

She sighed regretfully, and we studied the menus.

"I'll have the *avocat aux fruits de mer*," Dolly said, "and the *sole Véronique*."

I went through the ritual of ordering and tried not to think about what Mark would say when he saw the bill—fifty-dollar lunches for two brought out the worst in him.

Dolly batted her absurd eyelashes a couple of times and said, "But tell me about yourself, Mr. Cotter. What do you do?"

"Potter," I said. "With a P."

"Potter? *Mille pardons.* I'll think of ceramics. I adore ceramics. I knew Picasso, you know. Such a dear man. But tell me about your*self.*"

"I'm one of the partners in Price, Potter and Petacque. We're stockbrokers, in New York."

"Oh, dear. I'm afraid the name doesn't mean a thing to me, and I know it should. You're undoubtedly terribly important in your field."

The wine steward arrived. I ordered a modest Pouilly-Fuissé at an immodest sixteen bucks a bottle, then turned back to Dolly and said, "Well, anyway, that's who I am. Now tell me about you. The way you speak French, you must have spent a lot of time in France."

"How clever of you," she said delightedly. "Yes, I have." And we were off.

The next forty minutes were entirely hers. She used them to provide me with an extravaganza of jet-set and pre-jet-set activities the likes of which I'd never been exposed to. I don't know how many names she dropped—names of people, names of places, names of houses, names of yachts—but the total must have been well into the hundreds. In forty minutes she covered sixty years of European and American history, and did it all in terms of names.

The era she was talking about had seen the rise and fall of Mussolini, Stalin, Hitler; the Depression; the extermination of twenty million people in a global war; the defoliation of the rich in England and the spread of socialism everywhere else; the end of empires and the emergence of new countries; moon landings. Yet, listening to Dolly, you wouldn't have known that any of these events had taken place. To Dolly Whitcomb, the most significant development of the period she'd lived through wasn't the splitting of the atom, or the invention of the computer, or the discovery of antibiotics. Not by a long shot. To her, the twentieth century's principal contribution to human progress was the cocktail party.

I fell off the sled at the first turn. I simply couldn't figure out who she was talking about. A few names I recognized—Coco, Noël and Elsa, I deduced, went with Chanel, Coward and Maxwell. But I had no idea who dear Scotty was until she mentioned dear Zelda, and I couldn't quite differentiate Lady Mendl from Lady Peel, although evidently there had been some important differences between them. I didn't care whether Monique had bought the house at Cap after her divorce from Jean-Pierre or after her divorce from Nigel, or whether the Cap in question was Ferrat or d'Antibes.

Nothing that Dolly said indicated that she'd ever known Elissa Koberg, however. So, after forty minutes, I asked.

"Elissa?" Dolly said, surprised. "Do you know *her?*"

"No," I replied, "but the Wilson family and the Koberg interests . . ." I left the sentence uncompleted.

"Oh, I see what you mean." She speared the last grape from her plate, ate it and washed it down with some of the wine. "Poor Dwight. He *did* have to be nice to her, didn't he?"

I gathered that she didn't particularly like Elissa, and as the waiter whisked away our plates, I said so.

"Don't be naughty," Dolly reprimanded me. She fitted another long cigarette into the holder.

I lit the cigarette for her and was thanked, in French of course.

Dolly blew smoke out of the corner of her mouth. "I don't think it's wise to think too much about whether one likes one's friends. I mean, if one does, one might find that one doesn't have any friends. Then where would one be? Elissa could be amusing at times, but at other times . . . I remember once in 1938—or was it 1937? No, it was '38—we were in Capri. Have you ever been to Capri? It's simply lovely, and Mona's villa was divine— Mona was quite a gardener, you know. Well, we were in Capri, and Elissa was married to this perfectly dreadful German. She wanted to divorce him, but he wouldn't give her a divorce. Bunky and Crawford were there—I told you about them, didn't I? He's the one who had the horse, Galahad, that won the Grand National. Well, we were having lunch, and Elissa made an absolute spectacle of herself. She was drunk, of course, but still—"

"She drank a lot, I take it."

"Heavens, yes! And she was such a climber. Crawford predicted—"

"Her daughter was different, though, wasn't she?"

"Bonnie. *Mais oui, mon cher, très différent.* A nice, simple child. Pretty too. But naïve. She let herself fall into the hands of that fortune-hunter, and Elissa was simply beside herself. At any rate, Crawford predicted . . ."

Crawford's prediction had nothing to do with Elissa, however. It had to do with one of the Aga Khan's horses, to the extent that it had to do with anything. As with most of Dolly's anecdotes, there was little point to it; all that mattered were the names involved, and the Aga Khan, dear man, hadn't yet been mentioned.

I tried to bring Dolly back to the subject of Elissa and her daughter, but I didn't succeed. She rattled on from the Aga Khan to Peggy Guggenheim to Queen Juliana when she'd been merely a princess, and from Juliana to dear Wallis, dear Mainbocher, dear Cole and Linda.

The waiter recommended the lemon soufflé, but Dolly ordered half a grapefruit. I decided to have the soufflé, though. I figured I might as well get a good dessert for the time and money I was investing; I certainly wasn't getting any useful information.

But then Dolly departed from the main avenue of her life's story—the Avenue of Celebrated Friends—and entered a byway. She did so in connection with a Swede named Axel, who was one of the many men on the avenue who'd wanted to marry her. "I've never really regretted that I didn't marry," she said, suddenly pensive. "Some people shouldn't, I think. I was always attracted to the wrong sort of man, just as Elissa was. But at least I had sense enough to know it. Otherwise I'd have been in the same predicament she usually was—married to someone I'd been infatuated with but had turned against and was having an awful time getting free of." She sighed. "Poor thing. I really should call."

Mentally, I'd drowsed off. But suddenly I woke. "Call?"

"Elissa, I mean."

"Where is she?"

"But, *mon cher*, don't you know? I thought you did. She's just a few blocks from here, at Northwestern Memorial Hospital. The poor thing is terribly ill."

I felt my jaw sag. "She's in the United *States?*"

"Why, yes. Has been for months. Her husband's living at the Whitehall."

The Whitehall was no more than two hundred yards from where we were sitting. "Well, I'll be damned! What's his name?"

"Henri. The Comte de Garonne. I've invited him to my party, but I'm not sure whether he's coming. Everything is so uncertain, he said."

The waiter brought our desserts.

Dolly went back to 1951. She was on the Côte d'Azur. Dear Willie was giving a dinner party . . .

I dug into the soufflé with gusto. Mark was wrong about fifty-dollar lunches, I thought. Some of them paid off.

22

I stood at the corner of Walton and Michigan, buffeted by a wind that seemed to be coming from all directions at once, and tried to make up my mind. Across the street was the Drake Hotel; somewhere off to my right, Northwestern Memorial Hospital. I had a choice.

The traffic signal went from "WALK" to "DONT WALK" and back to "WALK." The wind tore at my coat, stung my face and made my eyes tear. Yet I continued to stand there.

I had plenty of time—I wasn't due at Wilson's for another two hours. But would anything be gained? How could the presence of the Koberg heiress in Chicago have any bearing on the price of Koberg stock? Would the Koberg heiress, if she was as sick as Dolly said, even know anything about what was going on in the company?

The traffic signal changed again.

"She never cared about the company," McDonald had said. "All she cared about were the dividends."

For most of her life she'd lived an ocean away from the company.

But she was Augustus Koberg's daughter and no doubt a major stockholder. Perhaps *the* major stockholder.

I hailed a taxi and got in. "Northwestern Memorial Hospital," I told the driver.

I'd reached no conclusion, arrived at no theory. I'd merely decided nothing ventured, nothing gained.

Within five minutes we were there.

"Wesley or Passavant?" the driver asked.

"What's the difference?" I said.

"This is Wesley. Across the street there—that's Passavant. And around the corner—"

"This'll do." I paid him and got out.

The lobby was lofty and forbidding, but the lady at the information desk wasn't.

"The Countess de Garonne," I said.

The lady consulted a computer printout. Watching her, I thought what a great democratizer the computer was; it treated rich and poor alike, reducing everyone to mere symbols.

"De Garonne, E.," the lady said, and gave me the room number.

"Which building is that?"

"This one."

I joined the cluster of people waiting for an elevator, and when one came, I got in with the others.

And presently I found myself looking at the closed door to the room which, according to the computer, was occupied by De Garonne, E. For a moment I hesitated. This wasn't research; this was invasion of privacy.

But I cast scruples aside and invaded.

A nurse was sitting in a straight-backed chair beside the bed, reading a magazine. She didn't look up.

My eyes shifted to the bed, and I almost let out a groan. I'd seen sick people before, but I'd never seen anyone sicker than this old woman appeared to be. She was asleep, her mouth slightly open, and snoring. Each intake of breath produced a rasping sound, each exhalation a grunt. Her hair was white and wispy and disarranged. Her face, shrunken and skeletal, was the color of a pumpkin. The one hand that was exposed resembled a chicken's claw. Saliva was trickling from a corner of the open mouth.

I just stood there, stricken.

The nurse at last looked up. She started to speak.

"Sorry," I said, and backed out of the room.

It took me a little while to recover. I knew that I hadn't actually seen the angel of death hovering at the foot of the bed, but I knew that I'd felt its presence. Elissa Koberg was a goner.

As soon as I reached the lobby, I lit a cigarette. The world began to seem normal again. I started toward the revolving door. But before I reached it, a man emerged from it. The man I'd seen first at the Brasserie, then at the Koberg offices. He was preoccupied and didn't notice me.

It had to be more than coincidence, I decided, and on the spur of the moment I went up to him. "I beg your pardon," I said.

He came out of his reverie, recognized me and turned pale.

"We've almost met twice," I said. "A couple of weeks ago in New York, when you were with Louis Glass, and again yesterday, at Koberg Chemical. I feel I ought to introduce myself. I'm Brockton Potter."

The color came back to his face. He made a show of trying to remember. "But yes," he said, after a moment, "*je me rappelle.* You are the friend of Louis. You say—Pot-aire?"

"Yes. And you?"

There was a flash of indecision, followed by a smile and a barely perceptible bow. "Henri, Comte de Garonne."

I was stunned. He couldn't be the husband—he was too young. He had to be a son or something.

"*Enchanté.*" He removed a pigskin glove and held out his hand.

I shook it. "The woman upstairs—?"

He turned pale again. "My wife. You—?"

"Heard she was sick." I tried not to show my bewilderment. The figure in the bed had been in her mid-eighties and looked a hundred. This man was at the most in his early sixties and possibly even younger. "I'm pleased to meet you."

Another smile. Another barely perceptible bow. Both stiff.

"I just had lunch with a friend of yours," I volunteered. "Dolly Whitcomb."

"Ah, yes. Dolly. An acquaintance of many years."

"So I gathered." I tried to figure things out. The husband of

Elissa Koberg would certainly be welcome at the Koberg head-quarters. And he just might be a friend of Louis Glass. But, as far as I knew, Glass didn't go in much for counts; scientists, generals and senators were more his bag. "Perhaps you and I can get together for a drink while I'm in town."

For an instant De Garonne's eyes were those of a stag at bay. He didn't seem to know what to say. But then he made up his mind. "*Avec plaisir*, Monsieur Pot-aire."

"How about this evening? I'm staying at the Drake. Why don't you come over around six thirty?"

"But no. You must come to me. I have a suite at *le* Whitehall. I insist."

What difference could it make? I wondered. But then I had an inkling. At the Drake, I would be in control. At the Whitehall, he would. "If you'd prefer," I said. "Around six thirty?"

He nodded, smiled, bowed and moved on toward the elevators.

Jesus, I thought, Freud would have a field day.

23

The house was a big, comfortable-looking old place. Red brick, with a couple of glassed-in porches, three chimneys, two television antennae. But there were signs of neglect, as if the owner had stopped caring. The paint around the windows was peeling, some tiles were missing from the roof, and the evergreens that flanked the front door were turning brown.

The tall, gaunt woman who opened the door said that she was Abigail Henning, Mr. Wilson's sister. She took my coat and led me across the foyer to a large living room.

Wilson was sitting in a wing chair, glowering at what was left of a fire in the fireplace. He got up with difficulty as his sister and I approached. "Potter," he said, offering his hand.

His hand seemed so frail that I was almost afraid to take it, but his grip was unexpectedly strong. I smiled. "How do you do, sir?"

"Price, Potter and Petacque. That's a new one to me." The querulous note I'd detected in the voice in the background when I telephoned was even more pronounced now. "Any relation to Price, Underhill?"

"Yes, sir. My partner Mark Price is the son of John Price." John Price *was* Price, Underhill. Mark couldn't stand his old man, however.

"I used to know John. He was one tough hombre."

"Still is," I said.

Wilson sat down and invited me to do the same. "You may enjoy standing," he said, "but I don't. My legs aren't what they used to be."

I settled into the nearest chair.

"Shall I make tea?" Abigail asked her brother.

"You usually do, don't you?" he replied testily.

She departed.

Wilson eyed me narrowly. "You told Abby you wanted to talk about Koberg Chemical."

"Yes, sir. I'm doing a study of the company."

"Have you talked to Carmichael?"

"No, sir. He doesn't seem anxious to give me an appointment."

"Damn fool."

"The stock has begun to rise, and I'm curious."

"Simple. It's been too cheap for years."

"Perhaps. But why has it begun to rise at this particular moment?"

"Someone knows a value when he sees it. Why won't Carmichael talk to you?"

"I don't know, sir."

"Damn fool."

"One thing I have learned. The company is buying up its own stock."

Wilson's eyebrows rose. But they came right down again. "Poke the fire, will you? I'm no good with fires, and Abby's worse."

I went over the fireplace, moved the screen aside and gave the one remaining log a few jabs with the poker. The fire came back to life.

"That's better," said Wilson.

I sat down again.

"Let's get something straight, young man. Are you here because you think I can tell you what's going on in the company or because you want me to get you an appointment with Paul Carmichael?"

"Well—"

"Because, whichever it is, you've come to the wrong place. Paul Carmichael won't give me the time of day."

"But—"

"A good man—Paul. Picked him myself. Had my eye on him for years. But he's a damn fool. Doesn't believe in the long haul. I'd hoped . . ."

"Yes?"

"I'd hoped . . ." The old man studied his hands, as if they were somehow responsible for everything. His expression became less irascible. "Before he died, Mr. Koberg picked my father to carry on the business. Then, years later, my father picked me. He'd brought me up in the business. Trained me himself. Between the two of us, we managed the company for almost sixty years. That's a lot of years, young man. A lot of years. We took the company through the wars, through the Depression, through everything. Kept it solvent when other companies were going broke. Never missed a dividend, never had a strike. For sixty years we kept Koberg Chemical going. Because we believed in the long haul. Not today, not tomorrow—the long haul. I'd hoped that one of my sons . . . But that wasn't to be. So when the time came for me to step aside—we all get old, young man; the time comes for all of us—I picked Paul. I thought—I hoped—that I'd still be of some use, that he'd consult with me. First Father, then I—for sixty years we led that company. Twice as long as Mr. Koberg himself. All that experience was worth something, I thought. But apparently I was wrong. Paul has chosen *not* to consult me. To exclude me. To dispose of my people. Not even to tell me what's going on. Not even to invite me to sit on the board. The board is all young men now. Young men like yourself. There's no room on the board for an old man like me. So you've come to the wrong place, Mr. Potter. I can't help you."

"I see."

"Do you? I doubt it." He raised his voice. "Where's the tea, Abby? How long does it take to boil water?" Then, in a lower voice, he said, "She's getting old too. Takes her forever to do anything."

The telephone rang. Someone answered it. Abby, I guessed.

"A good man—Paul," Wilson went on. "But he doesn't believe in the long haul. All he believes in is science. Scientists are what he wants." He shook his head sadly, as if scientists were of some lower order.

"I understand he's built a new research plant," I said.

"That's what he believes in—research. Bugs."

"Bugs?"

"That's what I hear. Bugs. Microbes."

"You must have *some* contact with the company, then."

He sighed. "A few old friends. They hear. They tell me. Microbes. Jungle rot."

"Jungle rot?"

"Some bug that caused jungle rot, in World War II."

"Odd."

"Odd, you say? Crazy, I say. Nothing to do with paint at all. Nothing to do with plastics. Good man—Paul. Good executive. Not a spendthrift. But I made a big mistake. He doesn't want my advice. And he wants to be another Pasteur."

I gazed at the fire. It was again close to going out. What it needed was another log. "Jungle rot," I mused. I'd have to tell Brian about that. Perhaps he could learn something about jungle rot from one of his contacts.

"Impellers, fermenters, centrifuges, refrigeration closets— God knows what he's doing out there," Wilson said. "None of it's expensive equipment. Paul's no spendthrift. The plant didn't cost more than a million, I hear. But, whatever he's doing with it, he's not making paint. And that's what Koberg is known for: paint."

"Sounds like biology," I ventured.

"Sounds like a lot of nonsense, if you ask me. Father would turn over in his grave. So would Mr. Koberg."

A diversion arrived. Abby with the tea tray.

"That was Dolly Whitcomb on the phone," she told her brother, setting the tray on a table. "She's all excited. She had lunch with Mr. Potter today. She considers him a find." She looked at me. "How do you take your tea, Mr. Potter—lemon or milk?"

"Neither," I said. "No sugar, either."

"A Spartan," she observed, and brought me the tea, along with a tiny plate of gingersnaps.

"Tea!" her brother snorted. "I hate tea. But my goddamn prostate's acting up, and the doctor won't let me have alcohol."

Abby gave him a cup and a plate of gingersnaps too. Then she served herself and looked at me again. "Dolly said something I don't understand, Mr. Potter. She said you told her you're a friend of Dwight's. Why did you do that?"

The old man almost upset his teacup. "You did that?" he demanded. "You used my name to meet Dolly Whitcomb? Who told you you could? You've a hell of a nerve, young man."

"I wanted to meet her," I said with what I hoped was disarming candor. "She's a friend of Elissa Koberg's."

"Elissa? What's she got to do with it?"

"She's a large stockholder, I imagine." I glanced at Abby and detected a gleam of satisfaction in her eyes. She'd got me in trouble and she was glad. She had a hard life, I decided. Cooped up with an irritable and bitter old man day after day. But perhaps she deserved it.

"Just what are you up to?" Wilson asked me suspiciously.

"Exactly what I said, sir. I want to know what's going on at Koberg Chemical. Carmichael wouldn't see me, and I didn't know how helpful you'd be."

"In other words, you're covering all corners. Even Elissa's."

"Yes."

There was a silence.

"Elissa!" Wilson snorted.

"Well, you see, sir, it's through her, in a remote sort of way, that Koberg Chemical came to my attention. Her grandson was engaged to marry my secretary's niece."

Abby put her teacup down and regarded me with interest, as if sensing the imminence of gossip. "Really?"

"The son of Bonnie Cadbury?" Wilson said. "Bonnie and that—that—what was his name?"

"James McDonald."

"That's it. McDonald. The crook."

"Crook?"

"Used to work for me. Took kickbacks. I found out about it and fired him. But meanwhile he'd married Elissa's daughter. I didn't care, though. I fired him anyway. And Elissa was glad. She hadn't wanted Bonnie to marry him."

Abby smiled. Her hopes were being fulfilled.

Wilson gave another snort. "Elissa. God, what a woman!" Then he became reflective. "Poor Amos. Her cables used to upset him so."

"Amos?" Abby said eagerly.

"Amos Fisher," her brother told her. "You didn't know him. He died before you moved in. Managed the Koberg estate." He turned to me. "Fine man, Amos. My best friend. I miss him. Elissa's cables used to upset him so, poor fellow. They always said the same thing: send money. Sometimes he just didn't know where to get the money. She never meant a little; she always meant a lot—several hundred thousand, a million dollars. The poor fellow didn't know what to sell first. And he was an old-line Yankee—it hurt him to sell anything."

"Was there that much to start with?" I asked.

"Thirty, forty million. The mother was already dead, and everything went to Elissa. It wasn't just her father's stock in the company. That was the smaller part of the estate, actually. There was stock in all kinds of other companies, and bonds, and real estate—Augustus Koberg was a good investor. Yes, there was that much to start with, young man. The Depression reduced it, of course. But Elissa didn't want to know about the Depression. All she knew was that her current husband was giving her a hard time and in order to get rid of him she needed money."

"Is that what the money went for? Husbands?"

"A good part of it. Lords and barons don't come cheap, you know. It cost her a lot to get them, and it cost her a lot to get rid of them. But no, that was only part of it. There were houses, too. She was always buying houses and redecorating them. She saw a house she liked, she bought it. Usually an old castle or something that needed fixing up. Well, that takes money, young man. You ever tried to fix up a castle?"

"No."

"I haven't either, but I know what it costs—what it cost even during the Depression. Amos showed me some of the cables. It cost plenty. And then there were the parties. I remember Amos telling me about one party she gave. Cost forty thousand dollars, that party did. And that was during the thirties, mind you. Flowers from God knows where, three orchestras, dozens in the kitchen and serving. Forty thousand dollars that party cost. And you know why she gave it? She gave it to get even with some lady who'd given a party and hadn't invited her. Elissa Koberg! I don't mind telling you, young man, I never had much use for that woman. She was spoiled, selfish and mean-spirited. Never did anything for anybody but herself. Didn't care about anyone's problems but her own."

"Dwight!" Abby cried happily. "I've never heard you talk like that about anybody before."

"Well," Wilson said, nodding in my direction, "he got me started."

"Sounds like most of the money must be gone by now," I said.

He gave the question some thought. "Most of it, I suppose. Amos gradually had to sell off the real estate. All except the Koberg Building—that belonged to the company, and what the company did was up to me. All I had to do was see that we never missed a dividend, and that I managed to do, although I don't mind telling you there were times when it wasn't easy. But Amos had to sell off the other real estate, and plenty else besides. Yes, I'd say most of it's gone."

"But not her stock in Koberg Chemical?"

"Maybe some of that too, by now. I don't know anymore. But I suppose Carmichael would know."

I thought of the old woman in the hospital bed. Soon she would have no need for money. "She's pretty sick now," I said.

"Of course she's pretty sick," Wilson snapped. "She's eighty-six years old and has cirrhosis of the liver. The only thing I can't understand is why she didn't die years ago. The way she drank, she should have."

"Then you've kept up with her?"

"Only through Dolly. Dolly was a friend of my wife's, and we see her occasionally. She's the only one around here who knows Elissa."

"Dolly keeps up with everyone," Abby put in.

And how, I thought.

"But I don't like having my name used, young man. I want you to know that. I don't like it."

"I'm sorry, sir." I looked at the fire. It had just about gone out. All that remained were a few glowing embers. And that, it seemed to me, was all that remained of the world of Elissa Koberg too. A few glowing embers. Dolly Whitcomb, Dwight Wilson, Elissa herself—the fire had never been bright, but before long not even the embers would be alive. The company itself, though—that was something else again. Koberg Chemical would endure. Koberg Chemical was anticipating the future, preparing in some way to deal with it. And someone who had contact with the Central Markham and Retailers Bank believed that Koberg was on the right track.

"Well, sir," I said, getting up, "I won't take up any more of your time. You've been most helpful." I turned to Abby and tried to smile. "Thank you for the tea."

"Helpful?" Wilson said. "I haven't been helpful at all. Nobody consults me."

I shook his hand. "*I* consulted you. And I appreciate the information you gave me. Every little bit helps, you know."

Wilson sighed dejectedly.

24

Sheridan Road snakes through the suburbs north of Chicago, more or less following the shoreline of Lake Michigan, skirting landmarks such as the Baha'i Temple and Northwestern University, wriggling around large houses and small parks, a main drag that in the age of expressways seems decidedly out of date.

But it's the shortest route between the Drake Hotel and the eastern edge of Winnetka, and I'd followed it north to Wilson's house. Now I was following it back to the city, slowly, deep in thought. I had the feeling that I was in a strange and somewhat incomprehensible country where no one spoke my language and where I didn't understand the system. Albania, maybe.

I should have been happy. I was beginning to make progress. Koberg Chemical was engaged in research that involved microbes and, ostensibly at least, was far outside the realm of paint and plastics. The company had been buying up its own stock. And an outsider who'd got wind of what it was doing was also buying its stock. To Price, Potter and Petacque and its customers, such information could be highly significant.

But I wasn't happy; I was somber. Because of the people I was meeting. I'd entered the odd world of the aged, of men and women who'd once had a certain importance but no longer did, who'd outlived their generation. Dwight Wilson and his sister;

Elissa Koberg; Dolly Whitcomb; even Amos Fisher, who was no longer around but who was in a sense also a new acquaintance of mine—all of them were people who had at one time figured in the scheme of things but now, as Dolly had put it, had no one left to lunch with.

Octogenarians had never played much part in my life. Compulsory-retirement policies kept most of them out of the active business environment, and my personal milieu was singularly free of them. My father had hanged himself when he was in his early thirties, and my mother had died when I was in college. I had a couple of aunts, but I hadn't seen them in years, and anyway they weren't yet in their eighties. Most of the people I knew were between twenty and sixty-five. But today, within a period of five hours, I'd had a look at another facet of the stone, and I didn't find it beautiful.

"The time comes for all of us," Wilson had said.

I shuddered.

The jaundiced woman in the hospital bed.

I tried to think of something else.

But my conscious couldn't get a grip on my unconscious, and my unconscious had a message to deliver about mortality.

Of them all, I sensed, Elissa Koberg was the most important. She hadn't given a damn about the company, yet she'd owned a large chunk of it, so in a sense everything had revolved around her, whether she cared or not. Selfish, social-climbing, callous, self-indulgent—no one had a good word to say about her. And I was in no position to dispute the general opinion. But during the few moments I'd been in that hospital room I'd felt, in addition to horror, pity. A squanderer she might have been; an unloving mother; an indifferent wife; a drunkard. I couldn't argue with any of that. I simply didn't know. Now she was dying, though. Dying of a lingering and cruel disease, far from wherever she called home, attended only by a bored nurse and a husband who couldn't help but find her—in her present condition, at any rate—repulsive. Children, grandchildren, great-grandchildren, friends? Nobody.

And yet there might have been. Her daughter might have

lived and been at the bedside. Her grandson, as well. Maybe other grandchildren too, if the daughter had lived longer.

Now there was nothing but an unborn fetus in Andrea Doyle's womb that Elissa Koberg certainly didn't know about and that, when it was born, would be illegitimate.

Did the old woman have regrets?

Couldn't help but have. No mother could cut an only child out of her life and not have regrets. Especially when the child subsequently died.

And what about Amos Fisher, the hard-pressed and disapproving lawyer, Wilson's friend and near neighbor? A lot in common, those two must have had. Both dependent on a woman they held in contempt. Alike in temperament too. My primary impression of Wilson was not merely that he was bitter and self-pitying but that he was tight-fisted. That was what "the long haul" was all about: not spending money. He'd admired Fisher for being reluctant to part with the Koberg assets.

Yet there had been a difference between the two men's roles. Wilson had been obligated not to a single stockholder but to many. Fisher, on the other hand, had had only one person to cater to—the Koberg heiress. So if both men disliked her, Fisher must have harbored the more intense dislike.

Fisher.

A thought flickered and became brighter.

Was it through Amos Fisher that James McDonald had managed to keep abreast of his former mother-in-law's marriages and whereabouts? McDonald and the Knights knew more about her than the distant relationship could explain. Fisher's hostility toward Elissa had made him sympathetic toward the man she scorned. Regardless of what McDonald had done, Fisher for as long as he'd lived had been McDonald's secret ally. He'd probably kept the alliance secret even from Wilson.

It was just a hunch on my part. But it was a strong hunch, and I regretted that Fisher was dead. He and I might have had an interesting conversation.

James McDonald. Had he lied to me about the kickbacks, or was Wilson the liar? Perhaps neither of them had deliberately lied. Each had had some thirty years in which to convince himself that he'd been in the right; each might have been telling me the truth as he'd come to see it.

None of this had anything to do with the bug that caused jungle rot, though, I told myself. I'd have to talk to Brian about the bug. I'd also have to talk to Harriet again. The answer to Koberg's future might lie not only in Chicago but in New York as well.

Jungle rot. That was just one kind of rot. There were many other kinds, including the kind that eats away at men's souls.

Sadly, almost morosely, I guided the car around the many turns that led back to Chicago and my appointment with the Count de Garonne. How he and Louis Glass had ever met was beyond me. But then, I suspected, everything about the Count de Garonne was beyond me.

25

Only four hours had passed since I'd last seen him, but he looked quite different. Mainly because of his clothes. He was dressed like a teenager. Slacks that barely covered his hips, a black turtleneck that when he leaned forward revealed four inches of bare back, and moccasins. What he was trying to convey, I gathered, was that he still had an abundance of lively hormones.

And in that he succeeded. I felt that I was in the presence of sex appeal. Which only made his marriage to the breathing skeleton I'd seen in the hospital harder for me to accept. In the few beauty-and-the-beast couples I'd met, it was the woman who was the beauty.

"May I give you a drink?" he asked.

"Scotch, if you have it," I said, not doubting that he had it—the desktop was a forest of bottles. "On the rocks."

"Avec plaisir."

He'd gone to the trouble of having a bucket of ice cubes ready, and I watched him as he made my drink. He was a true European—he put only two ice cubes in the glass and poured the whiskey as if it were worth a fortune. But what I noticed even more was the bare back with its prominent spinal column and the tightness of the slacks across his buttocks and thighs. I wondered for a moment whether he was putting on some sort of an exhibition for me, but decided that he wasn't. He was simply a man who admired his own body and flaunted it. He'd probably been doing so ever since, as a young man, he'd discovered its value.

For himself he made a vermouth cassis, with the same care. Then, drinks in hand, he turned around and caught me staring at him. "You have the—how do you say?—the curiosity?" he asked with a smile.

I was embarrassed.

He handed me the Scotch. "*À votre santé.*" He dropped into a deep chair, put his glass on the floor beside it and, with a show of casualness, extended his legs and crossed his ankles.

"Yes," I said, "I have curiosity."

He nodded. "Some hours ago I have talked with our friend Louis Glass by the telephone. He has told me that you have the curiosity. He has said that you are cle-vaire. You are *un voyeur?*"

"I've never thought about it. I suppose I am, by profession. Anyone who does investigative work has a streak of that in him."

"*Un voyeur* by profession." The idea seemed to appeal to him. "How—what shall I say?—*extraordinaire.*"

"Not really. News reporters, biographers, anthropologists— the world is full of professional voyeurs."

He sipped his drink.

"Why did you call Glass? To find out about me?"

"*Mais oui.* I do not understand your wish to meet me."

"That's easy. I'm doing a study of Koberg Chemical."

"Ah. But surely you do not consider *me* Koberg Chemical."

"Only in so far as you're married to it."

"No, no, Monsieur Pot-aire. I am not married to a company. I am married to a woman. You Americans confuse the two, I think."

"Perhaps. But tell me, how long have you and your wife been married?"

"Nine years."

I tried to picture Elissa as she might have looked nine years earlier. Even then she would have been seventy-seven. And a woman of seventy-seven, no matter how well preserved, seemed an odd choice for a man who, to judge by his present appearance, had probably looked forty.

My expression must have been a clue to my thoughts, for the Count colored slightly and said, "I am European, *monsieur*. I do not worship youth."

Again I was embarrassed. But it seemed to me that when it came to worshiping youth, Europeans were little different from Americans. Or, for that matter, when it came to worshiping money. "Do you like it in the United States?" I asked.

The Count treated me to a Gallic shrug. "I miss my country. I miss my home. But I can do nothing—no?"

"Where is your home?"

"We have a villa in Marbella. But we live most in Paris. We have an *appartement* there. *Seizième arrondissement*, if you are acquainted with Paris. But my family home is in Sauternes, near Bordeaux. We have vineyards. You are acquainted with Château de Garonne?"

"I'm afraid not."

He sighed. "It is not much sold abroad, unfortunately. But that is—how do you say?—my family enterprise."

"Tough business, winemaking. Or so I've heard. A lot of ups and downs."

He tipped his hand first to one side, then the other. "One cannot predict the skies. But we have much experience, my family. Many generations. Now the export, it is more difficult, yes. The United States—your California vineyards . . ." He made a face. "But, as you say, up and down. It requires much attendance. And *ma pauvre* Elissa is not happy in the country, so we have lived most in Paris and in Marbella."

I'd detected a flash of something when he'd said that Elissa wasn't happy in the country. It had come and gone so quickly that I hadn't been able to identify it, but I thought it was worth following up. "You don't like Paris?"

"*Mais oui, monsieur*. I love Paris. Everyone loves Paris. Paris is beautiful. But more I love my land, the land that has been in my family for three hundred years. I love my vineyards. I want to improve my vineyards. You Americans—forgive me, *monsieur*—

you Americans do not love vineyards. You do not love land. You love buildings."

I detected a chink in the armor. "Your wife is an American in that respect?"

He smiled with his lips but not his eyes. "My wife, Monsieur Pot-aire, loves neither land nor buildings, except perhaps *les châteaux*. She loves society. Parties, galas, *fêtes*, people. Paris, Marbella, *le* Côte d'Azur, St. Moritz—my wife is not happy to be *solitaire*."

She's pretty damn *solitaire* now, I thought. And will soon be even more so. "Your friendship with Louis Glass," I said, "is it long-standing?"

The Count frowned. "Long-standing? I do not understand. Do you mean, is he a friend of many years?"

"Yes."

"No. Not many years. He came to us in Paris with an introduction from friends. I have liked him. I have found him *sympathique*. And he is a very good businessman—no? I have for him much admiration."

"You're also friendly with Paul Carmichael."

The Count looked uncomfortable. "Monsieur Carmichael is the president of the Koberg company," he offered noncommittally.

I pursued the matter, but didn't get anywhere. De Garonne conceded that he knew Carmichael, but that was all. And when I questioned him about what the company was doing, he professed ignorance.

I finished my drink and wished that he would offer me another—I felt I needed it—but he didn't.

"When you were at the hospital this afternoon," he asked cautiously, "you met my wife?"

"Saw her," I replied. "Didn't meet her."

"Permit my own curiosity, *monsieur*, but why did you wish to see her? You are, from the past, a friend?"

"No. I thought she might be able to tell me something about the company."

"But *en vérité*—surely—*monsieur*, you must know that my wife is not *au courant* with the affairs of the Koberg company. My wife is not a woman of business. She is not—how shall I say?—sophisticated in affairs of business."

"To tell the truth, Count, I didn't know that. She's a stockholder, she gets reports. I assumed—"

"But she has lived most of her life, many years, in Europe."

"She's not in Europe now, though. And then there's another thing. A member of her family was at my house recently."

"A member of her family?"

"Her grandson."

"Ah." The Count's face became expressionless. "Her grandson. She has never met him, unfortunately."

"You know about him?"

He nodded. "She has told me. It is regrettable."

"What is?"

"That they have never met. She has wished it."

"Well, it's too late now. He's dead."

"*Juste ciel!* But that is not possible, *monsieur.* He is a young man." He reached for his drink, missed on the first try, connected on the second. He finished it in a gulp, then looked at me. He seemed at a loss for words. "*Mon Dieu!*" he exclaimed at last. "*Ma pauvre* Elissa."

I watched him. He was no longer the teenager. He was a middle-aged man in clothes that were too young for him. And for a moment he didn't even seem French. He was just a man—any man—with a problem.

He got out of the chair and went to the desk. "I must have a drink."

I followed him. He poured himself a stiff Scotch. His hand, I noted, was not quite steady. He took a long swallow. I held out my glass. "If you don't mind," I said.

"Forgive me." He gave me a refill.

We returned to our chairs. This time the Count made no attempt to appear relaxed. He sat with his back straight, holding the glass tightly. His face was no longer expressionless. It was grim. "I make you the confession," he said. "I tell you about my life, my—how shall I say *tristesse?*—my sadness? I have made the unfortunate mistake. I have married a woman I have not loved."

I nodded.

"It has not been a good marriage, Monsieur Pot-aire, that of Elissa and myself. For many years it has not been a good marriage. We have not been—how shall I say it?—we have not been close companions. There has been no love, no *confiance*. I have been a bad man. I have married a woman older than my mother because she is a woman of consequence. I was not sure, I have thought that we could . . . She did not have the appearance of a woman so old, and she wished to marry me. I was not seduced—I was a man of the world. But I—I do not know how to say it; it is most difficult—I seduced myself, if you comprehend. Many times I have regretted it."

"We all seduce ourselves occasionally."

He sighed. "Now it is almost ended. Elissa will die where she was born, and I shall return to where I was born. I shall return to France, to my vineyards. I shall be happy to go. I do not like the United States. I do not like the hospital. I wish to forget."

I glanced at all the bottles on the desktop. They made more sense to me now. "Hasn't your wife ever talked divorce? She has quite a history of divorces."

He finished his Scotch and spoke to the empty glass. "She has talked divorce. She has talked divorce many times." He shifted his gaze to me. "My family is very ancient, Monsieur Pot-aire. Many centuries ancient. You are an American. Such a thing is of no importance to you, perhaps. But I am not an American. To me, my family, my land—it is of great importance. My family—on the side of my mother's, my ancestors have fought at Crécy; on the side of my father's, my ancestors have been advisers to kings. To kings, *monsieur*. For centuries my family has been of consequence. But never—never, Monsieur Pot-aire—in all those centuries has there been a divorce. I am not willing to be the first."

I thought it over. No one in my family had ever advised a king, and if any of my ancestors had fought at Crécy, I sure as hell didn't know about it. "You're right," I said, "we come from different worlds." I drank the last of my Scotch, then got up. "I appreciate your hospitality, Count. I don't want to overstay my welcome."

He made no attempt to keep me there, and five minutes later I was out on Michigan Avenue, fighting the wind. The wind was quite an adversary.

And as I battled my way toward the Drake Hotel, that was what I thought about. Adversaries.

26

There was a message for me. Harriet Jensen had called at four fifteen. Please call back.

I dialed Harriet's home number, but got a busy signal. So I kicked off my shoes, loosened my tie and stretched out on the bed to evaluate the day.

A "C" was the best I could give it. I'd collected a lot of gossip but little solid information. Koberg Chemical was doing something with bugs—that was significant. But everything else I'd learned had to do not with Koberg Chemical but with a woman who'd spent millions chasing happiness and was about to die without having caught it.

Elissa Koberg, with all her titles and married names, was important simply as the beneficiary of other people's work. She mattered to Price, Potter and Petacque only to the extent that she could shed light on that work. And at this point she was in no position to shed light on anything.

A "C" just wasn't good enough, I decided. I'd made a mistake.

It was my own fault. I should have dug deeper before leaving New York. Also, I should have chosen a different week. The week before Christmas was the wrong time to go burrowing into the affairs of a company in which I had no friends and about which I knew next to nothing.

Well, this wasn't the first wild-goose chase I'd gone on. I'd miscalculated before—the people I'd thought would help me hadn't, the company I'd imagined was up to something wasn't, the rumor I'd believed to be true was false.

Yet in this case I'd heard no rumor, the company really was up to something, and I hadn't expected much help. Therefore I hadn't exactly miscalculated; I'd merely failed to bring the right key and was locked out.

I closed my eyes and tried to let my intuition take over. But my intuition had nothing new to say. All it did was repeat what it had told me before: stocks that have been becalmed for a generation don't suddenly begin to rise for no reason; new management means new ideas; companies that buy up their own stock often do so because they're threatened; big New York banks rarely make pointless purchases.

Big New York banks.

I rolled over and reached for the telephone.

But Harriet's line was still busy.

That might be my problem, though. I was researching in the wrong city. The answers I was looking for might be found more easily in New York than in Chicago.

And sometimes answers are hard to find, no matter where you look. It can take a long time. Weeks, months, even years. I was expecting too much too soon.

Possibly, also, my luck was changing. I'd had more than my share of successes. Perhaps I was now due for a few failures.

I didn't like that idea, though. I got off the bed and went to the window.

The rush hour was over. Traffic was moving normally on Lake Shore Drive. A thousand windows glowed in the string of high-rises along what Chicago called its Gold Coast. The windows were those of some of the richest and most powerful residents of the city which had spawned so many of America's great fortunes—fortunes that had flowed slowly, like molten lava, to all corners of the world. Even to villas in Marbella and apartments in the *seizième arrondissement* of Paris. But fortunes, I thought as I stood there looking at the lights, were like human lives; each had a definite beginning and a definite end. Everything had its cycle.

I went back to the telephone and dialed Harriet's number once more. This time there was no busy signal.

"You got my message?" Harriet asked excitedly.

"Yes. I've been trying to reach you for the past twenty minutes, but your line's been busy."

The excitement waned. "My sister called." But then it waxed again. "You were right, Brock. There *is* a connection."

"Oh?"

"I couldn't get the exact details. I think it's rather complicated. But Louis Glass has been borrowing money from Central Markham, and Central Markham has been buying the stock. I don't understand the details—my man didn't seem to know—but what it boils down to is that Central Markham is financing Glass's stock purchases. I believe he's put up some of his Interamerican Marine stock too, as collateral."

My pulse quickened. "Wait a minute, dear. Let me get this straight. You mean, it isn't Interamerican Marine that's buying the stock, but Glass personally?"

"As I understand it."

My thoughts quickened too. Not a merger of two companies, but a personal acquisition by one man, backed by a bank. The final step up the ladder. Glass was planning to leave Interamerican Marine. He was going to buy himself the controlling interest in Koberg Chemical. Interamerican Marine was owned by the public; Glass himself had no more than a fraction of one percent of the stock. A few bad years in a row, and he could be fired. But with a company of his own, and a company on the way up . . .

"Thank you, Harriet. You've done a magnificent job."

"Really, Brock?" She sounded surprised, but terribly pleased.

"Magnificent. Have a merry Christmas, dear. I'll see you Monday."

I hung up and sat on the bed, my mind racing. I was wasting my time in Chicago. Carmichael wasn't the man I had to see. Louis Glass was. Even though tomorrow was Christmas Eve . . . No, it was pointless. I couldn't accomplish anything until after the holiday weekend. Still . . .

Impatience got the better of me. I began calling the airlines. And it was the airlines that decided my course of action. I couldn't get a reservation on any flight to New York for the next forty-eight hours. So, whether I liked it or not, I had to stick with my original schedule.

But I felt vindicated. If I hadn't come to Chicago, I wouldn't have seen the Count de Garonne at the Koberg offices, or made the association with Louis Glass.

My luck wasn't changing. It was as good as ever.

27

The telephone woke me at nine fifteen. I'd been up earlier, had coffee, then gone back to bed, fallen asleep again and slept soundly enough to have a dream. I'd dreamed that Harriet, Joe and Brian were taking me to dinner but couldn't agree on which restaurant to take me to, and as the center of the controversy I was embarrassed. The whole thing seemed somehow to be my fault.

They were still arguing when the telephone rang.

"I hope I didn't waken you," Dolly Whitcomb trilled, "but I know what a busy man you are and I didn't want to miss you."

"Not at all," I said, rubbing my eyes.

"I'm so glad. I do hate to be an early bird, but I simply had to tell you how you captivated me. I get to meet so few new people these days, and when I meet one who's as fresh as you, I feel quite rejuvenated."

I stretched. "You'd better clarify 'fresh.'"

She gave a laugh that went up and down the scale. "Really, *mon cher,* you're much too shy to be *that* kind of fresh, though I wish you were—it's been years since anyone pinched me."

God, I thought. "You could have pinched *me.*"

This time her laugh went up and down the scale twice. "*Mon cher!*"

"Well."

"But I hope you liked me. It's so nice to be liked by the people one likes, and one so seldom is."

"Why, of course I did."

"Good. Then perhaps you'll be *my* guest for lunch today. I'd like to reciprocate."

"That isn't necessary, Dolly. It was a pleasure."

"But I *want* to. I know what a busy man you are, but a simple lunch—nothing elaborate; my cook is going off early today; Christmas, you know—just the two of us—I was hoping you could find an hour. Especially since you won't be able to come to my party."

"Really, Dolly—"

"We talked so much about me yesterday, we hardly had a chance to talk about you at all. And I didn't realize what an important man you are."

"Oh? I'm important?"

"Really, *mon cher*, you're much too shy. I told you that right away. Modesty is becoming, but in your case—"

"Who said I'm important?"

"Why, everyone. And you didn't even give me a clue. You *must* come to lunch today."

"O.K., Dolly. If you really want me to."

"But I *do*. You must tell me all *about* yourself. All the things you didn't tell me yesterday. Twelvish, shall we say? I told Mrs. Haupt she could leave at one thirty. She's going to her niece's, you see."

"Twelvish is fine with me."

"I'm so pleased. I'm dying to know you better."

We hung up, and I got out of bed wondering who "everyone" was.

I treated myself to an extra-long shower and shaved and dressed in slow motion, but nevertheless I was ready for action by ten thirty, and no action was available.

I went down to the newsstand and bought both morning papers, intending to sit in the lobby for a while, but the lobby was so deserted that I felt uncomfortable in it and went back to my room.

The newspapers were full of what the Goodfellows were

doing—distributing Christmas baskets—and of how the Christmas pilgrims were making out in Bethlehem and of the record-breaking crowds at O'Hare Airport. Nobody had blown up anything, and there were no guerrilla attacks anywhere in the world, apparently. Genocide, for the moment, was at a standstill.

Yuma, Arizona, was the hottest place in the nation, and International Falls, Minnesota, was the coldest.

Minnesota. Carol.

I put the newspapers aside. It was definitely time to make up with Carol. Our estrangement had gone on long enough. The least she could do was explain what she meant by "defeated."

So I called her at her parents'. But she didn't explain what she meant by "defeated," perhaps because something in her voice prevented me from asking. Although she didn't sound angry, she just didn't sound like the old Carol. She appreciated my call, she said, and she told me about what she'd been doing, and that it was nice to be home again. Not wonderful, I gathered; just nice. She was surprised to learn that I was in Chicago. Did I really have to go off on a business trip right before Christmas? Couldn't I have waited? But she was glad that I was going to visit Brian's family; it would do me good to be with a family for a change—I was so unfamily-minded.

It was one of those conversations that resolve nothing. I didn't feel any better after it was over than I had before. I merely wished that I'd kept my damn mouth shut about her being too old to have kids. Especially since she really wasn't too old. Yet I couldn't help feeling that, while I'd been wrong about the specific, I'd been right about the general; that Carol and motherhood wouldn't mix well. She wasn't like Andrea.

Andrea. What a terrible Christmas this was going to be for her. And for Helen. Those two distant links with the old woman who was dying out here in Chicago, unaware, probably, that they even existed.

Unaware?

I went to the window. Another gray day.

The problems of the world. Distant links. Isolated people. So near and yet so far.

My flight didn't leave until after six. Perhaps, after lunch, I'd go to a movie. Any movie. As long as it wasn't a love story.

Dolly's apartment was like Dolly—a mélange of periods. The 1920's, '30's, '40's were represented in abundance. But there were odd items from later decades, too. And there were a few valuable antiques mixed in—"Mother's things," she called them. Quick had been right about the tea service, either by accident or because he really did know the Dolly Whitcomb type. It was Sheffield and included more pieces than I'd ever seen in a tea service. There was also a Whistler painting and a number of Dutch canvases that weren't of museum quality but had no doubt cost plenty.

But what really made the apartment different from most people's apartments were the photographs. They were everywhere, in every kind of frame. In the living room alone there must have been thirty, and in what Dolly called the library, although it was bookless, there were even more. I was reminded of an athlete whose trophies were on display all over the house. And I guessed that in a sense the photographs were Dolly's trophies. They represented her many victories over friendlessness and anonymity.

The only photograph that really interested me, however, was one of herself with Elissa and Elissa's fourth husband, taken some twenty years before, on the terrace of the Carlton Hotel in Cannes. The husband—"Julio," according to Dolly—was a handsome man, very Spanish-looking, who gave the impression of being thoroughly bored and not at all pleased to be where he was. Elissa, on the other hand, was smiling brightly. A very different Elissa from the wasted creature I'd seen in the hospital. But even then, despite the bright smile, I sensed, perhaps because of all I'd heard, that she might have had problems. Not only because her husband appeared bored, but because he was obviously younger than she. And because of all the cocktail glasses on the table. They suggested a social afternoon that might soon degenerate into something sloppy.

I asked Dolly about the picture—or, rather, about the day on which it was taken—but she had no recollection of it. All she could remember was that the weather had been "heavenly" that year and that Julio came from a sherry family and was an expert horseman—he'd competed internationally.

The meal itself was a bit more than the "nothing elaborate" Dolly had spoken of. Consommé with warm cheese sticks, veal piccata, rice, a barolo that was one of the best wines I'd ever tasted, endive salad, apple tarts. And espresso, after the meal, in the living room, with cognac. Despite the fact that her cook was leaving early, Dolly had laid it on.

Furthermore, she was doing her best to be a *femme fatale*. In magenta velvet hostess pajamas, with the long cigarette holder and the vast eyelashes, she was rather like what Delilah might have become if Samson hadn't brought the walls down and cut short the lives of all of them.

What I wanted to know was who had put Dolly up to it.

I found out, too, for it wasn't really in Dolly's nature to be secretive. Abigail Henning had been the first, and the Count de Garonne had been the second. They'd called within an hour of each other, inquiring about me. And Dolly hadn't needed much encouragement. She'd concluded that I was someone really worth knowing, and that was evidently all that was required. I even suspected that if a photographer had been available on short notice, she might have had my picture taken. One more for the collection. Brockton Potter—such a dear man, and a very good friend of mine, you know.

To the best of her ability, she probed. My home, my business, the reason for my interest in the Koberg company—she was eager to know the entire story. And I saw no reason not to give it to her, within limits. I told her about the old house on West 11th Street that I'd bought; how it had been converted into apartments, and how I'd converted it back into a house. About the general nature of Price, Potter and Petacque's activities. About how my secretary's niece had been engaged to marry Elissa's grandson, and the chain of events that had brought me to Chicago. I didn't tell her about Louis Glass, or about Koberg buying up its own stock, or about the research that it was doing. But I told her enough to satisfy her curiosity, and to make it fair for me to do some probing of my own, once she got over the shock of learning that Elissa's grandson was dead.

She'd seen Elissa's grandson once, she said. When he was an infant. Bonnie had brought him to visit her. Bonnie, poor dear, had seemed rather "sad," but who in the world would have imagined that she would ever do away with herself? And one hates to interfere.

I pictured the infant Bob McDonald on his mother's lap in that very room, and for a moment I felt closer to the McDonald family than I had before.

When it came to Abigail Henning, Dwight Wilson and "dear Henri," Dolly at first was reticent. She handed me the same line she'd handed me at the restaurant—she didn't think it was wise to think too much about whether one likes one's friends. Apparently she had a genuine fear of judging people harshly and what that might lead to. But she also loved gossip and eventually she loosened up. Her acquaintance with Wilson went back further than I'd thought. They'd attended the same private day school as children, been members of the same club—the Fortnightly Club—as teenagers, and their parents had belonged to the same church. Later their paths had diverged, however. Wilson had gone into business and become, in Dolly's words, "frightfully stuffy," whereas she had gone off to pursue her "gadabout" existence.

Dolly had never much cared for Hazel, Wilson's wife, although they had belonged to many of the same organizations and had, during Hazel's lifetime, seen each other from time to time. I gathered that her present friendship with Wilson, such as it was, was due mainly to the fact that they had memories in common, but not to any real affection. And it certainly wasn't due to Abby, who, Dolly felt, was like a prune, poor dear—all dried up. "It's so sad when a woman has no money of her own," Dolly concluded. "It makes her dependent, and dependent old women, *mon cher*, make dreadful friends—you can't believe a thing they say."

But the Count de Garonne was another story. Dolly's attitude toward him was much more complex. He was a true predator— *un sauvage pur*—and she rather liked men of his sort. Not as husbands, of course—Dolly didn't care much for husbands of any sort—but as traveling companions and friends. They were exciting.

"I had drinks with him yesterday," I said. "He didn't seem particularly exciting to me."

"You're not a woman, *mon cher*. And, if you'll forgive me, you're not a man of the world."

The phrase rang a bell. The Count had used it to describe himself. A man of the world. "You're forgiven," I said, "but tell me, what *is* a man of the world? Because it seems to me that I've knocked around more than most people. I've sure had my share of experiences."

Dolly considered the question. "A man of the world, *mon cher*, is a man with different *kinds* of experiences. Especially with women. And a man who has often lived by his wits."

"I live by my wits. That's all I have going for me."

"No. You're shy."

"I wish you'd stop saying that, Dolly. A lot of people think I'm too aggressive."

"Come now, would you marry a woman twenty-five years older than yourself simply because she's rich?"

"No."

"Then you're shy."

"I'm afraid you and I use different dictionaries."

Dolly let the remark go by. "Henri wasn't in love with Elissa," she said. "He didn't even pretend to be. *She* was in love with *him*. Monique was at their wedding—I told you about Monique, didn't I? Well, Monique was there. It took place at the *mairie* in Nice. Henri had a cigarette in his mouth all through the ceremony. He looked, Monique said, like someone who's waiting for a train that's late."

"But what about Elissa?" I asked. "Didn't she *care?*"

Dolly sighed. "Poor Elissa. She was too *besotted* to care. He was handsome. He reminded me of Cary Grant in those days. In fact, he still does, a little. Elissa's whole life, *mon cher*, has been running away from facts, refusing to see things as they are. And by then—well, she had so much to run away *from*. Her conscience mainly, I think."

"Her daughter?"

"That bothered her in later years. Do have some more espresso, *mon cher*."

I nodded, and she poured.

"She seldom talked about it," Dolly went on. "I mean, what was there to say? But I think it bothered her. And the child. I can't tell you how shocked I am to hear about *that*. Crime in Chicago is bad enough, but I do believe New York must be worse. But the child—I think Elissa thought about him. I think she felt—I don't know—*deprived*."

"Well, it's too late now."

"How true. And perhaps it was too late a long time ago. But I can understand. Elissa and I, at least in a manner of speaking, are in the same boat. And poor Dwight too, come to think of it. We're the last of our line. When we die . . ."

"But in Elissa's case it didn't have to be like that. In a way, it's her fault that Bob McDonald is dead. If he'd been raised differently, elsewhere, he'd probably still be alive."

"Yes, *mon cher*, I daresay that's true. In my own case, I don't mind so much being alone. There's never *been* anyone—I never wanted there to be. At times I'm sorry, but at other times I'm not. I'd rather have had my life than Elissa's. But in *her* case—if that dreadful son-in-law of hers had let the boy visit her—she did want him to, you know—well, you might say that what happened is as much the father's fault as Elissa's."

The coffee was bitter and had got cold, but I drank it anyway. I pictured the Count smoking while he was being married. That too seemed somehow bitter and cold. "Elissa's present marriage," I said, "according to the Count, hasn't been the greatest."

"But what would you expect? Of course it hasn't. She realized immediately, I daresay, that it wasn't going to be. And she wanted a divorce. That was her pattern. Love, marriage, regret. But he wouldn't give her one—or, I suspect, he named too high a price—and she was old. I mean—I hate to sound unkind; after all, she *is* my friend—but she was definitely *passée*, and at a certain point, probably, even a bad marriage is better than no marriage at all. For someone like Elissa, at least. Except for a grandson she'd never seen and never would see, there was no one else. And in Elissa's case there always *had* to be someone else."

"I feel sorry for her."

"You're a kind man, *mon cher*. Shy, but kind."

I grimaced. "If you don't stop calling me shy, Dolly, I'm going to forget you're older than I and take you across my knee and spank you."

"*Mon cher!*" Dolly cried happily. "Perhaps you are *un sauvage*, after all."

And on that note the simple luncheon that had turned out not to be so simple came to an end. It was after two o'clock, and I decided it was time to go. Too late for a movie, but perhaps there was something good on television. And with the Christmas Eve traffic, I would have to allow myself plenty of time to get to the airport and turn in the car.

Dolly hobbled with me to the door, and as I reached out to shake her hand, she pulled me toward her and kissed me. "*Bon voyage, mon cher sauvage.*" I'm not sure I understand you, but I do like you, and if you ever come back to Chicago, I hope we'll have another lunch together."

"It'll be my pleasure," I said, and went out to the vestibule to ring for the elevator.

The elevator came. I stepped into it. And the door closed between Dolly Whitcomb and her dear savage.

28

The sky had turned the color of charcoal, and the air was decidedly moist.

Snow, I thought. At any minute.

Recalling the traffic I'd encountered on the expressway driving into the city, and reminding myself that today most offices would be closing early, I decided to head for the airport earlier than I'd planned.

There was no need to rush, however. My plane wasn't due to leave for another four hours. So, entering the hotel by the Lake Shore Drive entrance, I loitered in the arcade, window-shopping as I strolled toward the elevators. The jewelry, the china, the glassware, the tiny Christmas trees decorated with gingham bows—everything was attractive and tempting. And suddenly it dawned on me: I hadn't bought anything for Brian's family.

I backtracked to my starting point and studied the displays again, with deeper interest. I'd never met Brian's family; I wasn't even sure how many members it had. But one item, something that all of them could enjoy—that would be a nice gesture.

And in the window of the gourmet food shop I saw just the thing. A straw hamper filled with fresh fruits and imported delicacies—a tin of French *pâté*, two jars of Scottish marmalade and a large box of English biscuits.

I went into the shop for a closer look—and emerged, fifteen minutes later, lugging my purchase.

Even before I reached the elevators, I realized that I'd made a mistake. The package was too fragile to be checked and too big to fit under the seat of an airplane. Furthermore, it was heavy; it felt as if it weighed at least fifteen pounds. When I thought of all the walking I was going to have to do at the airports and of the hard time that the cabin attendant was bound to give me, I was sorry that I hadn't chosen something smaller.

It was too late, however. I'd bought the damn thing and was stuck with it.

The elevator was a long time in coming. When it finally did come, I put the package down, to give my arms a rest. But when we reached my floor, I picked it up again and started down the long corridor to my room, wondering how any kid, no matter how young, could be dumb enough to believe that eight lousy reindeer could pull a sleigh big enough to hold all those presents.

Lumbering along the corridor, I anticipated what the stewardess would say to me and what I'd say to her. The corridor seemed very long. And very still. The thick carpeting, the high ceiling—for a moment I thought about how comfortable the hotel was, and how pleasant it was to have it almost to myself. They didn't build hotels like this anymore. Large rooms, old-fashioned windows that could be opened from the top or bottom, walls that didn't transmit every sound.

Every sound.

I halted. A faint noise had registered to my right. I turned my head. I was parallel with the door to the service stairs. The door had creaked.

I took another step, then froze. The door was open. Only a few inches. But I could see the muzzle of a gun in the opening. The gun was pointed at me.

For a fraction of a second I was paralyzed by fright. Then instinct took over. I hurled the package at the door and ran.

Noise and motion were one. The crash, the clatter, my pounding feet.

Suddenly something happened to my right leg. It felt as if it had been stung by a bee. I stumbled and fell. "Help!" I shouted.

A piece of plaster flew from the wall at my left. I rolled sideways toward the shelter of the other wall.

A door slammed. A woman screamed.

I flattened myself against the wall.

The screams continued, then stopped.

Nothing else happened.

I hoisted myself to a sitting position and noticed that I was bleeding. There was a pool of blood on the floor, and the leg of my pants was soaked. I tried to get to my feet, but couldn't.

I stared at the door to the service stairs. It was closed. The package I'd intended for Brian's family lay on the carpet in front of it. I sat there, leaning against the wall, for what seemed a very long time.

And I was still sitting there when the house officer and a bellman arrived.

29

Unfortunately, I was conscious throughout. And I didn't know which was worse, the questions or the lights.

Even with my eyes closed, the lights bothered me, and I kept complaining. Finally one of the doctors said, "We have to see what we're doing."

What they were doing, I said, was hurting me.

"Sorry about that," he replied. "We're trying not to." And soon after that someone jabbed me with a hypodermic syringe, and the pain diminished.

The questions were something else again. Waiting for the ambulance, in the ambulance, on the way to the emergency room—the security officer, the policemen, the paramedics, the doctors—I thought they'd never stop badgering me for the facts.

To most of the questions I gave the same answer: "I don't know." I didn't know who, why or how. I was no longer even sure of when. And as for where, they knew that as well as I did. I was walking along the corridor on the way to my room, I heard a slight noise, I turned my head and saw the muzzle of a gun and I began to run.

After thirty years or so, someone gave me another injection, and I went to sleep.

When I awoke, it was daylight. At first I couldn't figure out where I was, but then I realized that I was in the hospital. Bits and pieces came back to me—I'd been shot, an ambulance had brought me to Northwestern Memorial, a lot of faces had hovered over me, the lights had been too bright, and now I was all by myself, which was a relief. My leg hurt a lot when I moved it, but only a little when I didn't, and I was sore in other parts of the body—my forehead, the bridge of my nose, my hands; evidently I'd bruised myself when I'd fallen. Still, I felt pretty good, considering. Just tired. Tired and peculiarly unconcerned. All I really wanted was to be left alone.

I went back to sleep, awoke, went to sleep again. Doctors came, nurses, a woman who cleaned the room. But mostly I just slept or dozed or stared at the ceiling, which had a funny spot on it that resembled a horse with wings.

At one point—I don't remember when it was—I realized that it was Christmas Day, and it occurred to me that I'd never expected to be spending Christmas Day in a hospital. But there didn't seem to be anything wrong with spending Christmas Day in a hospital. The only thing that worried me—and even that didn't worry me very much—was the gift I'd bought for Brian's family. The last I'd seen of it, it had been lying where it had landed, in front of the door to the service stairs. I hoped that someone had thought to pick it up—it was a nice hamper.

I also hoped that someone had notified Brian that I wouldn't be there for Christmas dinner. One of the nurses—or it might have been one of the doctors—had asked me who was my next of kin, and I'd said that I didn't have any next of kin, but to please call my friend Brian Barth—he was supposed to meet me at the airport in Richmond, Virginia. I couldn't remember his phone number or his mother's married name, but I remembered the name of the town and, in any event, they could have him paged at the airport.

I had a vague feeling that I ought to let someone know where I was. Tom, Mark, Irving—someone. But at the same time I had the feeling that I shouldn't. Tom and Mark were on vacation, and Irving was going out somewhere with his family, and why get everyone upset? Eventually things would straighten themselves out.

Time lost its meaning. Food came and went. I had no appetite and didn't even make a pretense of eating, although a couple of times I did ask for a glass of water. Other doctors appeared at my bedside, other nurses. They asked me how I felt. I said I felt all right. One of them brought me a pill, and I swallowed it without even asking what it was. Whatever it was, it was probably something that I needed.

Aside from members of the hospital staff, my only visitors were two nice-looking men who identified themselves as Detectives Brown and Grissom. They were handling the case, they said, and they asked me a few of the same questions I'd been asked before, but they didn't seem particularly interested in my answers. They gave the impression that they'd come to see me for social rather than professional reasons. They were in the room for less than ten minutes. What they were mainly concerned about, I gathered, was how I was feeling. I told them that my leg hurt when I moved it, and I was rather sore, but otherwise the only thing that was bothering me was my bladder—I wished that someone would bring me a urinal. Which induced them to leave. They'd be back later, they said.

A nurse subsequently brought me another pill, and I swallowed that one too. Then I went to sleep again.

But the next time I awoke, I saw a very familiar face.

Brian was standing beside the bed, looking down at me. And for a moment I thought I was still dreaming.

"Brian?"

He took my hand. "Thank God you're all right." He looked awful. Red-eyed, unshaved, exhausted.

"How did you get here?"

"The hard way. What in God's name happened, Brock? I've been going crazy."

For the first time in many hours I made a serious attempt to concentrate. It was difficult. "I'm not sure," I said at last, "but I think someone tried to kill me. I'm sorry about your present."

30

The next day they took me off medication, and everything was different. I was fully alert. And aware that my leg really did hurt. But the other pains that I'd been dimly conscious of were about gone. I had a slight cut on the bridge of my nose, and my right wrist was sore, but neither was worth mentioning. The only problem was the leg. The bullet had passed completely through the inside of the right thigh, about six inches above the knee and, luckily, near the skin surface. I'd lost a considerable amount of blood, and the doctor said something about shock and the danger of infection; but he also said that I'd been given plasma and enough antibiotic to discourage the germs.

All it amounted to, he assured me, was giving the wound a chance to heal. And by way of further reassurance he added that he'd sewn up people with worse gunshot wounds than mine and sent them home within hours.

"So why didn't you send *me* home within hours?"

"Because you said your home was in New York." He grinned. "And because you were such a damn nuisance while we were trying to treat you."

I apologized, and asked when I would be released.

"Let's give it another day," he said, "just to be on the safe side. Actually, you could go home right now if you had anyplace to go other than a hotel room. But since you don't . . ."

Brian, who was with me, nodded vigorously and said, "Keep him here."

The doctor's expression became more serious. "In point of fact, Mr. Potter, I wouldn't recommend your attempting the trip back to New York for another few days. And even then you'll have to stay off your feet for a while. I'll arrange for you to be fitted for crutches before you leave here, but—"

"Crutches?" The idea was somehow humiliating.

"Yes, crutches. You'll be glad to have them, believe me."

I turned to Brian. "Maybe I ought to stand on a street corner with a tin cup."

Brian didn't think it was funny, and neither did the doctor. "Crutches," he said again. "And plenty of rest. And if anything further develops, although I'm quite certain it won't, see your doctor in New York."

That was the sum total of his advice. For which, I guessed, Price, Potter and Petacque's insurance company was going to have to pay plenty, since the cost of getting shot had probably gone up, along with everything else.

"I refuse to be an invalid," I told Brian after the doctor left.

"Don't be ridiculous," Brian said. "I'm here."

And so he was. From morning until night. Looking better, too. He'd checked into the Drake, in a room on my floor, and had a good night's sleep. Prior to that, I gathered, he hadn't been to bed for some thirty-eight hours. No one had bothered to notify him that I wouldn't be on the flight, or if someone had bothered, he hadn't got the message. He'd waited until the last passenger was off the plane, checked with the airline, called the Drake, driven back to his mother's, made several more calls to the Drake—without getting any satisfaction. According to the hotel operator, I was still registered, period.

"So how did you find out?" I asked.

"Finally I called the police," he replied. "And when I finally got to the right guy, he told me."

Whereupon Brian had set out before dawn for Washington, D.C., where he'd thought he could get the best service to Chicago. But because it was Christmas Day, many of the flights weren't operating, and when he'd eventually got on one, it was diverted to Indianapolis.

"Indianapolis?" I asked incredulously.

"On account of the snow," he said.

"It snowed?"

"Eighteen inches."

"I didn't even know." But then it came back to me: I'd anticipated snow. "How long were you in Indianapolis?"

"Until the first bus left."

"You came here by *bus?*"

"I thought it'd be smarter than renting a car."

I just looked at him.

"I didn't tell Irving or anybody. Should I have?"

I shook my head. Brian, I thought. My piranha.

Anyway, Brian said, after leaving the hospital he'd gone straight to the Drake, told the desk clerk that he was an associate of mine and wanted a room on my floor, and when he'd been given one, he'd poked around. Without success. Except for a spot on the carpet and a faint odor of cleaning fluid, there was nothing to indicate that a shooting had taken place.

I asked him about the door to the service stairs and a bullet hole in the wall. He said that he'd found the service stairs and what might have been a spot of fresh plaster, but neither offered anything in the way of a clue. And when he'd asked around the hotel about what had happened to me, no one had been able or willing to give him any information.

"Hotels are like that," I said.

"I know. And it wasn't the hotel's fault. The same thing could have happened anywhere."

I nodded, and neither of us spoke for a while.

"What caliber bullet was it?" Brian asked at last.

"Damned if I know," I replied. "No one has told me."

But not long after that, someone did tell me. Detective Grissom. He and Detective Brown arrived just in time to spoil my lunch.

I'd had dealings with law-enforcement officers in the past. I wasn't proud of that fact, but it was true. In the course of the investigations that had earned me the reputation I wished I didn't have, I'd met police officers, sheriff's men, FBI agents and others whose duty was the capture and prosecution of malefactors. By and large, I'd found such men to be more or less like everyone else—concerned with doing what they had to do as well as they could, with as little trouble as possible, keeping in mind such matters as citations, promotions and pensions. Some of them had struck me as slightly paranoid, which, given the nature of their work and the public's attitude toward them, was understandable. Others had struck me as more satisfied with themselves than they had any right to be. But in general I'd found them a decent lot, and all had had one thing in common—a certain mental flexibility, a willingness at least to consider more than one possibility.

Not Brown and Grissom, however. They were unique. Their minds were closed. As far as they were concerned, this was an open-and-shut case and interviewing me was a mere formality.

According to them, I'd been shot more or less by accident. I'd simply got in the way of a jewel thief.

The intended victim of the theft was the woman who'd opened the door and then slammed it and started to scream—a Mrs. Mildred Forrester, widow of the late Harold Forrester, formerly of Chicago, presently of Fort Lauderdale, Florida. Mrs. Forrester had arrived in Chicago on Monday for a week of festivities that were to culminate in the wedding of her granddaughter. And had arrived with a $150,000 assortment of necklaces, rings, bracelets and other doodads, in addition to two mink coats—a long one and a short one—valued at $20,000. Between wearings, the jewels had been stored in one of the hotel's safe-deposit boxes, but the wearings had been frequent, and at the time I was shot most of them were in Mrs. Forrester's room—she'd just returned from a luncheon and would soon be dressing for a reception and dinner.

An armed robber had been about to invade Mrs. Forrester's quarters, but at the crucial moment I'd come sauntering down the corridor, and the thief, fearing that I'd spotted him and would be able to describe him, had panicked and shot me.

Mrs. Forrester was absolutely certain that that was what had happened, and she'd persuaded the police. Perhaps the police hadn't required much persuading, either—all they'd had to do was look at the jewelry, which Mrs. Forrester had showed them. Brown and Grissom were still, almost two days later, awed by it. "A diamond-and-emerald necklace like you wouldn't believe!" Brown exclaimed, his face turning pink from some inner excitement.

As soon as they found the would-be thief, the two men said, they'd have my assailant. They couldn't guarantee that they would find him, of course, but they thought their chances were pretty good; their file on jewel thieves was very comprehensive. Furthermore, they were getting cooperation from the police in Fort Lauderdale.

Their main interest in me had to do with my future whereabouts. They wanted to make sure that I'd be able to identify the clown, as they called him, if and when he was caught, and that I'd be willing to testify. They were annoyed when I said that I might not be much help—I'd merely seen a door that was open a few inches and the muzzle of a gun.

They weren't stupid men. They'd done some careful detail work. Two bullets had been fired, they said, and they'd recovered both of them. They were .22-caliber bullets and were in reasonably good condition—they would be useful to the prosecution. They'd also picked up the package I'd thrown at the door. It was now impounded as evidence. Their reconstruction of the shooting itself made sense and showed that they'd given the matter considerable thought. They believed, on the basis of what I'd told the security officer and the patrolmen who'd been the first to question me that I'd saved my life by throwing the package. It had either hit the gun or had hit the door hard enough to make whoever was holding the gun drop it. And it did seem likely to me that the gun had been dropped, for I'd been parallel to the door when I'd seen the muzzle and some thirty feet past the door when I'd been shot. The gun had been dropped, picked up and fired twice, in haste, without proper aim.

I couldn't argue with any of that. As I recalled the noise and movement of those few seconds, I felt that the detectives were quite right. What bothered me was their one-track theory that I'd been shot because of Mrs. Forrester's jewelry. And my own inability to come up with a better theory.

I couldn't disprove a single thing that Brown and Grissom were saying. But some instinct warned me that they just might be wrong. I had, I admitted to the detectives—and to myself—no murder-minded enemies that I knew of. Still, this same instinct said, I might recently have acquired one that I didn't know of.

Grissom did ask me what I was doing in Chicago. But he asked the question in a perfunctory way and didn't seem much interested in my answer—namely, that I was a securities analyst and that I was looking into a Chicago company, Koberg Chemical, about which I was preparing a report. However, when he inquired whether I'd learned anything about the company which might be damaging to someone in it, and I told him that I hadn't, he abandoned that line of questioning.

The detectives seemed already to know that I would be leaving the hospital the next day. They asked where I could be reached afterwards. I said that I intended to return to New York as soon as possible and gave them my home and office numbers there. They assured me that as soon as something turned up, I'd hear from them, either directly or through the police department in New York. Meanwhile they wanted a signed statement from me.

So, although the interview lasted a full hour, it ended more or less as it had begun, with the detectives convinced that, except for the identity of the thief, the case was solved.

I wanted to believe that they were right. And to a certain extent I could. Their theory was logical. But something that had nothing to do with logic argued that they were wrong.

Evidently Brian felt as I did. He'd offered to leave the room during the interview, but the policemen had told him that he could stay, and he'd listened to all that was said.

"Does it make sense?" he asked, as soon as we were alone.

I thought for a moment. "In a way."

"In a way," he agreed, sounding skeptical.

I looked at him. He appeared worried. "At any rate," I said, "let's hope so."

He nodded.

We didn't have to say more than that. Both of us knew that if the police were wrong, I could be in real danger. For whoever had tried once might be determined enough to try again.

31

Sometime during the middle of the night I awoke; and I remained awake for several hours, thinking.

Except for footsteps and low voices in the corridor when the floor nurses made their rounds, the silence was deep. The hospital, Brian had remarked, didn't seem crowded, and we'd concluded that this was the time of year when hospitals, like big-city hotels, had the fewest occupants. It seemed odd to me that I should be one of the few.

My leg hurt, but that, I knew, was something I was just going to have to get used to. Eventually whatever had been torn would mend and the pain would stop. But the fact that I was having pain was part of the general oddness—it was all so unexpected, so inexplicable. Part of an experience that most people went through life without having.

Why me? I wondered. And that was what most of the thinking was about: why me?

I spent a lot of time pondering the policemen's theory. It was entirely plausible. A woman seen repeatedly in public decked out in jewels worth a fortune. That woman, by coincidence, staying on the same floor of the same hotel as myself. And, by coincidence, about to be robbed at the very moment I stepped out of the elevator. A peculiar, one-in-a-million quirk of fate. But possible.

On the other hand, did thieves usually commit such robberies in the middle of the afternoon? They did not. Of course, as Brown and Grissom had explained, Mrs. Forrester kept her jewelry in a safe-deposit box most of the time. The thief might have known this, might have followed her, might have waited for the opportune moment—the moment I'd spoiled for him.

Would I have spoiled it, though? Would I have suspected anything? Would I later have been able to identify him? The fact was, I hadn't seen him at all. Why would he think that I had?

Brown and Grissom had taken some rather broad leaps in their reasoning.

Yet I couldn't develop a theory that was any better than theirs. I went over every move I remembered making during the two days I'd been cantering about Chicago. Analyzed them. Imagined inferences that might have been drawn from them. But I still couldn't come up with an alternative explanation. I hadn't learned anything about Koberg Chemical that could hurt the company or anyone in it. The only item of possible importance which I'd picked up was that the company was doing research on the bug that caused jungle rot. The other item, which was of more than possible importance—the crucial item—was that Louis Glass was trying to get control of the company. But I hadn't picked up that item myself—Harriet had picked it up for me. And she'd obtained it in New York, not in Chicago.

Could Harriet have dropped a careless word?

Not if I knew Harriet Jensen. I doubted that she'd dropped even one careless word in all the years since she'd first learned to talk.

The key figure in Koberg Chemical, Paul Carmichael, had refused to see me. The other figures I'd met were on the fringe—none of them were involved in Koberg's current activities. Dwight Wilson had been cast aside, and Dolly Whitcomb, as well as the Count de Garonne, had never had anything to do with the company to begin with—their relationships were with Elissa, who herself had never had anything more to do with the company than cash her dividend checks.

My thoughts lingered for some time on Elissa. Now we had something in common, she and I: we were fellow patients in the same hospital. But I was going to leave the place alive, and she wasn't. What was going through her mind as she lay in her bed, which in one way was so close to mine and in another was so far? Did she have regrets? According to Dolly, she did.

I decided to pay her one more visit before leaving the hospital.

Dolly, now—that was a different story. She'd invited me to lunch. She'd known at what time I would arrive and approximately at what time I would leave. She couldn't have known that I would go directly back to the hotel from her apartment, but she'd known more about my plans than anyone else.

She'd given me the impression that Abigail Henning and the Count had been indirectly responsible for her wish to see me again. That might have been the case. But then again, it might not.

In any event, what motive could she have had? What motive could anyone have had?

All possibilities had to be considered. Even the possibility that I hadn't told Brown and Grissom the truth when I'd said that I had no enemies. Actually—I had to face it—I did have enemies. I'd uncovered criminal activity and caused anguish to those involved. Some people no doubt hated me and always would. Had one of them caught up with me?

Conceivably. But how would any of them have known that I would be in Chicago when I myself hadn't known until almost the last minute? How would any of them have known at which hotel I was staying when I'd made the reservation myself, also at the last minute? Above all, how would any of them have known that I would be returning to my room at that particular time?

How long, I wondered, could a person stand in the service corridor of a hotel without being seen? Given the fact that the hotel wasn't crowded and that a large part of the staff had probably been laid off for the slow weeks during the holidays, I supposed that someone could stand there without being seen for quite some time.

But how could that person have known which corridor to wait in? This, it seemed to me, was the essence of the problem, the real reason I couldn't come up with a theory that was any better than that of the detectives. If someone had planned to shoot me, that person would have had to know which floor I was staying on and in which wing of the building. The only way anyone could know that was by asking for my room number. Hotels were cautious about giving out room numbers, however. I recalled what had happened a while back when, after visiting three cities in as many days, I'd forgotten my own room number. The clerk at the desk had made me sign my name and had compared that signature with the one on the registration card before giving me my key.

So how, damn it, could anyone have got my room number? Had I been followed? Had someone been bribed? Had I mentioned my room number to anyone? Philip Quick, Abigail Henning, Dolly Whitcomb, Dwight Wilson, the Count de Garonne—I went over the conversations I'd had with each of them, groping for every word that my memory had stored away. Not all of the words were reachable, but quite a few of them were. And I positively couldn't recall having told anyone I'd met in Chicago the number of the room in which I was staying.

But memory is a tricky thing. Long after I'd stopped trying to dredge up every act and every utterance, it came. I recalled that I'd given my room number to Paul Carmichael's secretary.

32

Brian helped me dress. It was a difficult process. I'd gone up and down the corridor a couple of times to try out the crutches, but I was clumsy, and the simple acts of sitting down and standing up were painful. My real problem, however, was psychological—the clothes themselves revolted me. I hadn't thought to tell Brian to bring me clean ones, and it hadn't occurred to him that I might need them, so I was putting on the same bloodstained outfit in which I'd been brought to the hospital, and the sight of it turned my stomach. I'd known that I'd bled, but I hadn't realized that I'd bled that much. Even my shoes had dried blood on them.

It annoyed me that Brian didn't share my feeling of disgust. He seemed intrigued by the vestiges of mayhem and examined the bullet holes in my topcoat and pants with great interest. "They aren't very big," he observed.

"Would you have preferred them bigger?" I asked dryly.

But he merely shook his head. "Not very big at all."

When at last I was fully clad and propped up on my crutches, I said, "I want to make a stop on the ninth floor before we leave. I'd like to see the Countess de Garonne again."

I'd given him a rundown, during the many hours we'd spent together the day before, of the people I'd met in Chicago and how they'd struck me. The Countess had been included in it. I'd told him what people had said about her, how she'd looked, the sensations I'd had after leaving her room. And in her case I'd emphasized the negative aspects, physical and otherwise. But Brian was Brian, and evidently he hadn't been in the least turned off, for he now asked eagerly, "Can I come too?"

"If you want," I replied.

He escorted me to the elevator, and we went up.

Everything was as it had been before. So much so that it was as if for the past four days time had, in that one hospital room, stood absolutely still. The same nurse was sitting in the same chair, reading what looked like the same magazine. Everything else was so unchanged that I had a fleeting impression that she was even reading the same page. Elissa was asleep, as before, in almost the identical position. Her appearance was unaltered. Her color, the degree of emaciation—there had been no deterioration, no improvement. And it crossed my mind that she might have been like that—might remain like that—for longer than I'd imagined. Death was unpredictable; sometimes it came very slowly.

The nurse looked up, as she had previously. But then differences set in. She actually did speak. "Yes?" she said.

"Is this the Countess de Garonne?" I asked.

"Yes," she replied. Her eyes went from me to Brian, but quickly came back to me. The crutches, the stains on my coat and pants must have puzzled her, for she frowned. "May I help you?" she said, more like a receptionist than a nurse.

"I'm a friend of the family," I said.

Her frown deepened. The family, it said, had no friends. "The Countess—" she began.

But at that moment the unexpected happened. With a sudden start and a snort, the Countess woke. For the first time I saw her eyes. They were black, and in the wasted face they seemed enormous. The whites weren't white, however; they were yellow. She seemed startled. "*Mon Dieu!*" she exclaimed.

I was startled too. I didn't know what to say.

Her gaze shifted from me to Brian. And lingered. Her eyes became even larger, and her face showed animation. She smiled. "Roe-bear?" she asked.

Brian said nothing.

The Countess continued to gaze at him, and her smile broadened. "You are Roe-bear?"

"No, Countess," I said. "My name is Brockton Potter, and this is a member of my staff."

"Not Roe-bear?" Her smile faded.

I shook my head.

The Countess turned away. "Leave me," she said. "I am ill."

I stood there a moment, wanting to say more, but not wanting to inflict further hurt.

"You'd better go," the nurse said.

I nodded, and shifted my weight to begin an about-face on my crutches. For an instant the Countess turned back, and I saw tears in her eyes. But then she closed them.

Brian and I left the room.

"God!" he said in a low voice.

I was unable to say anything at all.

33

The remainder of the day was just plain horrible.

First there was the matter of returning to my room at the hotel. I hadn't anticipated that I would have any emotional reaction to walking past the spot where the shooting had occurred. But when I saw the door to the service stairs, everything came back to me in a rush. In my mind's eye I saw the gun, and in my gut I felt the emotion. For some moments I was in the grip of a recalled terror that was worse than the original terror had been.

Then there was the matter of my statement to the police. I'd wanted them to come to the hospital, or, if not to the hospital, then at least to my room at the hotel. But they'd insisted—"We prefer" was the way they'd put it—that I come to their office, where "the facilities are better." They hadn't even offered to come for me in a car. On the theory, I suppose, that if I felt well enough to make the trip back to New York, I could damn well get myself over to a Chicago police station.

Giving the statement and waiting for it to be typed took much longer than I'd expected. It took almost three hours. And while the facilities might have been better at the police station than anywhere else, the atmosphere was infinitely worse. Even the smell—nine parts stale cigarette smoke, one part floor wax—

affected me. But the worst of the whole tedious ordeal was my own indecision as to whether or not to tell them I'd given my room number to Paul Carmichael's secretary.

In the end, I did tell them; and that was one of the reasons the session took as long as it did. For, having told them, I couldn't not explain. But, having explained, I couldn't come up with a plausible link between my having revealed my room number and my being shot. Had I ever met Mr. Carmichael? No. Had I learned anything about him that would cause him to want to kill me? No. Had I ever met Mr. Carmichael's secretary? No. To whom could either Mr. Carmichael or his secretary have given my room number that would want to kill me? Well, she could have given it to anyone. Where did that leave us, though? Nowhere, as far as the police were concerned. As for me, I was beginning to believe that there might be an answer to what seemed unanswerable, but in order to find it I had to go to New York. And these two polite but skeptical cops were delaying me.

They did say that they would "check out" Mr. Carmichael and his secretary, but they said it without enthusiasm, and I was certain that even if they did, they wouldn't uncover anything. To Carmichael and his secretary I would be merely someone who had requested an appointment and been turned down. End of relationship.

I was sorry I'd brought the subject up at all.

Then the true test of my stoicism began. The trip itself.

The long ride to the airport over snow-rutted streets and the icy expressway in a taxi that desperately needed new shock-absorbers was painful as hell. But the real hell was the plane ride.

Brian had questioned the airline and been assured that the runways were clear and operations were back to normal. That much was true. Our flight left on time. What I hadn't known, however, was that changes in air pressure could affect an unhealed bullet wound as much as they did. It was like flying with a head cold and getting an earache, only it wasn't my ears that hurt. And on this particular flight the pilot couldn't seem to find an altitude that suited him. We tried them all, and the pressurization in the cabin was such that I felt them all, acutely.

At first I blamed the doctor for not having laid it on me heavily enough; he'd told me not to travel for a few days, but he hadn't forbidden it. But I had to admit that even if he had forbidden it, I would have got on the plane. I'd had enough of Chicago; I'd almost been killed there; and I had a hunch that if I remained, I might be the victim of a second attempt. Furthermore, there was information in New York that I needed.

So I sat there and endured. I even made conversation.

Brian wanted to know why I hadn't told *him* about giving my room number to Carmichael's secretary. I replied that I hadn't done so because I hadn't yet thought the matter through. It might be important, it might not.

He informed me that in the past two days he'd spoken three times by telephone with his brother Keith. Keith had cut his Christmas vacation short and gone back to school.

"Why?" I asked.

"To find out about that bug you mentioned. The one that causes jungle rot."

"But the school is closed."

"The school may be, but most of the professors are still in town. They *live* there. And Keith, I've got to admit, is a pretty good digger."

"That was very nice of him," I said, "but why did he do it?"

"Because I asked him to. And," Brian added, with modest pride, "he kind of respects me."

"He must be scared to death of you."

"That too," Brian acknowledged.

Keith, it seemed, had already gathered some data, and Brian started to pass it on to me, but I just didn't feel up to listening to a complicated scientific explanation, and I told him so.

"You really don't look too good," he conceded, and lapsed into silence.

The silence lasted for maybe a hundred and fifty miles. But Brian was thinking—I could see that.

Finally he said, as the plane was somewhere over eastern Pennsylvania and, to my considerable anguish, was descending, "You know, Brock, I just can't help believing that you weren't shot because of that lady's jewelry. I think you were shot because you turned up something you don't know you turned up."

I nodded.

He presented me with a whole string of questions. They had to do with the people I'd talked to, their connections with one another, with the Koberg company, with me. The questions were penetrating and showed that he'd paid a great deal of attention to everything I'd told him in the hospital.

I didn't answer any of them individually—he didn't seem to expect me to—but when he'd exhausted the list, I did give him a sort of general answer. "I can't put it all together," I said, "but I have a nagging idea that if I wasn't shot by a jewel thief, then I was shot, somehow, as a result of *every*one I'd met and *every*thing I'd done. Only one person pulled the trigger, but other people may be involved."

"You mean a conspiracy?" Brian looked surprised.

"No, not a conspiracy, exactly. A—I don't know what to call it—a combination of factors is as close as I can come. But if that's the case, then it's possible that my being shot is related to Bob McDonald's being shot."

Brian registered even more surprise. "I don't understand."

"Neither do I, quite."

There was another long silence. We were over Manhattan before Brian spoke again.

"But, Brock, if what you said is true, then you were shot by an utterly determined killer who'll stop at nothing. New York, Chicago . . . You wouldn't be any safer in New York than in Chicago."

"It's just a nagging idea."

His expression became much more sober than it usually was, and he didn't say another word until the plane was at the gate.

And I didn't either, except once, when the plane touched down. It hit the runway too hard and bounced, and I let loose with a loud "Ouch, damn it!"

34

Usually Mark was the first one to arrive at the office in the morning. For reasons that had to do, I'd always believed, with the Puritan ethic.

But Mark was on vacation, and that Monday morning after the long holiday weekend I was the one who opened the joint. Not because of any Puritan ethic, but because I'd slept badly and been up since dawn.

I was beginning to get used to the crutches, and I felt stronger than I had the day before. I swung myself jauntily down the corridor, turned into the office, managed to get my coat off, and settled down at my desk to catch up on the accumulated mail and messages.

And that's what I was doing when, a few minutes later, Irving appeared in the doorway to see why the light was on. "Hi," he said cheerfully. "You're early."

He looked rested and wonderful, and just seeing him gave me a lift.

He came into the room. "How was the trip?" But then he noticed the crutches on the floor at my feet. "What's the matter? You hurt yourself?"

"A little."

"How?"

"I got shot."

"I mean, seriously."

"So do I."

Furrows appeared above the bridge of his nose. The corners of his mouth turned down. I could see that he was having trouble making up his mind whether I was kidding or not.

"I spent the weekend in the hospital, in Chicago," I said. "Brian came out."

Irving sank into a chair. "Why didn't you call *me*?"

"I didn't call anybody, Irv. Brian came because I failed to show up in Richmond as promised."

Irving was speechless. I told him briefly what had happened. Then Helen came in. She too looked better than she had before I'd left. "Mr. Potter!" she exclaimed, and glanced at her watch. "Am I late?"

"No, I'm early."

She was all smiles. "It's nice to have you back." But the crutches caught her eye also. "Is something wrong?"

"A slight mishap," I replied.

"Oh, dear. Can I get you anything?"

"No, thank you, Helen. I'm fine."

"Well, it's good to have you back." She went into her own office to take off her coat and hat.

And so the day started. I'd intended to make it as much like any other Monday as possible, staff meeting and all, but I'd known that it wouldn't be exactly like any other Monday, because I intended to tell the staff what had happened in Chicago. Without making it more dramatic than it had been, but at the same time without skipping any of the implications.

Which was what I did. Most of our meeting was given over to a discussion of Koberg Chemical. The preceding week had produced little in the way of new developments anyway. The market had gone up slightly, but we all knew why that was: a slight drop in interest rates.

Everyone except Brian was shocked, of course. Everyone had questions. I answered such questions as I could. There was a certain amount of idle speculation. A few opinions were expressed. But the mood of the morning, aside from one of shock, was one of caution. No one wanted to go off half-cocked.

I did observe, however, a sudden drawing together, a closing of ranks. It was the exact opposite of what had been happening while we were working on the annual forecast; and it occurred to me that by having got myself in jeopardy, I'd accidentally accomplished what I hadn't been able to accomplish previously on purpose.

When the meeting was over, I asked Joe to remain in my office. Irving said that he would like to stay too, and I nodded.

I told Joe that I wanted to meet with Louis Glass at the earliest possible moment, and that since Glass might be more willing to see him than me, he should make the appointment without telling Glass that I would be there too.

"I understand," Joe said briskly. "Will do." And he hustled off.

Whereupon Irving, with uncharacteristic hemming and hawing, stated what was on his mind. Could this, he wondered, turn into another of those situations that would affect my reputation?

I felt the blood rush to my face. "Do you mean, am I about to mortify Price, Potter and Petacque again by getting someone into trouble?"

Irving's face turned as red as I guessed mine was. He nodded.

"I don't know," I said. "I hope not. I've thought about that. About what Tom and Mark would say. About what everyone would say. When I was in the hospital, and again last night—I've thought about it, all right. My intention, when I started, certainly wasn't to make waves. But now that I'm in the thing, Irv, I have to see it through, if for no other reason than my own safety."

"I understand," Irving said. "That's really what I wanted to tell you. I understand, and you can count on me."

I smiled, and, still looking embarrassed, Irving left.

But almost immediately Helen reappeared, and she was no longer smiling. Evidently she'd had time to think, and now she was looking worried. "Er—Mr. Potter?"

"Yes, Helen?"

"I hate to ask personal questions, but it occurred to me, that mishap you mentioned"—her eyes went to the crutches—"could that have anything to do with—well, you know? I'd feel dreadful if in some way I were responsible for—well, you know."

Actually, I was beginning to think that Helen *was* responsible. But I said, "Not at all. And how's Andrea, by the way?"

Her expression didn't brighten. "About as well as can be expected, I suppose. The thing that bothers me more than anything else, Mr. Potter, is the baby. Do you think any of this, what Andrea's going through, could affect the baby?"

"I doubt it. Women have been through some pretty terrible traumas and still given birth to normal, healthy babies." I paused. "Incidentally, when I was in Chicago, I saw the baby's great-grandmother."

Helen looked bewildered.

"Bob McDonald's grandmother."

The look of bewilderment became one of pure amazement. Of utter awe. I couldn't have had a greater effect on her if I'd said that while in Chicago I'd stumbled upon the True Cross and the Holy Grail at the same time. "You didn't!"

"I did." And I told her of Elissa's circumstances.

She was wholly fascinated. "I had no idea," she kept saying. "No idea at all. I simply had no idea." Then she began to appear concerned again. But for a different reason. "The poor thing," she said. "The poor, poor thing. I wonder if Andrea ought to send her some flowers. A nice arrangement, with a card."

I considered. "I don't think so, Helen. She's really terribly ill, and I didn't see any flowers in the room. Possibly she isn't allowed to have them."

"A book maybe. Or my new afghan. I've finished a new afghan."

"No, Helen. Not just now, I think."

Helen didn't seem convinced, however, and I doubted that at that particular moment she was entirely convinceable. She got up. "I must tell Andrea," she said, "right away. I'm sure she'll be interested." And Helen hurried out of my office.

By then it was lunchtime and I was hungry. I picked up my

crutches, hoisted myself to my feet and went down the corridor, looking for someone to have lunch with.

That was when the day turned unusual. For there was no one available to eat with me. Every one of the researchers had gone out, Clair Gould informed me, without saying when he or she would be back.

"Did they go together?"

"No, separately."

There was nothing extraordinary about that. The researchers often went out separately, at lunchtime and at other times. But they usually left word where they were going or when they would return. And in this case not one of them had.

"Even Irving?" I asked.

"Yes, sir."

I went past the empty offices—Tom's, Mark's, Irving's, the others'. I felt lonely, and puzzled. I looked in on the salesmen. All of them were busy, and the salesmen often didn't eat until late anyway—they waited until the New York Stock Exchange closed.

So finally I sent out for a sandwich and ate it at my desk. Then I sweated to come up with something to put in the Tuesday letter and made a few phone calls to people who had left messages for me.

By three o'clock none of the researchers had come in. Or by three thirty either.

At that point my energy was beginning to give out, and I went home.

Louise, my housekeeper, was surprised to see me so early, and surprised to see the crutches. I explained that I'd hurt my leg over the weekend.

I had a joyful reunion with Tiger, who had been staying with Louise, in Harlem, while I was away. Then I took a nap.

It was seven thirty when I awoke, and there was a note from Louise on the hall table: "Meet loff in ovven. Dog is been out."

I ate some of the meat loaf and the things that Louise had left with it. I watched television for a while. But presently I began to think about one of the questions that had crossed my mind while I was in the hospital.

And at ten thirty, although I didn't really feel like it, I forced myself to put on my coat, go outside and hail a taxi.

"Claremont Avenue, near One Hundred and Sixteenth Street," I told the driver.

35

In the vestibule, I noticed for the first time, there was a row of buttons, with a name opposite each, and a speaking tube. I deliberately pushed the wrong button.

A voice spoke. "Whozzit?"

"Brock Potter," I replied.

And that was the end of the transaction. Nothing happened. No one pushed the buzzer that unlocked the door to the lobby.

I pushed the button opposite "D. CHAPIN."

The identical exchange took place. But this time, after a moment, the buzzer buzzed.

I entered the lobby, turned to the right and knocked at Chapin's door. He opened it on the safety chain, just enough to peer out. Then he unfastened the safety chain and opened it all the way.

"You again?" he said.

"Me again," I replied.

He saw the crutches. "What happened to your leg?"

"I hurt it. Can I come in?"

He stood aside, and I maneuvered myself into the living room. It seemed different. There was no Andrea, no despair.

"I don't remember a safety chain," I remarked.

"It's new," he admitted. "Since the murder. Just in case. What brings you here?"

"I need a consultant."

We studied each other. He hadn't changed much, I thought. The same jeans, or a pair just like them. A sweatshirt instead of the pajama top. Hair two weeks longer. The identical young man in the identical surroundings. But this time I made an assessment. Sandy hair; grayish eyes, rather serious; a generous mouth; scattered freckles. Basically nice, I decided.

"If it pays more than the cafeteria," he said, not smiling, "I'm interested. This is a crazy time to come visiting, unannounced."

"I know, but I was under the impression that you worked until about ten, and you said your phone wasn't connected."

"You have a good memory."

"The secret of my success, Dan."

He nodded, still with that serious expression. Then he remembered the safety chain and hooked it up again.

"Mind if I sit down?" I asked.

"Be my guest. You already are, anyway. How'd you hurt your leg?"

"I'll get around to that." I lowered myself into the ragged chair in which Andrea had sat. It was very uncomfortable, but I stayed there.

"And what's this consultant shit?"

"It's no shit. I need someone to talk things over with."

"Ha."

"You don't believe me?"

"No. I think you think you already have all the answers. Guys like you always do."

"Oh, for Christ's sake, shut up and make us some coffee."

I'd sized him up accurately. For he grinned and said, "Sure," and went out to the kitchen.

I glanced around the room. A large book was open on one of the tables, under a high-intensity lamp, and a sheet of tracing paper was spread over it.

When my host returned, I pointed to the book. "What're you doing?"

"Tracing a message to Garcia."

I frowned.

"I'm kidding. It's a message, but not to Garcia. It's about a corn harvest, *circa* 1350. Want to see?"

I got up, and we went over to the table, and I was given a lesson in Mayan hieroglyphics. Chapin really did know his stuff. He showed me the system of numerals, with its lines and dots, and explained various symbols. What he was dealing with, I realized, was economics—the economics of the strange and isolated people who had inhabited Guatemala and the Yucatán peninsula for centuries. Even to them, I learned, taxes had been a concern.

But my lesson was cut short by the whistling of the kettle. I sat down again, on another chair, and was given a mug of coffee. Chapin brought one for himself too.

"What I really want to talk about," I said, "is Bob McDonald and the day he was killed."

"Jesus!" Chapin exclaimed. "I've already been over that with the fucking Gestapo a hundred times. They keep coming back, the bastards."

"I gather you don't think much of the police," I observed.

"You gather? What the hell, man, I don't make any bones about it. I not only don't think much of the police, I don't think much of any authority figures. What I'd like to be is an anarchist, but I don't like anarchists either, so I'm just against authority figures. It's a hangup."

"Even Mayan authority figures?" I asked.

"Again, when I wasn't expecting him to, Chapin grinned. "They're excluded. Besides, they were so fucking exalted, those guys, that you can't call them authority figures—they were gods."

"All of them?"

"All the interesting ones. But go ahead, Mr. Potter, get on with the inquisition."

"Brock. Please. And it's not an inquisition. . . . You asked me about my leg, so I'll tell you. I was shot the other day."

Chapin's eyes almost popped out of his head. "No!"

"In Chicago. By someone with a twenty-two-caliber gun. Was Bob shot with a twenty-two-caliber gun?"

Chapin swallowed. "Honestly, Mr. Potter—Brock—I can't tell you. I don't know."

"Is that the truth, Dan?"

"I swear it is, sir. Nobody's told me. I suppose I could've asked. I just never thought of it."

"O.K. I believe you. But I have a hunch that he was."

"I'll try to find out, sir—Brock."

"I'd appreciate that. But don't 'sir' me. It makes me uncomfortable."

"Yes, sir. I mean, Brock. It's a habit I have when I get nervous, and you've got me nervous."

I smiled. "Was your father a policeman, Dan?"

"No, sir—no, Brock. A high-school football coach. Why do you ask?"

I shrugged. Then we smiled together. And Chapin stopped calling me "sir."

"Tell me about Bob," I said.

What followed was neither a monologue nor an interrogation, but a mutual exchange of information. He talked, I talked, and a picture emerged. In most respects it was the picture I'd had before, but in some respects it was different. Chapin and Bob McDonald, I learned, had occupied adjoining apartments for two years and had become reasonably close friends. They would have been even closer friends were it not for the fact that their schedules seldom coincided. What with classes, research projects and jobs, both of them were out much of the time, and when one was home, the other wasn't. Money was a problem for both of them, and at certain periods each of them, in addition to going to school, had worked at not one outside job but two. Nevertheless they had become buddies of a sort, and shared a certain intimacy.

The Bob McDonald that Chapin described was a conscientious, highly intelligent scholar and a thoroughly decent man. He was, according to Chapin, very much in love with Andrea, although Chapin was of the opinion that Bob and Andrea wouldn't have planned to marry for another year or two if Andrea hadn't got pregnant.

All of which jibed with the conclusions I myself had come to. But what Chapin also told me was that there was a dark side to Bob. He cited Bob's relationship with his father as an example. Bob talked freely enough about his aunt and uncle, but there was a certain tension between him and his father that caused him to shy away from any mention of "his old man," as Chapin put it. There had been friction between Bob and his father, Chapin said, over whether Bob should remain in school. His father had wanted Bob to quit studying and go to work at something that paid more than teaching English would pay. Bob hadn't agreed, and his aunt and uncle had taken his side.

Chapin was shocked when I told him about James McDonald's prison term and about the suicide of Bob's mother. Bob had never mentioned either of those events to him. "The poor son of a bitch," he said. "No wonder he always clammed up."

It also shocked Chapin to learn that Bob was the grandson of an extremely wealthy woman. Bob had never mentioned that either.

"Did he know?" Chapin asked.

I nodded. "I was with her just yesterday." And I told him of some of my experiences in Chicago.

He listened attentively, and when I finished, he said, "Sounds like you were with a bunch of rich creeps who didn't like each other very much."

Which, I thought, was a pretty good summation.

"It's too bad," he went on. "It's such an honest-to-God struggle to stay in school when you don't have money. You keep wanting to throw in the towel, but you know you have a good mind and you hate to waste it. Bob felt that way, and so do I. It's something we had in common. I wish I had a rich grandmother—I'd sure put the bite on her. But I guess Bob never did. I must seem like kind of an asshole to someone like you, but the fact is, I do have a good mind. I have an IQ of a hundred and fifty."

"I can believe that," I said. "And if you ever decide to quit Mayan hieroglyphics and waste your mind on something like selling stocks, I hope you'll give me a call. But let's get back to what we were talking about. Tell me about the day Bob was shot. Did anything unusual happen?"

Chapin insisted that he didn't know anything about the murder—he hadn't been at home when it happened; he'd been out for most of the day.

But then he did remember something that was unusual, after all. While shaving on the morning of the murder, he'd heard the sound of a vacuum cleaner in Bob's apartment.

"What was unusual about that?" I asked.

"Bob didn't own a vacuum cleaner," Chapin replied, and frowned thoughtfully. "He must have borrowed Iverson's."

"Iverson?" Then I remembered. "The history teacher who lives on the second floor?"

"Right. He has a vacuum cleaner. Sometimes I borrow it. Sometimes Bob did too. Neither of us was ever much on housekeeping. I guess you can see that." Again he frowned. "Come to think about it, he borrowed my kitchen cleanser too. He didn't have any. The can's still in his apartment. The Gestapo wouldn't let me in to get it."

"When did he borrow the cleanser?"

"That same morning. Just as I was getting ready to leave. He knocked on the door."

"Did he say why he wanted it?"

"Christ, Brock, you don't have to explain why you want to borrow kitchen cleanser. All you do is ask for it, and either someone gives it to you or they don't. He knocked on my door and asked for the cleanser, and I told him to help himself, and I left."

"In other words, he was housecleaning."

"Must have been. Which he didn't do often, and not so early in the day." He paused. "You think that's important?" He seemed worried. "I never thought to mention it to the cops. About the vacuum cleaner, I mean."

"I think that under the circumstances, Dan, it might be very important."

"I told them about the cleanser. I had to. That was the last time I saw Bob alive. But I never told them about the vacuum cleaner. Why do you think it's important?"

"Well, before I rang your bell, I rang someone else's. They wouldn't let me into the building. People these days are afraid.

Yet someone got into the building to kill Bob, and Bob was killed just inside his own front door. And that same morning he'd been cleaning his apartment—but not, apparently, because Andrea was coming over."

"No. She was used to the way the place looked."

"So he must have been killed by somebody he was expecting, somebody he opened the door to, somebody he wanted the apartment to look its best for."

Chapin's face lit up. "God damn!" Then the brightness left it. "You think I ought to tell the Gestapo?"

"Let your conscience be your guide." My private opinion was that it wouldn't make any difference.

Chapin looked at me. "What's *your* IQ, Brock?"

"I really don't know," I said. "It seems to fluctuate. Some days it's high, other days it's low."

Chapin laughed, and offered me another cup of coffee.

36

My staff, it appeared, had decided to hold a meeting without me. All five of them were gathered in Irving's office, just as they usually gathered in mine, and were having a serious discussion. I paused in the corridor, still in my topcoat, watched and listened for a moment, then said, "What's going on?"

"We're talking," Irving said.

"O.K.," I said, "don't let me disturb you." I went on into my own office to settle down for the day.

But before I could get properly arranged in my chair, the staff filed in, as if summoned, and took the positions they normally did at a staff meeting, pencils in hand, notebooks and other gear at the ready.

Irving was the spokesman. "We've been working on this Koberg thing," he declared.

I looked from one to another. All of them seemed tired and preoccupied. "Is that what everyone was doing yesterday afternoon?" I asked.

Irving nodded and said, "Each in his own way. And we have some ideas."

The next two and a half hours were without doubt the most amazing I'd experienced in my entire business career. I'd known that an energetic person could dig up a lot of information in a short period of time if he knew where to look. But I wouldn't have believed it possible that five energetic people, each working on his own but motivated by a common sense of outrage, could dig up so much so fast. The collective accomplishment of my team was without parallel, and I was dumbfounded.

Irving began with a complete analysis of Koberg's financial structure, down to the last penny. Harriet followed with a detailed account of Louis Glass's assets and liabilities. Joe spoke next, offering a portrait of Paul Carmichael that even included Carmichael's predilections in food—he liked lamb chops and hated calf's liver. George delivered a meticulous history of Dwight Wilson, boy and man. And Brian, who since I'd last seen him had made a trip to Virginia and back, wound up with an equally meticulous history of the bug that causes jungle rot.

Generally at our meetings I was the one to whom the others directed their remarks. But at this meeting I had the feeling of being merely the titular head of the department, that the other five members were really talking to one another and letting me listen, as if they were engaged in a project that concerned me but didn't really include me.

Koberg's financial structure was both complex and simple. There were four senior issues of preferred stock and one bond issue, which was soon due to be retired. But old Gus Koberg had been smart. Voting control of the company was vested entirely in the common stock, as it was in most companies, and Gus Koberg had seen to it that the amount of common stock issued was small. Not knowing how his daughter was going to turn out, he'd intended for her and her descendants to have the company reins in their hands. He hadn't lived long enough to learn that she would take no interest in the company and that, in a manner of speaking, she would have no descendants.

Wilson, for reasons of his own, had never seen fit to increase the amount of common stock, either by splitting it or by issuing more. With the result that there were still only 2,100,000 shares of common stock outstanding. In the old days, during the 1920's, that had made for some wild fluctuations in the stock, but as the company had diminished in significance, the fluctuations had come to an end.

The important fact, however, was that even at the present price of the common stock, the fifty-one percent of it needed for control could be purchased for just over $6,000,000. Which made it an incredible bargain, particularly if the company was about to go places.

But Louis Glass didn't have $6,000,000. Louis Glass had less than $2,000,000, a large part of which he'd recently acquired through stock options in Interamerican Marine. He couldn't sell his Interamerican Marine stock without attracting attention. All he could do was use it as collateral for loans, which was what he'd done. He was in hock up to his ears. So the big man with the fancy office and the company limousines and the company jets and the other trappings of enormous wealth really wasn't so wealthy. And there was no chance that he ever would be, for, no matter how much he earned in the way of salary, taxes would keep him more or less where he was.

The only means Louis Glass had of joining the ranks of the super rich was to acquire a company of his own. He'd chosen, with foresight and, no doubt, inside information, Koberg Chemical. He had to be careful, though. If the board of directors of Interamerican Marine got wind of what he was doing—using the money they were paying him, borrowing against the stock they were giving him at a discount, to buy a company that had nothing to do with Interamerican Marine—he'd soon be out on his ear. He now owned 105,600 shares of Koberg Chemical, but he needed a damn sight more than that in order to gain control. He needed at least one large block, and possibly two. Purchased secretly.

Paul Carmichael had got wind of what was going on. He knew that someone had begun buying Koberg Chemical stock in a large way. And all he would have had to do to learn who that someone was was ask the stock-transfer agent, which he'd probably done at the first hint that an unusual amount of stock was changing hands. So Carmichael was fully aware that Louis Glass was on the way to becoming a threat. What Carmichael didn't know was how to deal with the threat. He was dealing with it by using company funds to buy Koberg stock in the open market, thus forcing the price up even more, whereas if he'd had any degree of sophistication, he would have checked on Glass's position, learned that it was precarious and applied a little quiet pressure by warning Glass that if he went one step further, he, Carmichael, would announce to the world what Glass was doing.

But Carmichael had no sophistication. He hadn't worked his way up through the ranks of a business. He was an academic who'd hit it lucky. A professor of chemistry who'd risen to the post of dean, he'd been snapped up by a small drug company, where he'd been discovered by Dwight Wilson. Carmichael was an excellent scientist with a fair background in economics and considerable administrative ability. However, he wasn't a businessman in the sense that he knew how to defend his company against attack and cope with the likes of Louis Glass.

That, really, was why he'd refused to see me. Not because of any fearsome reputation of mine, or even because he was being secretive. He merely hadn't had much to do with securities analysts and didn't realize how much good someone in my position could do him. And in his eagerness to get rid of the Wilson cronies, he'd got rid of the only people who, whatever their faults, had the sophistication he himself lacked, the only people who could have set him straight.

That the Wilson cronies had needed to be replaced was without question. Dwight Wilson, according to everyone George had talked to, had never been more than a conscientious mediocrity, nowhere near as capable as his father. For over thirty years Dwight had run the company, doing his duty as scrupulously as possible but without inspiration. And he'd run it like a branch of the Union League Club, with plenty of comfortable chairs, leisurely lunches, convenient copies of the latest newspapers and sports magazines scattered about. No one had worked very hard, no one had made any bold moves. With the result that while Dwight Wilson had kept the company solvent and outwardly healthy, it had in fact, like a tree, been dying at the top.

For each thing he'd done right, Wilson had done ten others wrong. He'd let one opportunity after another slip through his fingers. The only opportunity he hadn't let slip through his fingers was that of awarding himself stock bonuses. Each year another, from the company's treasury of unissued shares. Until the supply was exhausted, and until Dwight Wilson owned a tidy block of 240,000, which made him, undoubtedly, one of Koberg Chemical's largest stockholders, along with the Countess de Garonne. Nobody knew how many shares she owned, but, based on what Wilson had told me, she probably didn't own more than he did. This was the primary reason Wilson had never increased the number of shares outstanding—he'd wanted to protect his own position. Furthermore, he'd known that there would be little demand for the shares if he did increase the supply. And the company hadn't needed cash, because it hadn't been expanding.

Wilson, with typical lack of foresight, had chosen Carmichael as his successor. Carmichael was his sort of man—"double-breasted suits and an interest in the Boy Scouts of America" was the way Joe put it. But Carmichael had surprised him. Carmichael had seen the decay and had quickly cut it away. Wilson had been given no chance to guide the company from the background, as he'd hoped to do. And he was too old and too preoccupied with his health to fight back.

No one knew the exact relationship between Carmichael and Wilson. It was probably less distant than Wilson had described it to me, but perhaps not. In any case, Wilson was a tempting target for Louis Glass, and Glass had been courting him, just as he'd been courting the Count and Countess de Garonne. George had learned that from the manufacturer who for years had been supplying Koberg Chemical with its cans, and who had remained Wilson's friend.

So, as my researchers speculated, there were two known large stockholders in Koberg Chemical—the Countess and Dwight Wilson—and there was one man who wanted their stock. Other large stockholders might exist also; there was no way of finding that out. But it was just as possible that the other large stockholders, over the years, had given up and got out.

Glass, Carmichael, Wilson and the dying Countess—the four corners of a rectangle. Four personalities, each with a different background and a different motive. Four human beings.

But none of them was the central figure in the future of Koberg Chemical. The central figure in the future of Koberg Chemical wasn't a human being at all. It was an inhuman but living organism so small that it could only be seen with the aid of a microscope. Its name was *Trichoderma viride*. And Brian told us about it.

37

After lunch Brian went home to pack. He was leaving for Chicago to check out his findings with Dr. William Titus, a pupil and protégé of Dr. Orville Green.

Brian's brother Keith had located Dr. Green, and Brian had already had a long talk with him. Dr. Green was a biologist. Titus had studied under him while getting a Ph.D., before becoming a professor himself and moving from the fertile pastures of Virginia to the fertile pastures of the University of Colorado—and, recently, to the even more fertile pastures of Koberg Chemical, where he was now second in command to the head of Koberg's new research facility. Titus was a biochemist and a brilliant one. His specialty was enzymes. Dr. Green had introduced Brian to him by telephone.

But Brian's trip was merely for the purpose of verification. He'd given us the clues, and the six of us were pretty sure that we'd come up with the answers. Although none of us was a trained biologist or chemist, all of us were trained analysts who knew how to weave facts together and make interpretations. And that was what we'd done.

It was going to take Brian several days. He intended to see not only William Titus, but others who worked in the Koberg research facility. With Titus' support and the judicious use of Dr. Green's name, he thought he could.

I had a talk with Irving about the annual forecast. The finished copies were due from the printer the following afternoon, and I wanted Irving to supervise the mailing of them. The job would require a lot of hands.

I also had a talk with Joe. A huddle, he accurately called it, for what we discussed was our next play. Joe hadn't been able to get an appointment with Glass for that day; Glass was out of town. In Chicago, interestingly enough, Joe said. But, according to the secretary to Glass's administrative assistant, with whom Joe had spoken, Glass would be back late that night. After discussing it with the administrative assistant himself, she'd set up an appointment. Joe was to see Glass at nine thirty the next morning.

Joe and I agreed on our signals, and I turned to other matters—principally, the Tuesday letter.

Helen had looked better that morning than she had in weeks, and now, when she came into my office with her notebook to take down my remarks for the week to our customers, I told her so.

"Why, thank you, Mr. Potter," she said with a smile. "I really do believe that I feel better too. Somehow, what you said yesterday—about seeing the baby's great-grandmother—well, somehow it's made a difference. Andrea and I discussed it for quite a while last evening, and today Andrea's sending her my new afghan, with a nice note. Poor woman, we thought it might cheer her up. It's yellow and orange."

I returned her smile. But then I thought of Chapin and stopped smiling. "Speaking of Andrea," I said, "have the police told her anything? I mean, have they come up with any evidence that points to who might have killed Bob?"

Helen stopped smiling too. "They're just awful, those men, Mr. Potter. They keep coming to the apartment and asking the poor child a lot of questions, and they've taken her to that dreadful police station twice to look at photographs of a lot of terrible people. But Andrea didn't recognize any of them—she doesn't know people like that, and she told them that Bob didn't either. It's almost an insult to even presume that she'd know people like that. The police are only doing their job, I keep telling myself, but I don't think it's nice to take a young woman like Andrea who's carrying a child and make her go to a place like that to look at pictures of known criminals. Think of the effect it could have on the baby."

"As you say, they're only doing their job. But they haven't gotten very far, I take it."

"I don't think so. They won't admit it, of course. All they say is they're working on it. But it seems to me that they don't really expect to find the person who did it. They keep saying that it takes time, but I don't know—there are so many terrible people in that neighborhood, so many people who are demented, or would be if they didn't take their pills, along with all the nice people, the professors and the students like Bob. Honestly, Mr. Potter—I don't think neighborhoods should be like that, with nice people living in the same neighborhood with people who have such terrible problems. When I was a girl, it wasn't that way at all. You knew who your neighbors were, and they were people like yourself. But up along Broadway there, mixed in with all the nice people, there are thousands and thousands and *thousands* of people who have the most awful problems and who aren't a bit reliable. I think that's why the police are discouraged, even though they won't come right out and admit they're discouraged. They say it might have been one of those crimes without a motive and those are the hardest to solve. Is that true, Mr. Potter? Are crimes without a motive the hardest to solve? I should think they would be."

"I don't know, Helen. I'm not a policeman, thank God. But I kind of believe that there is no such thing as a crime without a motive. In my opinion, there's always a motive. For *every* crime. At least in the mind of the person who commits it. The motive may seem irrational to others, but it doesn't seem irrational to the person who has it."

"Oh, dear. That's the word the police use: 'irrational.' "

"But there's something that's been bothering me, and maybe you can help me. Did Bob ever mention going to Chicago?"

"To Chicago?"

I nodded. "Or was he thinking of going there? He might have said something to Andrea about it."

Helen shook her head decisively. "I'm sure he didn't, Mr. Potter. With all the questions everyone's been asking, I'm sure

Andrea would have said something about it to someone, and she hasn't. No, as a matter of fact, the only things Bob had ever said about Chicago were bad things. Because of what happened to his parents, I suppose. No, I think that's the last place in the world he ever would have gone. Why do you ask?" Helen answered her own question immediately, however. "Oh, I see what you mean. Because his grandmother was there and she was sick."

"Yes."

"No. He didn't know that. I'm quite positive he didn't. He would have told Andrea if he'd known. And when I told her yesterday, she was as surprised as I was. There were family problems, you see—his grandmother hadn't treated his mother very nice—and even if he'd known that his grandmother was out in Chicago, I don't think he'd have gone." Helen paused. "Still, a gift, I thought—a nice afghan—well, it just seemed like a friendly thing to do, and Andrea agreed with me. After all, no matter how badly Bob's grandmother treated his mother, she hasn't done any harm to Andrea. And you said she *is* sick." Helen's expression was becoming increasingly bleak. "That poor, unhappy family. Bob never complained, but I know now that he'd really had an awful lot to live through in his short life."

"You know who impressed me?" I said, to cheer her up. "The young man who took Andrea into his apartment that night. What was his name? Chapin? Even with all that was going on, I noticed him and was rather taken by him. This may not be the time, and I certainly wouldn't want to suggest anything, but someday Andrea will come out of this horrible period she's going through. She'll become interested in other men. And Chapin struck me as rather nice. Intelligent too. I imagine he has a high IQ."

It worked. Helen brightened. "Do you really think so? I was so beside myself that night, I didn't notice. But the other day, when he came over—"

"He came over?"

"The day after Christmas. To see how Andrea was getting along, and if there was anything he could do."

"Well, now."

Helen and I exchanged a look. She smiled and said, "Perhaps, later on, I should invite him to dinner. To thank him."

"Good idea," I said, "but let's get on with our work."

Helen put pencil to paper, and I began to offer Price, Potter and Petacque's customers the latest opinions of Price, Potter and Petacque's research department.

It was the shortest market letter I'd ever written. Less than a page. But it was also one of the most important. For the last paragraph was devoted to Koberg Chemical.

"It is our belief," the paragraph said, "that Koberg Chemical Co. (6⅞–7⅛) has become worthy of consideration. We feel that research which the company has been conducting will soon bear fruit, and we are making a comprehensive study. Meanwhile, we have learned that outside interests have taken a position in Koberg stock and are seeking to acquire more. It may well be that Koberg Chemical Co. is one of those special situations that represent an exceptional opportunity for profit."

I signed the letter, as usual, "Brockton Potter, Head of Research, Price, Potter and Petacque."

And of course, as usual, the letter would go to all our customers. Whose aggregate assets were approximately $21,000,000,000.

38

In the taxi, as we were on our way to the Interamerican Marine Building, Joe confessed. "I think I ought to tell you," he said, "that Glass has been trying to hire me."

I attempted to register mild surprise. "Oh? And what have you told him?"

"First no, then yes, then no again. But I've sort of been keeping my options open. Today, I guess, I'll be closing them once and for all."

"It may be for the best, Joe. If you ever do decide to leave Price, Potter and Petacque, I think you'll be able to do better for yourself than a job with Louis Glass. He'd exploit you, then drop you."

"Maybe. That isn't what decided me, though. When I said yes, we'd just had that big fight and I was mad at everybody, but now I'm not anymore. We're a good group, Brock, and I want to be part of it."

"And I hope you always will be," I said. Which ended the discussion.

The Interamerican Marine Building was located on the Avenue of the Americas, a stone's throw from the CBS Building, which it resembled. It had all the accouterments of late-twentieth-century Manhattan glory, including an outdoor fountain with water shooting in all directions from a bronze abstract sculpture.

But that morning the fountain was turned off. The weather was too cold.

Glass's personal suite was on the forty-second floor. In fact, it *was* the forty-second floor. No one else occupied that floor, except Glass's executive assistant and a few secretaries who looked like movie stars. The secretaries were grand and glorious creatures, fully worthy of the building and of a company that was rapidly approaching the top of *Fortune's* list of the five hundred largest.

Everyone seemed to know Joe. No one knew the fellow on crutches who was with him. Joe had to explain. He said I was one of his co-workers and slurred my name.

Glass received us precisely at nine thirty. When he saw who Joe's co-worker was, he looked absolutely furious. Someone, his expression said, was going to pay dearly for this piece of carelessness. But the look only lasted for a fraction of a second. Then Glass was all smiles.

"Joe, you've brought Brockton Potter himself! I'm honored!"

"Remember the last time we met?" I said, all smiles myself. "I promised I'd pay you a visit one of these days."

"So you did, so you did." The smiles were discarded. "But, good Lord, man, what happened to your leg?"

"I was stupid enough to come between a jewel thief and his loot."

"But that's incredible. Such things only happen on television."

"Well, CBS, ABC and NBC are all neighbors of yours."

We shook hands. I was getting good at balancing myself on one crutch while shaking hands, closing doors and brushing my teeth.

Suitable arrangements were made for my comfort. On a leather-upholstered couch that had cost Interamerican's stockholders at least $8,000. Under a Klee painting, and hard by an Epstein sculpture.

"I wish you'd chosen a different time to come, Brock," Glass said. "You happened to pick one of those rare days when I have no important statement to make."

"Oh, I didn't come for news," I said, "although I must admit that that was my original intention. I thought, a few days ago, that I was going to have to ask you all kinds of questions. But I found out yesterday that I'd made the mistake of underestimating my own staff. They gave me the answers I was looking for. No, what I came for today was not to get information but to give it."

"Really?"

I reached into my pocket and took out a copy of the market letter. I handed it to Joe, who handed it to Glass. "This went out to all of Price, Potter and Petacque's customers yesterday," I said.

Glass began to read. Suddenly he turned pale. But his voice didn't falter. "I'd heard that you were looking into Koberg," he said equably.

"From your friend Henri de Garonne, no doubt. I saw him up at the Koberg offices. I suspect that he's been keeping you informed as to what the company is doing. A charming man, really. So French."

"An old and very *dear* friend. But tell me, Brock, this research that Koberg is doing—what did you find out about that?"

"Quite a bit, actually. At this point I probably know more about it than you do, although you must know a lot. But I really ought to let Joe give you those details; after all, he's a member of the team that did most of the digging."

Glass turned to Joe.

"Koberg is doing research on a bug called *Trichoderma viride*," Joe said. "A microbe." He paused and crossed his legs. He looked quite distinguished, I thought. Much less like a not-too-bright tackle than usual. But then, he'd never been not too bright, even during his football years.

"It all goes back to World War Two," he continued. "During World War Two our troops in the South Pacific were losing more tents and cartridge belts and socks and skivvies to jungle rot than to the Japs. It was a terrible problem. Finally the Army decided to see what was causing it. It sent a cartridge belt or a piece of tent or something that was full of jungle rot picked up in New Guinea to its lab in Natick, Massachusetts, for analysis. And *Trichoderma viride* was found to be the culprit. So research began on him."

Glass nodded, but said nothing.

"Very well," Joe went on. "So *Trichoderma viride* is the cause of jungle rot. We, up at our office, call him Tricky for short. Brian Barth—he was with us that day at the Brasserie, although I don't think you met him—he came up with that name yesterday. Anyway, Tricky loves glucose. He survives on glucose—and Tricky is one of the world's most durable survivors. He breaks down cellulose, degrading it into glucose. That's what he was doing with all those tents and socks and everything—breaking them down into glucose."

I recalled the meeting and had a sharp twinge of embarrassment. I'd been the only one in the room who didn't know what cellulose was. And it had been Harriet, of all people, who'd explained it to me. "But Brock, dear heart, *ev*eryone knows what cellulose is. It's what exists in all plants and in everything that's made from plants. Trees, grass, geraniums, spinach—every single thing that can be called a plant. And everything that derives from plants—cotton shirts, paper, wooden chairs, butcher blocks. *Ev*erything. They all contain cellulose. So actually a large part of the world is made up of cellulose. And, if I remember my college chemistry correctly, cellulose is a polymer of glucose—a bonding together of glucose molecules."

But I kept the recalled embarrassment to myself. I merely watched Joe.

"In other words," he was saying, "all those items that Tricky was destroying in the South Pacific had one thing in common: they contained cellulose. The socks, tents, cartridge belts and khaki pants—they had cotton in them."

Glass nodded again and said, "There's nothing new in any of that."

"Right," Joe agreed. "Nor is there anything new in Tricky's importance to mankind. He's essential to nature's balance. If plants were allowed to manufacture cellulose unchecked, within twenty years all the available carbon on earth would be bound up in cellulose. The plants would begin killing each other off, and without plants there wouldn't be animals, and without plant life and animal life there couldn't be human life. So Tricky and all his little relatives keep us alive by breaking down cellulose. In his own determination to survive, he makes it possible for us to survive too."

204

Glass was beginning to look bored, as if all this was too elementary for him.

Joe paid no attention, however. "What's important to Koberg," he said, "is that in order to break down cellulose Tricky produces enzymes. And these enzymes are the key that unlocks the door to the huge reservoir of chemical energy in biomass. You probably know that. But what they're doing at Koberg is getting Tricky to work harder. Left to himself, he'd produce just enough enzymes to convert the cellulose into glucose for his own needs. But at Koberg they're working on getting him to produce a surplus. And since more enzymes turn more cellulose into glucose, and since glucose is energy, what they're doing is coming up with a new source of energy."

The expression on Glass's face was becoming one of greater interest. But he wasn't about to give anything away. "Cellulose," he said dryly. "There's nothing in the least modern in the discovery of its energy potential. The cavemen discovered that when they burned their first tree and learned that it produced heat and light. And enzymes are nothing new to the scientific community."

Joe wasn't in the least daunted. "Perhaps that's so. I can only tell you what George Cole said. George works at Price, Potter and Petacque too, and we've been friends for years. He said that the fossil fuels—oil and coal, for example—are actually compressed cellulose and lignin. Compressed leaves and trees and plants that have been in the ground for half a billion years or more. The sun's energy that's trapped in those leaves and trees and grass, which, as you say, the cavemen discovered when they burned their first tree, and which was discovered by later men in another form when they discovered that coal and oil are nothing but leaves and trees and whatnot that have been in the ground for a few hundred million years and that these products too give heat and light."

Joe stopped abruptly and turned to me.

I nodded and said, "In other words, Lou, what Koberg is doing is finding a way around fossilization. By using microbes to release the sun's energy that's contained in plant life, they've found a way to do in a few hours what it takes nature half a billion years to do. The microbe, manufacturing enzymes, turns the cellulose into glucose, the people at Koberg ferment the glucose into ethyl alcohol with baker's yeast, and the ethyl alcohol becomes fuel. There's nothing new about any of it, except the method."

"How utterly fascinating," Glass said. But it was impossible to tell whether he meant it or not.

"Irving Silvers," I went on, "—he's my chief assistant—has deduced that what the people at Koberg started out to look for was a substitute for one of the ingredients of paint and plastics which has become terribly expensive. I mean petroleum. And the consensus among us is that that's exactly what they did find. A substitute for oil. Also for coal and natural gas and atomic energy and good old hydroelectric power. Even trees. After all, you can't burn logs in your gas tank." I paused. "We think that their research is quite important. Wouldn't you agree?"

"You think," Glass replied. "You don't know."

"True. But, as I said in that letter you're holding, we're making a comprehensive study. We believe that the study will bear out what Joe and I have been telling you—and it may even contain more of the specifics. Now as to the other remarks in the letter . . ." I shifted position on the couch, and in so doing I knocked off one of my crutches, which had been resting against it.

Joe picked up the crutch and put it back, and while still on his feet he said, "Really, Brock, I should be going. I didn't know we were going to be here so long, and I have another appointment."

"Don't let me detain you," I said.

Joe offered his apologies to Glass for not being able to stay and made a hasty exit.

I took a chance. "O.K., Glass," I said, after Joe had gone, "now you can turn off your recording machine."

39

It was one of those times when I was right.

Glass got up from the armchair in which he'd been sitting, went to his desk and reached under the kneehole. Then he came back to the armchair. "It's off," he said.

A memory popped into my head spontaneously, and I became even more certain of who had killed Bob McDonald and had tried to kill me. "Good," I said. "Now as to the other remarks in the letter, the outside interests I mentioned are, of course, yourself, Glass. You currently own, as I understand it, one hundred five thousand, six hundred shares of common stock in Koberg Chemical Company, unless you were able to make a deal with Wilson in Chicago yesterday. Were you?"

Glass kept a poker face, and gave me a card-player's answer. "You're going to have to show me your hand first, Potter."

"Glad to," I said. "And intend to. But it doesn't really matter. I'd just as soon guess. I don't think you did. You may have reached an agreement with Wilson, but I don't think you even did that. If Wilson had wanted to make a deal, he would have made one before. Furthermore, you don't have the money to buy Wilson's stock. You're going to have to arrange another loan first. I have no doubt that you can do it; a man of your reputation can raise all the money he needs. But you're already a bit overextended, I believe, so it will take time. And in this case you're not going to get the money to buy Wilson's stock or the Countess de Garonne's stock or anybody else's stock—not because of the money, but because I'm going to plant myself in your way."

"Am I to understand that you're threatening me, Potter?"

"That's one way of putting it, I suppose. But what I'm really doing is not so much threatening you as accusing you of conspiracy to commit murder. Or of being an accessory before the fact. It doesn't make much difference which you are, in legal terms, because my accusation could never be proved in court anyway."

Glass smiled. "I'm glad you added that. But the mere accusation is outrageous."

I didn't smile. "You did your bit to cause the murder of a very nice young man. You also did your bit to cause me to be shot. I'm no righter of wrongs, Glass. The righting of wrongs is important work, but I'd rather leave it in other people's hands. It's too easy, in my opinion, for the righter of wrongs to get carried away and turn into a megalomaniac, and there are enough megalomaniacs in the world without me. So I wouldn't make any open accusations against you even if I could prove them. And I'm going to let you make a nice profit on the Koberg shares you already own. But I am not—and please don't make any mistake about this, Glass—I am not going to let you buy any more shares."

Glass managed another smile. "What astonishing vindictiveness."

"Vindictiveness? I don't think I'm being vindictive. I've already told you that I'm no righter of wrongs. Yes, it makes me mad as hell to think that Bob McDonald is dead. He was a good human being, with a good life ahead of him. And he was about to marry a young woman who's also a good human being and of whom I'm quite fond. What's more, someone shot me, and that makes me mad too. I don't like being shot. It hurts."

"And you claim you're not being vindictive?"

"Correct. I'm not. I'm merely trying to avoid being shot again, and maybe killed."

"And you expect me, after this morning, to care whether you're killed or not? Come now, Potter, I'm beginning to hope that you will be."

Until then I'd felt something, but it hadn't been anger. At that moment, however, it became anger. Still, I kept my voice low. "That's the trouble with you, Glass. You don't care whether someone gets killed or not. You can even hope that someone *will* get killed. And you don't mind saying so. That's why Bob McDonald is dead. That's why I was shot. Because you didn't care and you said so. You may not have made the specific suggestion—you're the only one who'll ever know whether you did or not—but you planted the idea. You suggested that it would be convenient, and it probably didn't take much more than that—the killer had probably been toying with the idea already. But, aside from that, even if you didn't come up with the idea of killing Bob McDonald, even if you didn't know I was going to be shot, even if you're not an accessory before the fact or a conspirator, you're still in the wrong, because you know who the guilty party is and you've said nothing about it, done nothing about it, and been happy about the way things turned out. Well, you can stop being happy, and regardless of whether you hope that I'll be killed or not, you're going to see that I stay alive. For your own sake."

For the first time Glass showed emotion. He turned the color of a blanched almond. I had to give him credit, though. He kept his voice as low as I was keeping mine, and gave me another of those gentlemanly smiles. "Perhaps I ought to turn my recorder on again," he said. "This is beginning to sound like attempted blackmail."

"Go ahead," I replied, "but, frankly, I wouldn't recommend it. You said that I'd have to show you my hand first. O.K., that's what I'm going to do." I proceeded to tell him everything I knew about his holdings of Koberg stock, his loans, and how I thought the board of directors of Interamerican Marine would react if I made my knowledge public.

But that wasn't enough. "The board of directors isn't interested in my private investments," Glass said. "The board of directors is only interested in one thing: how well I manage this company. And I've been managing it quite well, thank you."

So I went on. "There's also the matter of conflict of interest," I said. "I don't know whether that could be established, but questions could certainly be raised. However, let's say that you're right. Let's even say that a conflict of interest couldn't be established—although I think it could. The board of directors may be satisfied with you, but what about Price, Potter and Petacque's customers? The last time we met, you thanked me for the nice things I'd been saying about you. Well, some of our customers acted on the nice things I'd been saying about you and bought a lot of Interamerican stock. It would annoy them to know that you aren't devoting your full attention to protecting their investment."

But that wasn't enough either, for Glass said, "I really don't think I have to worry about the opinion of your customers, Potter. Their primary concern is whether the price of the stock goes up or down, and it's been going up."

So I was forced to say, "We also have to consider the price of Koberg stock. By the time I get through, it's going to be so high that you won't be able to afford to buy the big blocks you need."

Even that didn't do it, however. Glass hesitated briefly, but he had a ready answer. "I doubt that. The banks like me. As, apparently, you've learned."

At that point there was nothing for me to do but voice the ultimate threat. "Everything you say may be true, Glass. The board of directors might not care. The funds might be indifferent. The banks might go all the way with you. But there's one group of people you're forgetting: your own underlings."

Suddenly Glass appeared to be truly alarmed. His bald head began to glisten with perspiration.

I let the words sink in, then continued. "No one can reach the position you have without finding out a thing or two about corporate infighting. Hell, you're probably a master of it. In the black-belt category, I'd say. So you know how dangerous a jealous underling can be. And a setup like this—which I must say is really beautiful; someone has excellent taste—a setup like this, with all the nice furniture and paintings, to say nothing of the limousines and private jets and other fringe benefits, arouses enormous jealousy, Glass. Hell, there must be at least twenty people in this building who would love to have all that, and who think, moreover, that they could run Interamerican Marine as well as you do. Those people would like nothing better than to stab you in the back and twist the knife, and you know it as well as I. All they need is the knife." I paused. "I don't know any of those people personally, but I believe that Joe Rothland does— and if he doesn't, I'm certain that he'll make it his business to find out. So will my other researchers. They'll locate those underlings if anything should happen to me. You can count on that. And they'll supply them with all the knives they need. Those underlings, whom you can't get rid of because you can't run Interamerican singlehandedly, will fix you so that you'll never hold another responsible job as long as you live." I paused again. "So please don't tell me how invulnerable you are, Glass. Just tell me that I have your full cooperation."

"You have it," Glass said instantly.

And I knew he meant what he said. For his head was decidedly wet.

Whereupon I told him what I expected him to do, and he agreed to do it.

We even shook hands. His hand was as wet as his head.

I thanked him for his time and for his openmindedness. He replied graciously. We parted on the best of terms. But I couldn't help saying, as he held the door for me, "Oh, and by the way, Lou, please don't try to hire any more of my people. It irritates me."

40

I didn't go directly back to the office. I detoured to my doctor's. The dressing on my leg had become messy and needed to be changed. The doctor changed it, but not until he'd expressed his disapproval of my having been shot and of my behavior in general. "Really, Brock," he said sternly, "you ought to stop getting yourself mauled the way you do. I'm beginning to think you have a personality defect."

"You sound like my partners," I told him.

"There must be something about you that antagonizes people."

"So help me, Jim, every time it happens, it isn't my fault."

"That's not possible. But, I must say, you have a great capacity for healing. Considering that the injury is only six days old, you're doing fine."

"The crutches have made me sore under the arms."

"Well, you still need them. But don't use them any longer than you absolutely have to—you don't want to get dependent."

I assured him that that was the last thing I wanted, and he returned my file to the filing cabinet.

When I did get back to the office, Joe nailed me as I was going down the corridor. "How'd it go?" he asked anxiously.

I gave him a detailed account, leaving out only the part about telling Glass to lay off my people. He grinned, then frowned. "You think he'll keep his word?"

"Yes," I replied, and went in to see Irving.

Irving had his chair tilted back and was reading a copy of our annual forecast. The printer had beat his deadline by three hours.

"Looks pretty good," Irving said, handing the booklet to me. "I think it was worth the effort."

I sat down and glanced through the thing. "The printer's done a nice job," I said, "but whether or not *we* have, only time will tell."

"Not one telephone call yet," Irving said in a puzzled tone.

"Telephone call?"

"About Koberg. Our customers must have the letter by now."

"Good grief, Irv," I said, "nothing's going to happen so soon. The fact that we're all worked up about it doesn't mean that anyone else will be."

"I suppose you're right. Still . . ."

"Tomorrow's New Year's Eve. There's another long weekend coming up. Half the people we do business with are out of town. We won't get any inquiries until next week at the earliest, and then we won't get many. After all, this is just one more Price, Potter and Petacque recommendation—it isn't going to shake the world. And, frankly, I hope it doesn't. Not until after Brian's done all his checking, at least. Once he has, and if we're right, we'll recommend Koberg again. Our competitors will pick up on the item and *they'll* start checking. Whatever happens will happen gradually. But the price of the stock will go up. You can be sure of that."

Irving sent out for sandwiches, and we had lunch in his office. I described my conversation with Glass. Irving seemed pleased by the way it had gone, but at the same time he expressed anxiety. "For the next week you're going to be in a certain amount of danger. I'd be careful if I were you."

"Don't worry," I replied. "I've thought about that. And for the next week I'm going underground."

"Meaning?"

"I'm not going to be home. After tonight I'm going away. I'll be at the office next Monday and Tuesday, but I don't intend to take calls. Tom and Mark will be back by then, and any calls that come through for me I'll have referred to them or to you."

"Great idea. Now I feel better."

I went into my own office to telephone the three people I had to speak with.

First I called Abigail Henning. She was in a hurry. It was an hour earlier in Chicago, and she was busy getting her brother's lunch ready. His prostate had been giving him no end of trouble, she confided, and he was awfully difficult to please.

Then I called Dolly Whitcomb. She too was in a hurry. Her hairdresser had moved her appointment up an hour, because it was the day before New Year's Eve and every one of his customers wanted to have her hair done.

Both women, however, told me what I'd expected to hear.

When it came to the third call, I hesitated. I dreaded what I was going to have to do and tried to think of an alternative. But there was no alternative.

Still, I couldn't bring myself to pick up the telephone. I didn't like kicking someone who was already down, even when it was necessary.

Was it necessary, though? I'd told Glass that I was no righter of wrongs. I'd denied it when, less than two hours ago, the doctor had accused me of antagonizing people. Had I on both occasions been mistaken about myself? Was there some quirk in my nature that I didn't understand or wouldn't admit?

I spent quite a while wondering.

In the end, however, I decided that I couldn't avoid the confrontation; that I had to do what I had to do.

But as I reached for the telephone, it rang. The person whose number I intended to dial had dialed mine.

"James McDonald is on the line," Helen said nervously. "I can't imagine what he wants."

"O.K.," I said, and Helen put him through.

"I understand you saw Elissa," McDonald said.

"That's right," I replied, "and I think it's time for you and me to have a talk."

41

By the time McDonald arrived, I'd had dinner, given Tiger his evening airing and packed. I'd also made arrangements with Louise to board Tiger at her house from the next afternoon until the following Wednesday.

I was watching television, but I turned off the set when I heard the doorbell.

McDonald was wearing the same suit he'd worn at my party. He'd shaved and put on a clean shirt and a necktie. Yet somehow he didn't look much better than when I'd seen him at the Knights' apartment. Still haggard, gaunt, pale and hostile.

I apologized for not being able to take his coat because of the crutches, but he merely said, "I heard you had some trouble," and threw the coat onto one of the chairs that flanked the console near the stairs. There was no sympathy in his voice.

Leading him into the den, I said, "Help yourself to a drink. It's over there."

But this was one time when McDonald didn't want a drink. "Skip the hospitality. All I want is to know who killed my son. You said you'd tell me."

I settled myself in the chair I'd been sitting in before and put my crutches on the floor. Tiger made himself comfortable at my feet. "All right," I said, "I'll tell you who killed your son. *You* did."

McDonald had seated himself on the settee, but he immediately jumped up. "I dare you to repeat that."

"*You* killed your son, McDonald. If it weren't for you, he'd be alive today."

He took two steps toward me, his hands out as if to strangle me. Tiger sprang to my defense. Hackles raised, he bared his teeth and growled. He seemed totally unaware of how small he was.

"Sit down," I said to McDonald, "before you make a fool of yourself."

McDonald didn't advance any farther. But he didn't sit down either. He stood there, glaring at me. "Is that what you got me over here for?" His voice was quivering. "To tell me I killed my own son?"

"Among other things, yes. You didn't actually pull the trigger, but you helped make it possible for the one who did. You simply didn't know what you were doing."

He dropped his hands, but continued to stand there. "You're out of your mind."

"For heaven's sake, sit down. I'm not an enemy."

He hesitated, then went back to the settee. Tiger relaxed.

"Every now and then, McDonald, we need a little truth in our lives, and there's been too little truth in yours. I've appointed myself to remedy that. I feel I have the right to. It's partly on account of you that I'm on crutches. . . . You know goddamn well that you contributed to your son's death. That's why you look so miserable. Your own guilt is eating away at you."

He lowered his eyes.

"You know how you came into my life, McDonald? You came into it because Helen didn't like you. She wanted my advice. She said you frightened her. She knew you'd been in prison, although she didn't tell me that at the time, and it bothered her. But I don't think it bothered her as much as your personality. She said you never smiled, and she was right—you hardly ever do smile. Because there hasn't been much in your life to smile about. She didn't know how else to put it—all she could say was that you never smiled and you frightened her. I thought she was being—well, Helen has her peculiarities, and I didn't take her seriously. What I didn't realize was that beneath the peculiarities lies a pretty good sense of values. She may be narrow-minded, she may disapprove of too many things, but basically she's a sound person, and if she doesn't like someone, chances are there's something about him that isn't good. And that's true in your case. You're a man who always wanted the wrong things."

McDonald looked up, but only for an instant.

"What you wanted was money. And you wanted it the easy way. I didn't set out to make a study of you, and there's an awful lot about you that I still don't know, but in the past week I've run into a number of people who've had things to say about you, and everything they've said points in one direction: you've always wanted to be rich. And you've always been disappointed. You married for money, and your wife was disinherited. You took kickbacks and got fired. You robbed the store you worked for and were sent to jail. You wanted your son to visit his grandmother, but he wouldn't go. You tried to get him to quit school and go to work, but he insisted on sticking to his goal. And you wanted him to get a nice check as a wedding present, but instead he got killed. You contributed to your son's death, McDonald. No doubt about it. Because you made the mistake of letting his grandmother know that he was about to be married."

"Damn her!" McDonald cried. "Damn her, damn her, damn her! I hope she rots in hell!"

"Don't damn her," I said. "Damn yourself." But that, I knew, was what he'd been doing for the past two weeks. Suspecting that he'd made a mistake, wondering what it was, half guessing the truth, but not being sure that it was the truth, blaming himself, but not quite knowing what to blame himself for. Alone, unable to confide even in his sister and brother-in-law, he'd been trying to work it out, feeling worse and worse, hating himself, hating everyone else, and never fully understanding the reason. Now I was giving him the reason, but I wasn't enjoying it. I wanted to stop. He'd been through enough already. I knew I had to go on, though.

"That's what made me begin asking myself questions about

you, McDonald. When I was up at your sister and brother-in-law's apartment after Bob had been killed, you said, 'It's all Elissa's fault.' That didn't strike me as odd at the time, but when I thought about it later, it did. What would make you think that your former mother-in-law, whom you hadn't seen or been in touch with in all those years, could still affect your life? How could she have any bearing on what had happened to your son, or on anyone connected with you? And how did you, an ocean away, know about her marriages and divorces? Then, when I was out in Chicago talking with Dwight Wilson, the answer hit me. You had a friend in Chicago. For years. Or half a friend. Amos Fisher. He was the one who kept you posted. He must have liked you, if for no other reason than because Elissa didn't. His feelings about her were almost as strong as yours. She represented everything he didn't believe in."

McDonald finally looked up. His eyes were two chips of basalt. "Don't say anything about Amos. He was a good man."

"I don't intend to say anything about Amos, although personally I don't think much of a man who spends his entire life carrying out the orders of a woman he holds in contempt. Anyway, he's dead. For the past couple of years someone new has been handling Elissa's affairs. Someone who doesn't give a damn about you. So you didn't really know where she was, but you took a chance. You wrote to her old law firm, saying that her grandson was about to be married. You hoped that she'd do what you'd *always* hoped she'd do: come across with some money. If not for you, at least for your son. Was your letter ever acknowledged?"

McDonald was staring at the carpet again. He didn't answer.

"Was it?"

"Damn you, Potter."

"Was it?"

He nodded.

"So you knew she was in the United States, in a hospital in Chicago?"

He nodded again.

"And you wrote her there?"

He shook his head.

"You didn't write her there? Why? Because the acknowledgment said that your letter was being forwarded?"

He nodded.

"Well, it was. She got your message, all right. And her husband killed your son."

42

I'd expected a reaction. The man had a lifetime's accumulation of anger, frustration and bitterness stored up, and I'd tampered with it. So I sat there braced, ready for the abuse, the vituperation which, since De Garonne wasn't around and I was, was likely to be directed at me.

And a reaction came. But not the kind I was expecting. Suddenly McDonald began to cry.

It wasn't mere crying, however. It was a storm of grief the likes of which I'd never seen. He made no attempt to cover his face or stifle the sobs; and instead of lowering his head, he raised it. He appeared to be expressing his grief to the ceiling, or to some region far above the ceiling. His body shook, his face turned red, tears streamed from his eyes. Gasping, he tried to speak. "I loved her. . . . Nobody believes me, but I loved her. . . . I loved him. . . . I wanted him to be happy. . . . I wanted him to have a good life. . . . I loved her. . . ."

I knew that I wasn't the one he was explaining it to, and I passed no judgment. Something inside me was crumpling too. I didn't want to cry—I realized I had nothing to cry about, except maybe life itself—yet it was all I could do to keep from breaking down.

Tiger, who'd never heard such noises before, became alarmed and looked up at me for reassurance. I petted him.

Finally McDonald left the room. I guessed that he was hunting for a bathroom and I wanted to tell him where one was, but I had no voice. He did find the ground-floor bathroom, though. I heard the door close. But even then the sobbing continued—the sounds carried halfway across the house.

He was gone a long time. I eventually managed to get up and, with shaking hands, pour myself a drink.

By the time McDonald returned, I'd finished three ounces of Scotch and the urge to cry had left me.

His face was chalk white, and he seemed weak. "Sorry," he said. "I couldn't help it."

"You'd better have a drink."

He nodded, and helped himself to some bourbon. Then we began to talk again. But it was a different kind of talk now. We were two friends discussing a serious matter that concerned both of us and about which each had knowledge that the other lacked.

I told him how it occurred to me, while Wilson was describing the way Elissa bought houses and disposed of husbands, that she must have had a European law firm representing her. More than one European law firm, in fact—different law firms in different countries, since lawyers from one country can seldom practice in another. Amos Fisher had handled her investments, which were in the United States, but not her day-to-day legal problems. Her wills had been drawn up, signed and witnessed in Europe, for that was where she lived. And she'd probably made new wills often, since she'd often been married and divorced.

McDonald admitted that he'd tried to find out from Fisher whether Elissa had made provision for her grandson in her will, but Fisher hadn't been able to tell him; for the will, or wills, had indeed been drawn up in Europe. McDonald had always hoped, desperately, that his son would someday come into the money that he himself had been denied, but he'd doubted that it would happen. After all, her grandson was a stranger to her; the two times she'd tried to make contact with him, she'd been rebuffed. He described how, without telling the Knights, he'd taken it upon himself to write a letter to Koenig, Koenig, Dempster and Fisher, asking them to inform Elissa that her grandson, Robert

McDonald, was to be married in New York on December 21, and even giving Bob's address and telephone number, in case she might want to get in touch with him. It was this last that had made him wonder, after the murder, whether he wasn't somehow responsible. And he described the letter he'd received from one of the young Koenigs in reply. Unfortunately, it said, the Countess de Garonne was currently in poor health and was hospitalized in Chicago, but she would be duly informed of the approaching marriage.

We talked about Elissa's personality. He told me things I hadn't known, and I told him things he hadn't known. But they didn't change the profile: she was a woman who'd made no close friends, outlived most of her acquaintances and given nothing to charity. I explained that I'd spoken only hours before with Dwight Wilson's sister and with Dolly Whitcomb. The first had said that she didn't know that Dolly was going to invite me to her apartment, and Dolly had said without hesitation that it was the Count de Garonne who had suggested she find out more about me and who knew about the luncheon. Dolly had also confirmed something else for me: that, except for buying tickets to charity balls, Elissa had never contributed a cent to any cause in her life.

"So, with no close friends and no interest in philanthropy," I said, "who would she leave her money to? The two people with ties to her—her husband and her grandson. And she certainly wasn't going to leave much to her husband, in my opinion. What kept them together was her age. She'd grown very old and tired. She may have felt that a bad husband was better than no one at all. Besides, *he* wouldn't give *her* a divorce—he told me so. He damn well intended to wait it out and inherit."

Together, McDonald and I did some speculating. Had Bob really been the principal heir? Had De Garonne known? If so, for how long? But that was all it was—mere speculation. My belief was that the Count had known for a long time that Elissa was going to leave part of her wealth—probably the bulk of it—to her grandson. As far as I was concerned, that wasn't important. What was important was that the Count wanted everything Elissa had and figured that, in the absence of any other heir, it would be his. I also believed that Elissa's illness had given him the opportunity he'd been waiting for—to come to the United States, locate Bob and kill him. But he hadn't known where to look. Or perhaps he'd known where to look but had had second thoughts. Then, when he'd learned from Elissa of McDonald's letter to the lawyers and the impending marriage, he realized that he had to act quickly or not at all. Time was running out. Elissa couldn't live much longer, and if Bob was killed after the wedding, his widow would get his share of the estate. So he flew to New York, called Bob early in the morning, made an appointment—and kept it.

McDonald and I had several more drinks and talked far into the night. Not because the information we had to give each other required so much time, but because we simply needed each other's company. We'd been through an experience together, an exorcism, and neither of us wanted to be alone after it was over. For me it had been a hard day, a hard week, a hard month. I was feeling the strain. I was more tired than I'd been in a long while. But companionship was more important to me, that night, than rest. And although McDonald had been through far more than I had, and was more exhausted than I was, he didn't want to leave.

I confessed that I hadn't set out with any intention of tracking down his son's murderer, that all I'd been interested in was learning about Koberg Chemical. What had happened, I said, wasn't that I'd found the murderer but that the murderer had found me. De Garonne had been afraid that I would tell Elissa of Bob's death, afraid that I suspected him, afraid of God knows what. At any rate, he'd seen me as a threat that had to be eliminated. And Glass had probably thrown a scare into him by presenting me as a determined investigator.

I told him about Glass and how I believed Glass had manipulated the Count by inciting first his greed and then his fear. Glass had let him know that Elissa's stock was more valuable than supposed, but not how much more valuable. And he'd made me out to be more dangerous than I was. I very much doubted that Glass and the Count had ever openly discussed murder—Glass was too smart for that—but I suspected that Glass had brought up the matter of other heirs and had hinted at how nice it would be if the Count inherited the entire estate. For the Count was someone he knew he *could* manipulate and make a deal with; other heirs might be more difficult to handle.

"All it really adds up to," I said, "is that Louis Glass and his friend the Count discussed the future—what would happen if. But that was enough."

McDonald nodded. "Still," he said, "the Count was lucky. Poor Bob had all day to tell someone that he'd had a telephone call from his grandmother's husband, and that his grandmother's husband was coming to see him, and yet he didn't tell a soul."

"We don't know that he didn't tell a soul, Jim. We only know that he didn't tell you or your sister or brother-in-law, or Andrea, or Dan Chapin. He may have mentioned it to someone else, someone who hasn't associated it with his death and hasn't come forward. Or perhaps the Count told him not to mention it to anyone, or maybe Bob was merely waiting to see what would happen before talking about it. But you're right, the Count was lucky in a lot of ways. Lucky that Bob didn't talk, lucky that there were no eyewitnesses, lucky that Bob didn't hang up on him when he called—if he told Bob who he was, that is; we don't even know whether he did. Sure, he was lucky. He's been lucky right along. Until now."

McDonald looked at me, then at Tiger, who had long since fallen asleep at my feet. "That's a nice dog you have."

So for a while we talked about dogs. McDonald said he'd always wanted one, but Rosemary didn't like them. I said that it was amazing how you could get attached to them and they to you. I told him how Tiger, no matter where he was in the house, always seemed to hear me when I came home. The minute I put my key in the door, he raced into the foyer, yapping hello.

McDonald smiled. "He likes you. He wants to protect you. I think he was ready to bite me."

I smiled too. "To himself he's a big dog."

"You gave him the right name," McDonald said, and his smile broadened. But then it vanished altogether. "What did you mean, a little while ago, when you said 'until now,' Brock? You're going to the police?"

"Eventually, sure. But I don't think that they'll be able to establish a damn thing, Jim. Even if they recovered the bullet that killed your son, and can match it up with the bullets that the police recovered in Chicago, even if they find the gun, they have nothing more than circumstantial evidence. With no witnesses, no fingerprints, they couldn't prove that the Count fired the gun; and a good lawyer could easily get an acquittal. No, what I have in mind is to see that the Count doesn't get what he's so desperate for—his wife's money. Partly for Bob's sake, and partly for mine. I don't believe that the Count has changed his mind about me. I believe he still sees me as a threat. So I'm kind of nervous. Do you happen to have your marriage license?"

"I'm pretty sure," McDonald said, with a puzzled frown. "It's in the box with Dick's insurance policies and everything."

"Well, what I think you ought to do is get it out, and get a copy of Bob's death certificate and whatever other documents you can think of, and take Andrea and go out to Chicago. I think the two of you ought to have a long talk with Elissa's lawyer. Tell him everything that's happened. I think that when he, and Elissa, find out about it, and that Andrea's going to have Bob's child— well, I think Elissa might make a new will, naming Andrea. If Andrea and Bob had already got their marriage license, so much the better."

"They did."

"Good, but I don't think it would matter much if they hadn't. What matters are the facts and how well the two of you present them. Are you willing?"

McDonald took his time, and for a moment I was afraid he was going to say no, but he didn't. He said, "You know I am, Brock. But what about the Count?"

"You won't have to worry about him. Louis Glass is going to insist that he come to New York. He's going to offer him an irresistible price for the stock and keep him here until next Wednesday afternoon. The price doesn't matter; the Count doesn't yet own the stock, and Glass isn't going to buy it anyway. But it will get the Count out of Chicago. If you need money for the trip . . ."

McDonald refused to take any money, however. He had a little saved, he said—what he'd planned to give Bob and Andrea as a wedding present. But he was still worried about me.

"You don't have to lose any sleep on my account," I assured

him. "I'm going out of town, and until next Wednesday I'm going to be kind of hard to locate. I'll come out to Chicago next Tuesday night to lend a hand. I don't know, Jim—I just have a feeling in my bones that everything is going to work out all right. There is such a thing as justice. Sometimes it needs a push, that's all."

"You can count on me," McDonald said.

We had a final drink and made plans.

And eight hours later I took off for Minneapolis.

43

It was a good weekend. Far better than I'd anticipated. I arrived at the psychological moment, just as Carol was beginning to feel that she'd been with her family long enough. And seeing me on crutches shook her up. For the first time, she said, I looked incompetent, and that was nice for a change.

The weather was extremely cold, but that didn't bother us. We spent most of the three days indoors, at my hotel or at her parents' house. And I had ample opportunity to prove to us both that I wasn't as incompetent as all that. Sex is more difficult when you have a recent bullet wound in your thigh, but it's not impossible.

Carol's family was hospitable. I celebrated New Year's Eve with all of them and had dinner with Carol and her parents alone on Saturday night. Her father reviewed his investment portfolio with me and showed me his bowling trophies. Her mother told me confidentially that she'd once wanted to become an actress.

I explained to Carol that I didn't *really* think she was too old to have a baby, and she said she was glad to hear it, but she still intended to discuss the matter with her analyst. What brought us together more than anything else, though, was my willingness to talk about my recent doings. Carol had often complained that when it came to my business activities, I kept too much to myself—it made her feel that I didn't respect her intelligence. She was right too; there was a lot that I didn't tell her. Not because of her intelligence, but because she wasn't a customer. Now, however, I told her everything I'd learned about Koberg Chemical and about the people involved, for she knew so many of them.

And I had to admit that she grasped it all very quickly. She asked good questions and seemed to see certain things even more clearly than I did. It was quite logical to her that De Garonne would want to kill me. He knew that I'd seen him in the Koberg offices and with Louis Glass; he was afraid that I'd tell Carmichael about his friendship with Glass. And when he learned that I knew about Bob's death and wanted to see Elissa, he became doubly afraid of me. Carol agreed with me that he'd got my room number from Carmichael's secretary, but believed that I was making too much of the recording device.

I still thought I was right about that, though. De Garonne had insisted we meet in his hotel rather than mine, because Glass had warned him that I might have my room bugged, just as he had his own office bugged.

The Count interested Carol more than anyone else. What made a man like that tick? she wondered. We discussed his motives at length. Greed, I said. Pride, she said; the family estate was going to pot, and he wanted to restore it. I differed with her. In my opinion, he'd married late in life, for money; and money was all he was interested in. He was still young enough to look forward to years of being both rich and free.

"What a terrible, deceitful, but fascinating man he must be," Carol said, almost wistfully.

"You wouldn't have thought so if you'd been in his suite at the hotel with me," I replied. "He didn't seem terrible or fascinating or even deceitful. He seemed simply a good-looking middle-aged man with a streak of exhibitionism a mile wide—vain about his looks, vain about his ancestors, smart enough to be honest about himself when it served his purpose and when he got rattled, but not extraordinary in most respects. You wouldn't have guessed that he was a murderer, and you might have liked his accent, but I doubt that you'd have been charmed off your feet."

"I didn't mean that," Carol said hastily. "Although," she added, "Elissa was."

"Only for a little while."

"He must be daring, though. Look at the chances he took."

"Look at the stakes."

"Even so."

"He took the chances he had to take. Mainly, though, he was lucky. There's an element of luck in any crime, because there's always the possibility that the victim or some bystander will do something you didn't expect. Or"—I smiled—"that a door will squeak."

Carol sighed. "The stakes," she said. "That's what worries me, Brock. They haven't changed. You're as much of a threat to the Count now as you were before. I wish you weren't going back to New York."

"I know I'm still a threat. That's one of the reasons I'm doing what I'm doing. To minimize the threat. But I don't think there's anything to worry about. Glass will keep him busy. And I don't intend to sleep at home; I intend to sleep at a hotel, just in case."

"I don't see how you can be so sure of that man Glass. Suppose he double-crosses you. Suppose he—"

"He's someone I understand, Carol. He'll do exactly what I told him to do, because it's to his own self-interest. I scared the hell out of him, and he knows I meant every word I said."

Carol didn't appear to be convinced, however. "I know you think you're smart, Brock. And in your own way you *are* smart. But I can't help thinking that at times you're not as smart as you think. You're naïve about people."

"Cut it out, Carol. I'm not a researcher for nothing. I'm always a little bit doubtful."

"Yes, in a way you are. But you're also naïve. You don't realize what people will do when they want something bad enough. That's why you sometimes get in trouble."

"You're beginning to sound like Tom and Mark and everyone else. Well, you needn't worry. Nothing's going to happen to me. And Tom and Mark won't have to worry either. There'll be no wild stories about me in the newspapers or on television. Eventually I'll go to the police, but it'll be Bob McDonald's murder that'll get the attention, not me. I won't even have to testify in court. So quit frowning and call room service—I'd like a drink. I'm beginning to enjoy this room-service bit."

"All right, but put on your pants. I don't want to be embarrassed."

So I struggled into my pants, and we had drinks and we watched the second half of the Orange Bowl game.

And on Sunday night we flew back to New York together.

On the way in from La Guardia we argued about my going to a hotel. Carol wanted me to stay at her place, but I didn't think I should expose her to even the remotest danger. The odds that I'd miscalculated, that something would go wrong, were practically nil, but they did exist. I therefore stuck to my original plan, and after dropping her off at her apartment, I checked into the Tuscany Hotel, which was far enough from my usual haunts to give me a feeling of safety.

Monday and Tuesday were almost like any other Monday and Tuesday. To the extent that they were different, they weren't different because of anything that concerned me. It was just that everyone was settling down after two long holiday weekends in a row and getting used to the idea that a new year had begun. Tom and Mark were back, both tanned, both full of energy, both shocked to find me on crutches. When I told them what had happened, they were more sympathetic than I'd expected. The news about Koberg excited them, and we talked about buying some Koberg stock ourselves. We didn't spend as much time over it as we might have, however, because each of them had a lot of catching up to do in his own department.

Apparently everyone else had catching up to do also, for most of the people who usually called me during the early part of the week didn't; and the few who did were referred to Irving.

We had our staff meeting on Monday morning, as always. It wasn't entirely devoted to Koberg Chemical, but part of it was. Brian had returned from Chicago on Thursday and gave us a long report. He was bursting with information, including the information that he'd accomplished what I hadn't been able to accomplish—he'd seen Paul Carmichael. No trouble at all, he said modestly. Titus had called Carmichael and made the date. Brian and Carmichael had spent an hour together, discussing Koberg's prospects.

"We didn't go into anything about a takeover," Brian said, "but we talked a lot about Tricky."

According to Brian, the six of us had hit the nail on the head. Koberg's research had produced a substitute for petroleum and petroleum byproducts. We hadn't got all the details right—the process was simpler in some respects than we thought, and more complicated in others—but for a bunch of nonscientists we'd come remarkably close. The main thing we'd overlooked, Brian said, was that the new product was also an answer to pollution problems. Koberg's process was partly a recycling operation. Tricky liked, in addition to such things as tree bark and plants, old newspapers, worn-out cotton pajamas, used-up cereal boxes and a wide variety of other waste materials.

"God's gift to mankind," Harriet remarked.

"Just about," Brian agreed.

He said that he wanted to go to the United States Patent Office on Tuesday to see if he could verify what Titus had told him: that Koberg had already applied for patents—formula patents as well as process patents. If so, it wouldn't be long before the product could be put into commercial use.

I told Brian to go ahead, and I felt sufficiently confident to recommend Koberg again in Tuesday's letter.

The only one who behaved peculiarly during those two days was Helen. She was so nervous that she even misspelled my name.

"There's nothing to worry about," I assured her repeatedly. "Everything's going to be all right. I have a feeling."

"I hope you're right," she said. "I do so hope you're right, Mr. Potter. But I can't help it. I know you're trying to do the right thing, and I'm more grateful than I'll ever be able to tell you, but I just can't help it. Every time I think of Andrea out there with those—those *people*, I get the most awful fluttering."

"Think of silver linings, Helen. Things do have a way of righting themselves, you know."

"Oh, I hope so. I do hope so."

But Helen continued to have flutterings, even though I continued to reassure her. My reassurances weren't mere words, either; they were backed by information supplied by McDonald and by Andrea herself. I talked to them four times during those two days—twice on Monday and twice on Tuesday.

Both of them said that things were working out even better than they—or I—had imagined. Lance Koenig, Elissa's lawyer, was the nicest sort of man. Much nicer than Amos Fisher, according to McDonald, and more conscientious too. He was stunned by their story of the crime, but he believed them. The matter would have to be turned over to the police, he said— McDonald and Andrea were withholding information about a most serious crime. But he would be more than glad to draw up a new will and do what he could to persuade Elissa to sign it. Under the circumstances, he felt, speed was essential.

By Tuesday afternoon the will was ready and Koenig had visited his client. So had Andrea. Elissa had shown considerable interest in Andrea and seemed to like her.

"What about you?" I asked McDonald. "Have you seen her yet?"

"No," he replied, and after a pause he added, "I'm scared, Brock. Facing her again, after all these years."

"Well," I said, "it's time you did. But we'll face her together. Tomorrow." And I asked him whether there was any sign of the Count.

"Not so far."

"Good."

We made arrangements for the following day. He and Andrea were staying at the Holiday Inn on Lake Shore Drive, and I intended to stay there too. We agreed to meet at ten o'clock in the morning, in the lobby.

I reported the gist of our conversation to Helen, who said, "Bless you."

"Silver linings," I reminded her.

And I caught the seven-o'clock flight to Chicago.

44

Andrea left for the hospital ahead of us. She went in the car with the lawyer and two young women he'd brought from his office to witness the signature.

McDonald and I followed in a taxi. He was so tense that he was literally rigid. He sat on the edge of the seat, his back ramrod straight, his feet flat on the floor, his hands clenched.

"Relax," I said.

"I've hated her for so long," he replied in a husky voice.

I said nothing further, and neither did he.

We walked in silence through the hospital's lobby, and in silence we rode up in the elevator. When we started down the corridor toward Elissa's room, McDonald hesitated for a moment and closed his eyes, then opened them, drew himself up and accompanied me as silently as before.

The door was open, and the small room seemed crowded. Andrea and the lawyer were standing on the far side of the bed, the two witnesses behind them, and the nurse was cranking up the bed so that Elissa could see better.

There had been no improvement in Elissa's condition. Her skin still had that terrible orange hue, and the whites of her eyes were almost amber. But someone had done her hair for her, and she was no longer wearing the hospital gown. She was wearing something pink and lacy and a bed jacket to match.

On the dresser was an arrangement of fuji mums, and across the foot of the bed, folded neatly, was the afghan Helen had described.

Elissa looked our way just as McDonald and I came through the doorway. McDonald stopped in his tracks as their eyes met.

No one said a word. All of us simply waited.

Then Elissa smiled. "James," she said.

He nodded. "It's been a long time, Elissa."

"Come closer."

He moved toward the bed. She held out her hand. He took it. Neither of them seemed aware of the rest of us.

Finally Elissa glanced at a picture on the bedside table. It was a picture of Bob. It hadn't been there before. "He looked like you," she said.

"Yes," McDonald said, "he did."

"I wish I'd met him."

"You would have liked him."

"He chose a nice girl."

"The best."

There was a silence. Elissa turned her eyes from the picture. For the first time she took notice of me. And, to my surprise, she recognized me. "You were here before," she said. "With a young man."

I nodded.

"You must be the stockbroker. Andrea's told me."

"I am."

She turned back to McDonald. "Bonnie—was she happy at all?"

"At first," he replied. "But I wasn't a good provider."

"Nor was I a good mother."

"It was all so long ago, Elissa."

"Yes, so very long ago." Tears appeared in her eyes.

"But there's going to be a new generation," Andrea said cheerfully. "And soon. The first week in May."

Elissa brightened. "The first week in May." The brightness dimmed. "How far away that seems."

"Well, now," the lawyer said, "shall we get down to business?"

He proceeded to read the will aloud. It was a short document and simply written. The gist of it was that after her funeral expenses were paid, Elissa's entire estate was to be placed in trust for Miss Andrea Doyle, the intended wife of her late beloved grandson, Robert William McDonald, and, in the event of Andrea Doyle's death, for her offspring.

The lawyer then asked Elissa whether she understood the terms of the will.

She said that she did.

And so, at five minutes to eleven in the morning of a cold Wednesday, the sixth of January, in a crowded hospital room at Chicago's Northwestern Memorial Hospital, Augustus Koberg's daughter signed her last will and testament in my presence and in the presence of James McDonald, Andrea Doyle, Lance Koenig, two women from Koenig's office and a nurse. Koenig added his own signature, as did the two women he'd brought with him.

I had a feeling of enormous satisfaction.

Shortly after the signing, Koenig left and took the two witnesses with him. And moments later Elissa's lunch tray was brought in.

"The doctor really doesn't approve of all this excitement," the nurse suggested tactfully. "He only agreed . . . for a little while."

"We'll go," I said.

"I'll stay," Andrea said.

The nurse had no objection to that arrangement.

"Will you meet us?" I asked Andrea.

"No," she replied. "I plan to spend a few more days here."

Elissa nodded and smiled, and McDonald and I prepared to leave. Both of us shook hands with her. She and McDonald exchanged a look, and he said, "Goodbye, Elissa."

"*Adieu*," she said.

But then, as we started for the door, she called him back. "You will look after the baby, won't you, James?"

"You know I will."

And with that, he and I departed.

It was after five o'clock when our plane touched down at La Guardia.

The flight had been ordinary enough in most respects, but unusual in that McDonald and I had only spoken once during the entire trip. That once had been shortly after our takeoff from Chicago, while the plane was still climbing.

"I wish I could repay you, Brock," McDonald had said.

"Don't be silly," I'd replied. "I'll be repaid—plenty. Price, Potter and Petacque stand to make a lot of money out of all this."

"That's not what I mean," he'd said.

I'd suddenly become sober. It hadn't been what I'd meant either. "I feel somehow as if I already have been repaid, Jim."

The conversation had ended, and neither of us had said another word until the plane was on the ground. McDonald had sat with his shoulders slumped and a dreamy expression on his face, and I'd guessed that in his imagination he was reliving large chunks of his life. And I'd had plenty of thoughts of my own—about him, about Andrea, about happy endings. My expectations had been completely fulfilled, which was something that rarely happened to me. The Count de Garonne had been, if not legally punished, at least legally deprived, and it was as if he'd ceased to exist. Not once had his name been mentioned in the hospital room. He was finished.

As the plane was taxiing to the gate, we began to talk again, for it was snowing, and this was the rush hour, and there was the problem of our getting to our respective homes. This caused a long discussion about who should drop whom off and who should pay for the cab—a discussion that turned out to be pointless, because when we emerged from the airport there were no cabs and about fifty people in line waiting for the first one that showed up.

Eventually we settled for the airport limousine, which took us to 42nd Street and Park Avenue, where the discussion resumed. But again there were no cabs. It was a good ten minutes before McDonald managed to flag down a vacant one. He helped me in and got in after me, and before I could say anything, he gave the driver my address, which effectively ended the matter of where we would go first.

The streets were slippery, and the cab driver was disgruntled. He didn't like the traffic, he didn't like New York, he didn't like his work, and it was all the government's fault. He wished he could move somewhere else.

When we reached my house, McDonald and I had another discussion about the cab fare, but he refused to take my money. "It's the least I can do," he said.

I invited him to stay for dinner. My housekeeper usually went home around four thirty, I said, but she knew I was due in and she'd probably left something in the oven.

He declined. Rosemary was expecting him, he explained. But he offered to help me up the steps, and I had no objection to that. I couldn't manage the crutches and my small suitcase at the same time.

So while the cab waited, McDonald accompanied me to the door of my house.

"Sure you won't stay for at least a drink?" I asked as I put my key in the lock.

"No, thanks," he replied.

And it was then that I realized that something wasn't as it should be. I could hear Tiger barking, but the noise didn't seem to be coming from the foyer, where he usually met me. "That's funny," I said.

"What is?" McDonald asked.

"It sounds like Tiger's in the basement. Louise never leaves him in the basement—she says it's too damp."

"Think something's wrong?"

"I don't know."

"I'll come in with you."

I turned the key and opened the door. The foyer was dark. I reached for the switch and turned on the light.

And saw that something was very wrong indeed.

Louise was bound and gagged on one of the chairs beside the console. The Count de Garonne was standing directly in front of me. He had a gun pointed at my stomach.

45

He glanced at McDonald, but his eyes swung right back to me. They were wide with rage.

"*Sale bête!*" His voice came from deep in his throat. He uttered more words in French.

I had no conception of what he was saying. I had no conception of anything. My mind had jammed. It had locked around a single thought—Carol was right—and wouldn't budge.

The Count went on speaking, rapidly, in French, as if not knowing or caring whether I could understand him, as if speaking not to me but to some picture of me that existed in his head. His eyes darted to McDonald, darted back, but if he felt any surprise that two men had come through the doorway instead of one, he gave no sign of it. It didn't seem to matter to him that there were two men, and in that first instant of shock it didn't matter to me either. I forgot about McDonald. I was aware only of the Count and of the gun in his hand and of the fact that Carol had warned me.

But the intensity of the shock diminished. My mind began to work again. I realized that McDonald was by my side, that Louise was tied to the chair and probably had been for hours, that Tiger was barking, that the door to the street was partly open, that the taxi was waiting, that if the Count shot me he would also have to shoot McDonald and possibly Louise too. But, above all, I realized that the Count didn't care, that he was beyond caring.

It was all there in his eyes. He'd had a goal, he'd pursued it relentlessly—through murder, through attempted murder. Across an ocean, back and forth between Chicago and New York—one goal, one hope, one expectation. And one man had caused him to fail.

I'd underestimated him. I'd underestimated Glass. I'd overestimated myself. Carol had told me I didn't realize what people would do when they wanted something badly enough. Well, the Count had wanted something badly enough, and because of me he hadn't got it. The rage in his eyes was fired by disappointment, but it was real and it was heedless of consequences and it was lethal.

He stopped speaking.

And then I heard my own voice. "It's too late," my voice said, sounding, it seemed to me, like it always did. "She signed a new will this morning. It won't do you any good to kill me now."

His expression didn't change. He just barely looked at McDonald. He kept the gun pointed at my stomach. He was holding it with both hands, as if afraid of some unsteadiness; but there was no unsteadiness.

"You'll be caught, De Garonne," my voice continued. "There's no way you can get away with this. Put the gun down. Go home. I won't call the police. Nothing will happen to you. You're angry, you're disappointed, you're . . ."

My voice continued. I was only partly conscious of what it was saying. I knew what I wanted it to say. I wanted it to say the sort of things policemen say to people who are about to jump from rooftops, to people who are holding hostages, to people who are about to destroy themselves or others. But whether those were the right words, I didn't know. I could feel the cold air at my back, though. I was aware that the door wasn't completely closed and that on the street a taxi was waiting, with its meter running and an irritable driver in the front seat. De Garonne might not be deterred by one unexpected presence, but he might be deterred by two. I hoped for a miracle.

And it happened.

239

I could hear shoes scraping on the steps.

I began to talk more urgently, more earnestly.

I wondered whether McDonald also heard the shoes, whether he was thinking what I was. And whether De Garonne could hear them too.

Two seconds, one second . . . I felt more cold air as the door was opened wider. Then I heard the taxi driver's voice behind me. "Hey, you—"

But it wasn't a miracle.

"Oh, my God!" the taxi driver gasped.

De Garonne didn't pay any more attention to him than he had to McDonald.

The taxi driver paid attention to De Garonne, though. His retreating footsteps were very rapid. A metal door slammed. A car roared off.

"He's going to call the police," I said.

"*Fermez la porte*," De Garonne said.

"You'll be caught," I told him. "You'll—"

"Close the door," he said, seeming to realize for the first time that he'd been speaking in French.

I made no move, but McDonald did. I saw him from the corner of my eye. He was still holding the suitcase. He closed the door.

"You killed my son," he said softly.

De Garonne glanced at him.

"You killed my son," McDonald said, more loudly.

De Garonne frowned, glanced at me, glanced back at McDonald.

McDonald threw the suitcase, and De Garonne fired, and McDonald leaped at him—all, it seemed, at the same time.

I saw the blood, heard the gun fire again, saw the suitcase on the floor, the gun still in De Garonne's hands. The blood was reddening McDonald's coat, but McDonald was still moving, reaching for the gun. I raised my right shoulder. De Garonne pointed the gun in my direction. McDonald reached him and grabbed the muzzle of the gun, pointing it toward himself. I felt the crutch slide away from my body. I seized it and raised it. The Count fired again. McDonald uttered a strange sound and slumped to his knees. I brought the crutch down across the Count's left shoulder. He cried out and dropped the gun.

McDonald was on his knees. A pool of blood was forming around him. I lifted the crutch again. De Garonne knelt to retrieve the gun. I brought the crutch down across his head. He grimaced, and his eyes seemed to cross, but his hand kept moving toward the gun. I raised the crutch a third time.

At that moment McDonald slid forward, covering the gun with his body. I aimed at De Garonne's wrist, but only hit his arm. Then McDonald rolled onto his side, gun in hand, and fired.

The Count looked up in great surprise. And the surprise was still on his face when he died.

McDonald lived until shortly before midnight. I was with him until he was wheeled into the operating room. For a while I thought that he might pull through. He'd been shot twice in the left lung and once in the stomach, the doctors reported. Others, they said, had survived similar multiple gunshot wounds.

James McDonald, however, was one of the ones who didn't.

I wasn't with him at the end. I was still in the corridor where I'd been sitting for the past five hours, talking with the police. But the Knights were at his bedside—they'd arrived at the hospital shortly after eight o'clock.

I asked them whether at any point he'd regained consciousness. They said that he hadn't.

So he'd given his final message to me and to no one else. He'd given it to me in the ambulance as we were pulling away from the curb in front of the house. He'd asked me to look after the baby. I'd promised that I would.

46

And, of course, I've kept that promise. From a distance, but with great pleasure. It's been one of the most enjoyable responsibilities I've ever assumed.

Andrea brought the baby to the office yesterday for the first time. I'd been urging her to let everyone have a look at him. I hadn't realized what a commotion he would cause.

Unfortunately she arrived at an awkward moment. I'd been sitting in my office, kibitzing with Joe and George. We hadn't been talking business; we'd been talking vacations. Joe was planning to take his family to California, and George and his wife were going on a cruise.

But suddenly Tom burst into my office. "Have you heard the news?"

"What news?" I asked.

"About Interamerican Marine," Tom replied. "Louis Glass has resigned."

"No kidding?" I said. "Any reason?"

"For reasons of health is what they say. He seemed healthy enough to me, the last time I saw him."

"Who's going to replace him?" I asked.

"Neil Terman is who I heard. His executive assistant."

I glanced at Joe and George. Both of them looked decidedly uncomfortable.

"One never knows," I said to Tom.

He eyed me suspiciously. "Did you have anything to do with this, Brock?"

"Are you kidding?" I replied. "What gave you that idea?"

"Well, you've been recommending that our customers sell Interamerican Marine. And there was that business with Koberg Chemical."

"One thing has nothing to do with the other," I said. "We just feel that Interamerican Marine's too high."

Tom didn't appear convinced.

"If you don't need us," Joe said, and he and George got up to leave.

And it was at that moment that we heard the commotion. It seemed to be headed toward my office.

Andrea had arrived with the baby. And was being followed down the corridor by every female who worked for us, along with most of the males.

Joined by Helen, the entire crowd piled into my office. Tom, Joe, George and I got up to inspect our young visitor.

"Good grief," Tom exclaimed, "he's the best-looking baby I've ever seen!"

Helen beamed. So did I. I'd thought he was an extraordinary infant from the day he was born.

"And see how active he is," I said. "That's a good sign."

Clair Gould edged her way to the front of the circle. I gathered that at that moment the switchboard was unattended, but that no one cared.

"I knitted his suit," Helen said.

I held out my finger. The baby considered it. Then he reached.

"He weighs ten pounds," Andrea said.

I looked at the little guy. He seemed to be enjoying all the attention. But he gave no indication of knowing how rich he would someday be. Along with other odds and ends, he was the eventual heir to a house in Marbella, an apartment in Paris and, since his great-grandmother had outlived her husband, a vineyard not far from Bordeaux. In addition to 210,000 shares of Koberg Chemical, which, the last time I'd checked, was 19 bid, 19¼ asked.

Mark appeared in the doorway. "What's going on?" he wanted to know. Then he saw, and came in for a closer look. "Splendid child," he proclaimed.

"Probably make a great salesman," Tom speculated.

"Looks more like the financier type to me," Mark said.

I said nothing. The way things were shaping up, I thought, it was more likely that the baby would someday develop an interest in Mayan hieroglyphics.

"What's his name?" Clair asked.

"Koberg McDonald Doyle," I said. "But we call him Koby." It was all I could do to keep from adding proudly that Carol and I were his godparents.